"A new life in a new town, the promise of security, the ever-present mill that dominates and defines all their lives, *Cotton Mill Girl* provides an honest, authentic, personal look at life in the small-town South of the early 1900s. You'd need a time machine to experience it more vividly. Avoid the Great War, the Spanish Influenza, and let this enthralling book show it to you from a distance. You'll find that distance isn't far at all."

Jerome Norris
writer and retired civil rights attorney
New Bern, NC

"Flora Ann Scearce weaves a compelling story of rich characters in poor times set in the textile culture of piedmont North Carolina. As a native of Gastonia, I found myself enthralled by the description of life around the 'mill hill,' and could almost see the locales and hear the melodic hum of spinners and clatter of looms. *Cotton Mill Girl* is a captivating peek into a culture and a time worth remembering."

Dr. Jerry Cloninger
Pastor, Tabernacle Baptist Church
New Bern, NC

"*Cotton Mill Girl* evokes a family's journey, each choosing a path by circumstances. The family descends out of the mountains of North Carolina with simple attitudes, language, and traditions clinging to what is left of their memories. With a will to survive the changes in her life, a young girl's story captures the essence of the early 1900s during first airplane flights, World War I, and silent movies. The author brilliantly brings a flavor of the South into view for this West Coast reader."

Diana Schlepp
freelance artist

"Though a 'little mountain hooger turned linthead,' who at the tender age of twelve reluctantly left school to work in a Gaston County cotton mill, Selena (Sippy-gal) Burzilla Wright Sanders led a full and rich life, worthy of being remembered not just by close kin, but by a wider audience. Through this well-written and carefully researched biographical novel, Sippy's daughter, Flora Ann Scearce, turns back the calendar to another place and period, allowing her readers to enjoy the 'good ol' days' of early 20th century America in the South while suffering their hardships only from the safe distance of empathy. Sippy worked twelve-hour shifts in the cotton mill for sixty cents a day, but the richness of her experience and the poetry and faith in her soul, as chronicled by her daughter, will bless and inspire lives far removed from her own."

Dr. Donald W. Hadley
Pastor, First Baptist Church, Havelock, NC

"Flora Ann Scearce's *Cotton Mill Girl* makes me want to join in the fellowship on 'Corned Beef and Cabbage Night' at the boardinghouse and stick around for Jeff Davis Pie. I know World War I was going on in the background; however, I still want to know who stole Selena's new red and black coat."

Fran Phelps
retired French teacher
New Bern, NC

COTTON MILL

Girl

For: Brenda + Brad

All the best to

COTTON MILL

Girl

my good Christian

friends —

FLORA ANN SCEARCE

Flor Ann

12-1-13

Tate Publishing & Enterprises

TATE PUBLISHING
& Enterprises

Tate Publishing is committed to excellence in the publishing industry. Our staff of highly trained professionals, including editors, graphic designers, and marketing personnel, work together to produce the very finest books available. The company reflects the philosophy established by the founders, based on Psalms 68:11,

"THE LORD GAVE THE WORD AND GREAT WAS THE COMPANY OF THOSE WHO PUBLISHED IT."

If you would like further information, please contact us:
1.888.361.9473 | www.tatepublishing.com
TATE PUBLISHING & Enterprises, LLC | 127 E. Trade Center Terrace
Mustang, Oklahoma 73064 USA

Cotton Mill Girl
Cover design by Lindsay Behrens
LORAY MILL image provided by Lucy Penegar, Chair Gaston County Historic Preservation Commission, Gastonia, NC
Interior design by Elizabeth A. Mason

Published in the United States of America

ISBN: 978-1-5988671-8-3
07.01.17

This book is dedicated to the
children, grandchildren,
and great-grandchildren of
Selena "Sippy" Wright Davenport
Sanders, my mother.

F. A. S

Acknowledgments

My mother, Selena W. Sanders, never forgot those growing up years in Gastonia, NC, and Maysworth (now Cramerton). She left a wealth of material, some oral, some written, some published in *The State* magazine, (now *Our State*), as well as in newspapers such as *The Roanoke Rapids NC Herald*. Pursuing such avenues led me to the Gaston County Library where Librarian Janet Lee Robinson mined info about the streetcar system and sent copies of old *Gastonia Gazette*s, one describing in detail the history making July 4, 1912, parade. Others related events of the Great War and the Spanish Influenza pandemic.

Visiting the lovely town of Cramerton, I purchased at Town Hall a copy of *Cramerton, North Carolina, "The best place I ever did live," A Pictorial History*, by Autrey VanPelt, and lingered to check out the portraits of the handsome Cramers that graced the walls. I learned how father and son "grew the town." Mildred Gwin Andrews' *The Men and The Mills, A History of The Southern Textile Industry* outlined how it all happened.

Dr. Donald W. Hadley, First Baptist Church, Havelock, NC, and Dr. Jerry Cloninger, Tabernacle

Baptist Church, New Bern, NC, provided help and advice with Grandpa Spencer's sermons.

A writer's group led weekly by Maxine Harker, Grifton, NC, critiqued and spurred me on along the writing trail. Thank you all so much!

And my husband, Herman, put up with the hours on end I spent at my computer keyboard. "Supper's ready" were the sweetest words I ever heard.

TODAY'S RESOLUTION

'Tis said, "Tomorrow never comes,"
Then I shall fill this day
With gentle words and kindly deeds,
To help some pilgrim on his way.
Forgetting not, lest I should cause
Some fellow traveler sorrow–
I have no claim on another day
For contrition on the morrow.
And when at last the long night comes,
And I've said my last good-byes,
My soul shall be light and my pillow soft,
And no tears need curtain my eyes.

S. W. S

Foreword

The family saga of Selena Burzilla Wright Sanders begins with Flora Ann Scearce's first novel, *Singer of an Empty Day*, published in 1997. Selena or "Sippy-gal" tells her own story, moving from 1907 to 1912. In *Singer of an Empty Day*, Selena introduces readers to her Mama Rachel, Papa Jim, sister Marietta or "Met," Grandma Robinson, and to life on Utah Mountain where family ties are strong and survival is often on the edge.

Early in Selena's life, she remembers her family's cabin burning down, her Papa grieving as he smelled all his meat and corn burning, and her family going to live with Grandma Robinson who still had three children at home—Tom, seventeen, George, thirteen, and Effie, ten. Another son, Alex, had gone to work at a railroad depot in Asheville.

Flora Ann Scearce's impulse to write from the eyes of Selena, who is modeled after her own mother, is rooted in memorabilia as well as in her desire to get her mother's life in the mountains down as part of the history of American development. What stirs the heart in *Singer of an Empty Day* repeats its pull in this second novel, *Cotton Mill Girl*. Though this novel stands on its own as a story of mountain survival and the burgeoning textile industry of North Carolina in the early twentieth century, the story of Selena Wright deserves a full look. The reader is reminded to go back to *Singer of an Empty Day* and to move through *Cotton Mill Girl*, only to finish this installment hoping for a third where Selena goes on to love, marriage, and her own family.

In *Singer of an Empty Day* we learn specific things about Selena Wright. She has come up the hard way physically, with her father as a good-looking but poor mountain man with red hair and blue eyes. Her Papa was a tenant of Mr. Jacob Kingsley and worked by cutting timber, building split-rail fences to keep cows out of planted fields, hunting rabbits, quail, and deer. Selena's Mama was in the kitchen cooking roasted cornmeal bran, molasses gingerbread, sauerkraut, chicken dumplings, wheatbread, beans, pork, pickled pigs feet, and tea from sassafras roots.

Singer of an Empty Day becomes not only an in-troduction to the life of Selena Wright through her eyes, but also a social record of medicinal herbs, songs, and mountain culture of the early twentieth century. Among the medicinal herbs Granny had in her black bag are pennyroyal, shepherd's purse, squaw vine, and Shawnee plant. Among the folk songs sung in the cabin and around the mountain community are "The House Carpenter," "Lord Thomas," "Fly Around My Pretty Little Miss," "There Was A Little Boy," and

"Ole East-Bound Train." These songs are recorded both with sheet music and lyrics—a prize possession for a reader.

Also captured in the first part of Selena Wright's story is the mountain culture with the rural strength of its dialect and colorful imagery. Readers are introduced to the Pat and Mike Irish jokes, mountain cabin walls papered with newsprint, eighteen children in a one-room schoolhouse, eleven-hour work days in a cotton mill in Greenville, South Carolina, hot lye water as a disinfectant, dangers of diphtheria, echoes of the Spanish-American War, Tarot cards with Callie Dock explaining them to seekers, the power of Nature with snows, fires, and winds, clearing land in Tuscola.

Amidst all the hardships and struggles for survival, Selena Wright learns the strength and force of family. The cow, Cherry, wants to stay with the family and the mule, Buck, wants to die on the mountain. Selena's friend, Nellie Sue Muckle, is humiliated by her pregnancy and outrages her father only to find herself facing suicide. The crook, Rance Hoaghan, leads the Wrights to a shanty at Saunook Mountain only to have them almost starve to death.

The second novel, *Cotton Mill Girl*, Selena Wright's saga begins in 1912 in Gastonia, the "Boomtown" of the textile industry. Selena's Mama has died and her Papa has married Clemmie. Selena is twelve and loves school, but she is forced to work in the cotton mill. The crushing noise of the cotton mill machines, the family debt to the cotton mill store, and the big looms of belt-driven wheels remind readers of America in a time when capitalism was not checked by child labor and worker safety laws. Selena's job is to keep the threads moving onto the spools. She was called a "linthead" because so much lint sprinkled into her hair, on her face, and in her clothes. The novel creates a social commentary as we see owners from the North treat laborers unfairly, abusing them, thus giving rise to union leaders coming down from Massachusetts to arouse the workers. One child, Marvelee Davis, has her scalp pulled clean off her head while a union sympathizer, Sudie Hailey, has her house at 819 Lee Street burned to the ground.

Selena gives readers a sense of a two-story schoolhouse with Miss Lulu Whitesides as the teacher who encourages her to write. The importance of the Callaway Boardinghouse as a magnet of social reality looms large in this novel. Selena's best friend is Doreen Callaway whose mother runs the boardinghouse. The star boarder is Mr. Winfred Gentry whose love of corned beef and cabbage establishes it as a weekly meal. Mr. Gentry adds life to Callaway's Boardinghouse as he brings in new piano rolls and chocolates for all. Songs around the piano include "My Wild Irish Rose," "By the Light of the Silvery Moon," and "By My Side." Mr. Gentry's love affair with the popular schoolteacher, Miss Lulu Whitesides has its light and dark sides as does Selena's father's difficulties with his wife, Clemmie.

Selena's exuberance at the 1912 Independence Day parade in Gastonia enriches the social dimension of America in the early twentieth century. Readers are also made aware of the European conflict with Germany. Conversations occur about Woodrow Wilson as an idealistic isolationist, about the German submarine sinking the Lusitania, about women perhaps voting as a political move by Wilson to get re-elected, about U-boats off the North Carolina coast. When America declares war in 1917, Selena gives us a view of how the mill town reacted and how personal lives were affected. War songs become popular— "Keep the Home Fires Burning," "Don't Take My Darling Boy Away." Americans were going to make the world safe for democracy.

As Selena Wright begins to move from age seven to age twelve and older, readers see her life through her eyes. Selena and her best friend, Doreen, love to go down Main Street in Gastonia, eat ten cent Cherry-Berry ice cream sodas with two straws, and watch movies with Mary Pickford (Selena's favorite,) and Mabel Normand (Doreen's favorite). Work at Loray Mill gives them spending money and a hard life.

Dangers abound with the rise of the Spanish Influenza in 1918, the war, and unchecked capitalism. The blasts of the mill whistle rumble through the novel just as Selena's prayers to her Mama echo in Selena's mind. Selena's talks to her deceased Mama are powerful reminders of the validity of love present in a child. Selena's imagined words from her Mama comfort her, help her with her problems, and strengthen her as she grows into young adulthood. Mama says to Selena: (1) Do the best you can, honey. (2) God knows how much you love learning, sweet girl. He'll find a way. (3) 'Member how the evening sun looked in the mountains when we saw the rays from our cabin, how it just about took our breath away till it fell beyond the gorge? God's like that, only his light don't never set. (4) And God opens doors for them that trust Him.

Religion undergirds Selena's life, for it is her Mama's faith and the Loray Missionary Baptist Church that remind Selena of what it means to love and to forgive. Selena's imagination is rich and straightforward.

Flora Ann Scearce offers her readers a chance to leave the computer-thick landscape of modern America and enter the mind of the cotton mill girl until she reaches eighteen and is at Roanoke Junction—another junction in her life.

Now we await the third prong of the family saga.

Pepper Worthington, Ph.D.

Professor of American Literature

Mount Olive College

Mount Olive, NC

Preface

More than a century ago North Carolina was mostly a rural society consisting of those who owned land and those who farmed it for the owners. Then the textile industry revolution began. Mills were built. Recruiters scoured the countryside, hiring dirt farmers and lumberjack mountaineers to leave lives of poverty and grubbing for an existence. "Greenhorns" became "lintheads" as they came in droves, happy to exchange hard work and loyalty for the security of weekly wages. Mill owners provided a system of paternalism–jobs, houses, churches, schools, health care, markets–and life in the mill villages became "like family." Though millwork was a step up for most, dissatisfaction fermented when mill owners became too far removed from worker unrest.

For Smoky Mountaineer Jim Wright and his family, a cotton mill job was the means by which they moved from dire poverty to an emerging middle class. There were no work laws protecting children, however, and Selena Wright at age twelve was put to work in Loray Mill, Gastonia, NC. By today's standards this seems shocking, yet it was the norm for the times.

Still children will be children. They will always find a way to have fun and learn lessons.

Selena Wright was my mother and *Cotton Mill Girl* is part of her life's story.

FLORA ANN SCEARCE

Chapter 1

If I were blind as a cave bat I'd know I was in Waynesville Depot. The odors: discarded orange peels and chewing tobacco, pungent in shiny spittoons, boot black and lemony shoe wax, cigarette smoke and apple-scented pipe smoke pulled me in like Granny's apple cinnamon cakes drew me to her kitchen. And roasted chestnuts—my, how I loved 'em!

"Chestnuts, chinquapins, five cents a string; chestnuts, chinquapins, five cents a string."

I'd heard that rag-tag's high-pitched chant a thousand times. Like me and my sister, Met, he was there every time a train was due.

Since I was knee-high to a toad, I couldn't stay away from Waynesville Depot when that shrill whistle split the quiet of our Smoky Mountain town. The train was rounding Holcomb's Knob. We hightailed it fast as our skinny legs would go with only minutes to spare before the giant locomotive chugged in, hissing, groaning, spewing her steam onto silver tracks, like a steel dragon.

It was Friday, May 10, 1912. Papa, Met and I were taking the Charlotte Special to Gastonia, a city Papa called "Boomtown." Papa and Clemmie, Papa's new wife, had jobs there at Loray Mill—newest, biggest cotton mill in the entire world. We'd live in a company house, he bragged, and Met and I would go to company school.

"Papa, Papa, can I spend my nickel now?" I begged.

"I'll be dern, Sippy, if that nickel ain't burning a hole in your pocket. But don't waste it on chestnuts. Wait and see what five cents'll get you in Boomtown."

"Shoeshine! Shoeshine! Shine, mister?" The bootblack was my friend.

I tugged at Papa's sleeve. "Don't you need a shine?"

"Naw, Sip." He glanced down, barely missing a stride as he swiped the dusty toes of new brogans on the backs of his trouser legs. "Ain't wasting my greenbacks in Waynesville Depot."

It was a half hour till train time, but once we'd packed, we were too jittery to hang around Granny's. Our train was due at half past twelve and we'd brought bag lunches to eat on the train. I'd packed mine; Papa'd packed his and Met's. Times past Granny did that. Now Aunt Mary was spoon-feeding Granny like a little, bitty baby. Propped in a chair, eyes glazed, Granny looked for all the world like my crazy old ragdoll, Liddy. But nothing about Granny was funny.

Watching Aunt Mary trying to spoon broth into Granny, Papa just moaned. "She ain't long for this world, Mary. When they quit eating, it's like a pact 'tween them and the Almighty—'Lord, I'm gonna help you git me up yonder to the place you done prepared.' God knows wherever that is, Granny'll be a heap better off. Her life ain't never been no picnic, but she's too dern proud for this."

I was eleven and a half years old, old enough to know if my Granny wanted to die—which I didn't doubt since Papa said so—it had to be the complete turnaround of her world. Never, if she could help it, had Granny Wright, midwife and doctor of mountain medicine, been "beholden" to anybody for anything.

"*Waynesville Courier! Asheville Citizen!* Get your *Saturday Evening Post* right here!" The newsboy's dingy bag stuffed with papers sagged on his skinny shoulder. He was my friend, too, but I knew Papa'd never waste money on a newspaper.

He plucked an *Asheville Citizen* from a bench while Met and I strutted about pretending to be children of well-to-do tourists. Real tourists avoided us mountaineers like the plague, but we didn't care—not today. Today we were paying passengers and on our way to Boomtown.

When the Charlotte-bound chugged in, folks spilled to the platform: businessmen in derbies and pinstripes, women in feathered hats and big skirts. Most were tourists who came for the pure crisp coolness of mountain air. Their children scurried in middies and ruffles and white stockings.

Steam belched from the monstrous train's belly. She groaned and spat as if raring to get on with the rugged journey. Baggage was loaded, redcaps checking and rechecking. When the mad rush was over, the conductor yelled, "All abo—ard." We filed into passenger coaches. With everyone settled on red velvet seats, the conductor signaled the engineer.

I perched on the edge of my seat when a lurch with a loud *whoosh!* almost toppled me to the floor. I grabbed the arm of my seat with both hands.

"Watch out, Sippy-gal. You'ns better sit back, else you ain't going noplace."

Papa pulled Met to his lap, holding her tight as the train built up speed.

The station house, with WAYNESVILLE in block letters, inched past as I pressed my face against the window. People outside were waving and I waved back. Faster and faster we went till trees were flying by. My heart raced. My throat constricted. A factory flew past, black smoke curling above tall stacks. Through Holcomb's Knob we sped, bright clouds shining among green and russet hills, row on row of shanties with lines of laundry blowing like tiny flags in the wind.

The whistle shrieked a startling wail and I grabbed Papa's arm. My stomach was in knots, but I tried not to let on.

Papa laughed. "Ain't scared, are you, gal?"

"Naw."

I knew what to expect. When Mama was alive we rode the train to Greenville, South Carolina. Still, it got me tingly all over—like riding the Ferris wheel at Haywood County Fair.

Clickety-clack, clickety-clack. You're Boomtown-bound and you ain't going back. Clickety-clack, clickety-clack. You're Boomtown-bound and you ain't going back. The rhyme whirred inside my head. Smoke billowed, filtering through windows; smelly, gritty.

Clickety-clack, clickety-clack. You're Boomtown-bound and you ain't going back.

Papa opened his lunch bag and motioned to me, but I couldn't eat. When he finished he rolled a cigarette, lit it and leaned his head back, blowing smoke in the air. Met nibbled on a hard biscuit smeared with apple butter. She kept licking her fingers and picking crumbs from her lap. Watching made my stomach queasy, but I didn't dare tell Papa. He'd tell me to quit looking out the window.

"Better open that poke," he said.

"I still ain't hungry."

"You'll starve to death 'fore we hit Charlotte."

Papa's mind was on getting to Boomtown. It was all he could talk about. He wasn't the kind to look back, always talked about what lay ahead, what he hoped would happen. Mama wasn't like that. She'd dream about old times, how things used to be. At night I'd listen to Mama's stories till I could hardly hold my eyes open, her voice sweet and calm. She made the whole world seem right.

I dare not tell Papa I missed Waynesville already. He wouldn't understand. I loved Waynesville—everything about it—my school, my cousins. Even in our hand-me-downs, my cousins and I were treated same as children of the well-to-do in their pretty dresses and starched shirts. We wandered all over town. We knew every street, every alley, all the merchants on Main Street and Frog Level by name—the ones who drove us "street bums" away and the ones who gave us candy.

"D-double-dare-you," my cousins would challenge, and we'd sneak to the blacksmith's shop where the smithy cursed us for getting close to his fire, and the tannery where the smell made us gag and spit and laugh ourselves silly.

Once a lady came down in a hot air balloon with free tickets to Haywood County Fair. My cousin was the first one there and got us all tickets.

My Aunt Mary and cousin Burzilla lived on the creek where Depot Street angled from Main to Water Street. One block off Main on East Street was where we had lived with Granny, Uncle John, and two cousins—and my kitty-cat, Nelse, that I wanted to bring in a special box I'd made with plenty of airholes. But Papa said no, it would be too much trouble, changing trains in Charlotte and all. I cried one whole day for Nelse, but Papa's mind was made up. He didn't understand crying for a "flea bitten kitty-cat."

The only time I ever saw Papa cry was when Mama died. He cried for days till his eyes puffed out, and nips from his whiskey bottle were all that kept him going.

"What am I goin' do with two little gals to raise?" he said to Granny.

"Well now, Jim, don't worry none about that," she said. "They got a home with me long as they need one."

But before the flowers on Mama's grave dried up he was seeing Clemmie Pollard, and in six months they were married. He was working at Waynesville Tannery, a job he hated, when a recruiter came from Loray Mill in Gastonia. Papa signed up right away. No, he didn't mind leaving Waynesville. Not one bit.

He was excited about Gastonia. "Got us a two-bedroom millhouse," he bragged. You young'ns ain't never had it so good. In Boomtown there's a job for every man, woman, and child."

"But Papa, I don't want a job," I said. "I want to go to school. You promised."

Papa laughed. "We'll see. We'll see."

Met was sound asleep, her head against Papa's arm, her curly hair clinging to his sweaty shirtsleeve. On her lip dried apple butter looked like a brown mustache. Papa's eyes were closed.

Beyond my window sheep and cows were grazing on a grassy knoll. There were fodder stacks and wooden fences that zigzagged over rolling hills. With each mile, the distant line of blue mountains on the horizon faded into haziness. I strained my eyes to make them out.

Clickety-clack, clickety-clack. You're Boomtown-bound and you ain't going back.

Charlotte's station was the biggest, most crowded place I ever saw. You had to shout to be heard. But it wasn't magical, not like Waynesville. At Waynesville Depot a rag-tag could hob-nob with the rich, and in make-believe, hop a coach to a swank hotel high in the mountains. It could happen, but only at Waynesville.

From Charlotte we boarded the Piedmont and Northern to Gastonia. The cars were airy and bright with tall windows, "How mill folk 'round these parts traveled," according to Papa.

"Y'like this?" he asked.

"Uh-huh. Better'n a horse and wagon."

"Well, Boomtown's getting a streetcar line that'll take you anywhere you want to go, east to west and back again. Be rolling in a month or so. Won't cost but a nickel, they say—cheaper'n any horse and wagon or even a buggy ride."

"I like trains best of all," Met piped up.

Her curly hair was matted, her mouth smudged with dried vegetable soup from our meal at Charlotte's station.

"Wipe that mouth," I told her and she raked her dress sleeve across it. "Here, let me," but she twisted her head and looked out the window.

Maybe Clemmie could do something with Met, she'd stopped listening to me. I was tired of being in charge. Oh, Papa was still Papa, but he didn't know what to do with Met or me, admitted such to Granny. He was lost without Mama. Things would be different in Gastonia, though I wasn't sure how.

"Papa, I been thinking," I said.

"Watch out. Them brains is been resting up too long. They're 'bout to explode."

"Don't make fun."

"I ain't making fun, Sippy-gal."

"That's exactly what I been thinking about."

"What?"

"*Sippy.* I don't want to be *Sippy* anymore. Selena's my real name. It's what I want to be called."

"Well, I'll be a knock-kneed cowboy."

"Mama said Selena means moon goddess. She said the moon goddess was so beautiful. She rode across the sky in a chariot pulled by white horses."

"Well, now, ain't you done said you rather ride an electric streetcar."

"*Papa!*"

"Selena Burzilla Wright. That's the name your mama gave you all right. I 'member like it was yesterday. You looked more like a crawdad than a moon goddess. What about Met? Plan to call her 'Marietta'?"

I looked at Met, cranky from sleeping a big part of our trip. Met knew less of what to expect in a cotton mill town than I did. She wasn't but four when we lived in Greenville, South Carolina, where Papa worked in a cotton mill and Mama was still living. She could barely remember any of it.

"If she wants to be Marietta, it's all right with me. And, Papa, don't forget—*I want to go to school.*"

Clickety-clack, clickety-clack, you're Boomtown-bound and you ain't going back.

Chapter 2

The house was dark when we got there. Clemmie was working the second shift and wouldn't be home till midnight. She'd left a pot of pintos on the stove. Papa got a bowl and fixed himself a big helping to eat cold. Met and I split a hard biscuit and sprinkled each half with sugar.

Like Papa promised, we had our own room, something we'd not had since Greenville. There was an iron bedstead with a store-bought mattress on top of wooden slats. I set our valise in the corner on a pile of quilts and got ready for bed. Before I switched off the light bulb hanging by a cord from the ceiling, Met's mouth had dropped open and her breathing was deep.

I lay for what seemed hours. The front door latch clicked. Clemmie was home. I heard her and Papa talking. Soon their voices got loud like something was wrong. I imagined they were discussing Met and me. Maybe Clemmie didn't like us, didn't want us here. Papa and Mama never argued. I ached for Mama, especially when things went wrong and I didn't know what to do. Mama could soothe with words, or with gentle hands that patted away the hurt. I knew she was in heaven. She told us that's where people went that loved Jesus, and Mama loved Him.

"Mama, what if Clemmie doesn't like us?" I prayed. *"What should I do?"*

"Do the best you can, honey." The voice was soft as if she were right by my bed. *"That's all a body can do."* I imagined her hands were smoothing the cotton spread beneath my chin.

"I will, Mama. I promise."

———

Papa worked the day shift from 6:00 a.m. to 6:00 p.m., and half a day on Saturday. Clemmie went in at 3:00 p.m. and worked till midnight. She slept each morning till nine, so Met and I were quiet as mice till she got up.

If Papa gave us money, we'd go to the market in Loray or Albion Grocery on Main Street and buy something to fix for supper. Papa ate anything we fixed, but Clemmie called my beef stew, "Not fit for nothing but slopping hogs." Three times a week hog farmers picked up slop from buckets hanging from posts behind the millhouses. After Papa ate a big helping of my beef stew for supper, Clemmie dumped the rest in our slop bucket.

Clemmie didn't say much and I couldn't figure what she was thinking most of the time. She didn't ask Met or me where we were going or where we'd been. She spent her time reading dime novels women at the mill passed around. Sometimes when she was gone, I'd read parts of them. The ladies in her books were rich with handsome lovers in brocade vests and lace-trimmed sleeves, sporting dark mustaches. The lovers came calling in plush coaches with liveried drivers, bouquets of flowers in hand for the beautiful, yet shy, mademoiselles. The stories made me think of songs Mama used to sing, about "Lords and Ladies in Londontown." The songs were sad. At the end someone always died and I'd cry. But Clemmie's books had happy endings. The handsome lover would kneel and beg for the lady's hand in marriage. She'd fold her fan, drop her eyes, and say "Yes." He'd sweep her into his arms and smother her with kisses. That's the part I liked.

Met and I began roaming the streets, anywhere we wanted to go. If the weather were nice, we'd stay all afternoon. On rare days when Papa gave us each a nickel to "Keep the house clean and stay outta Clemmie's way," we'd walk the mile and a half to town and see a movie show. Afterwards we'd window shop till time to go home and fix Papa's supper before he got there at six.

Mill Street was crowded with traffic to and from Loray Mill, so we'd head straight for Main Street. That's where the best shops were.

J. M. Belk Company store was so big, you could find anything you wanted.

"Belk's is my favorite store," I told Met.

"*Huh*," she said. "Mine's Efird's."

Met's favorites were always different than mine no matter what we chose. We'd eaten ice cream only a few times and I preferred vanilla.

"*Chocolate's* the best," Met claimed.

"Doreen Callaway's my very best friend since we came to Gastonia," I confided to my sister. "She's so nice."

"I hate Doreen. She's stuck up."

"All right," I proposed one lazy afternoon when our chores were done and Clemmie was sleeping. "If Efird's is your favorite store, you can go there. I'm going to Belk's. We'll meet in front of Citizens National Bank when we're ready to head home."

Papa wouldn't like letting Met out of my sight, but Papa didn't need to know. I was tired of her disagreeing and wanted to call her bluff.

Met poked her lips out. "I don't care." She marched into Efird's and I crossed the street to J. M. Belk.

I felt uneasy, like when I left my kitty-cat, Nelse, back in Waynesville. But I had no choice in that. At Belk's I strolled each aisle, breathing deep of lemon drops and lavender, feasting my eyes on lace-trimmed teddies and exotic perfumes. Clerks never asked if we needed help, knowing Met and I weren't serious shoppers. Instead they kept close watch that grimy hands weren't caressing silk dresses, or squashing plumed hats onto unwashed heads. Sometimes we got a smile, but it was surely not the rule.

Looking cost nothing so I filled my eyes with all the things I'd buy if Papa had money. That white middy blouse with matching pleated skirt—I'd take that. Trimmed with navy blue, the blouse had a hand-embroidered anchor on the left pocket. To go with it, I chose a pair of white patent shoes and white silk stockings. Topping it off, I'd have *eau de cologne* sprayed on my wrists from a silver-filigree atomizer resting on its mirrored tray.

My fantasy-shopping spree ended with a return to the lavender toiletries, where once again I filled my nostrils with the scent to carry out the door. I crossed the street to The Citizens National Bank, but Met was not in sight. I hurried into Efird's.

"No, it's mine! It's mine!"

Oh, God! There was no mistaking the shrieks. It was Met. I raced to the front of the store's office where she stood, flailing angrily. A man gripped her upper arm while she tried to pull free.

"What is it, Met? What's wrong?"

She turned away.

I looked at the man. His face was red, his waxed mustache twitching. "Who is this child?"

"She's my sister, Marietta Wright."

"Well, *Marietta* took this bracelet from our display case and tried to conceal it on her person."

He exposed her arm. High on her left arm was a jade-green bracelet, rich-looking, yet the color of one Papa bought Mama the year before she died.

"Take off that bracelet," I ordered.

"It's mine. Mama said I could have it."

"Take it off this minute, or I'm telling Papa and he'll never let us come to town again."

She pulled the bracelet off and thrust it toward the man.

He scowled and turned to me. "Young lady." He spit the words. "I want you to see that this child never again comes to Efird's unattended. Do you understand?"

"Yessir."

"Shoplifting's a serious offence. We could hold her parents responsible."

"Yessir," I repeated. "She won't come here again."

We went outside and turned toward home. A cool wind was blowing and it was starting to rain.

"Please don't tell Papa, please," Met whined. Her voice screeched like a rusty hinge, "Papa'll beat me for sure."

"I won't tell," I promised, but I knew something had to change. Mama taught us never, never take things that didn't belong to us.

In bed that night, Mama's face came clear as the day she lay peaceful in her casket in Granny's front room. I wanted to reach out and touch her soft skin.

"I'm scared, Mama, scared for Met and me, scared she'll get in trouble again and I won't know what to do."

Mama's voice was soothing as plantain leaves on a bruised knee. *"Give 'er time, honey. Met ain't but eight years old. Just you be honest and be kind, 'specially to your little sister. I'm with Jesus now and I can't be there. But don't forget the things I taught you. Recollect how we walked and talked on the trails of Utah Mountain?"*

"Yeah, Mama. I remember times like when we had to sell Cherry, our cow. She loved us so good. When that smart loving cow came traipsing home, you sent her right back to her new owner. Me and you cried and cried for our sweet pet. 'We got no claim on 'er,' you said. Is Met too young, too young to remember about Cherry? Maybe it's my fault she tried to snitch that bracelet. Or maybe it's Papa's."

I didn't know. But I knew I didn't want Met with me anymore when I went to town. I tried sneaking off, but if she caught me she'd cut such a shine I'd have to take her. Met claimed she hated Doreen Callaway. So I began planning my trips to town on pretense of going to Doreen's, though it meant walking two blocks out of the way and circling back.

Doreen stayed busy helping her mother run a boardinghouse for mill hands. I loved it at Doreen's. Such interesting people stayed there or ate supper at Mrs. Callaway's large table.

There was "Grandpa," Mrs. Callaway's father, Doreen's grandfather. He was a lay minister and often preached at Loray Missionary Baptist Church. Mainly he felt duty-bound to keep tabs on all of Mrs. Callaway's roomers, especially the single girls, giving them short sermons on sins like gossiping or staying out late. Still, on rare occasions, he might take their side with a little white fib.

Stroking his fuzzy graying beard, he'd say, "Libby," Libby was Mrs. Callaway, his daughter, "I reckon those girls got home 'fore eleven." Curfew-time at Callaway's was 11:00 p.m. "Clear as day I heard the stairs a-creaking just as the hall clock struck the hour."

No one dared dispute Grandpa's word. Since the stairs creaked when the wind blew, or thunder clapped, and lots of times for no reason at all, Grandpa figured the Lord didn't count that a lie.

Gaunt and refined Mr. Winfred Gentry who came down from Rhode Island to work at Loray mill shared the biggest room in the house with Grandpa. He slept in the very best bedstead, carved from oak by Mrs. Callaway's carpenter brother. It wasn't hard to tell Mr. Gentry was Mrs. Callaway's star boarder. His favorite corned beef and cabbage was a meal served up weekly without fail. No one complained. Hands down, Mrs. Callaway was the best cook in all of Loray Village.

Mr. Gentry had a book of "Pat and Mike" stories and knew them all by heart. In his Yankee accent they were funnier than told by anyone else. Mrs. Callaway'd heard every joke a dozen times, but she'd grab her sides and do her shrill cackle neighbors could hear two doors away.

On payday Mr. Gentry came with boxes of candy for Mrs. Callaway's parlor. "Sweets for the sweet," he'd say, and we'd wonder which *sweet thing* he meant. Other times he'd bring a new piano roll for the player piano. Doreen and I could hardly wait to gather with others to sing "In the Gloaming," or "Danny Boy," or

learn the new lyrics of "By My Side." At Mrs. Callaway's Boarding House, I'd lose all track of time.

Chapter 3

Clemmie stood over the kitchen table, ironing Papa's shirts and two muslin pinafores she wore to work. It was early June, hot and humid. Moist curls at her temples made her blonde hair look darker.

"Lordy me." She sighed, mopping her brow with the back of a hand. "Sure hope it comes up a storm soon, cools things off. Lord help, I'm purely done in."

I knew when she finished the job she'd spend the rest of her day on the porch with a big glass of tea and a fly swatter, devouring her latest novel, *October's Girl*. Papa was down at "Greasy Corner" with his Loray Mill buddies, smoking and shooting pool or whatever they did. It was his only recreation. Clemmie could complain all day long, it wouldn't make a speck of difference.

"Gets all over me how he cain't wait to get down there," she said, "like they waren't all together in the weave room an hour ago."

"How come they call it 'Greasy Corner?'" I asked her.

"Cain't say it's purely true," she said, "but an old timer bent my ear how a freight carload of lard wrecked off the siding one day. Dumped barrels of it onto that street corner in the blazing hot sun. Well, that red mud got greased up to beat the band. Say a person couldn't hardly stand up."

I pictured people slip-sliding, trying to make it into Nesbitt and Gilliam Grocery or Loray Drug.

Papa came home earlier than usual—excited, more excited than I'd seen him since he got signed up for Loray Mill. At the Corner he'd picked up a *Gastonia Gazette* with news of a big Independence Day Parade less than two weeks off.

"Gastonia's the rising star of the Piedmont," he read from the front page. "Mill owners and merchants alike are ready to let the world know it with the biggest celebration this town has ever seen."

Clemmie asked, "Ain't that a Thursday?"

"Makes no difference," Papa said. "It'll be a holiday for everybody, young and old. Says so right here in *The Gazette*. Mills'll be closed right through the weekend."

Thinking on it gave me goose bumps. A real parade, with marching bands. Met and Clemmie and me had never seen a real parade.

"*Huh*, parade ain't all," Papa said. "Says here a man'll be flying in an aeroplane, a Curtiss Biplane, going to circle this entire town." His eyes fairly danced. "Call him a 'barnstormer.' Ain't *none* of us seen nothing like that. A biplane—means it's got two wings. Well, ain't that something."

"I want to see it, Papa," I said, praying Doreen wouldn't have to work so we could go together.

"Me, too. Me, too." Met was jumping up and down. "Ain't never seen no aeroplane."

Met could spoil a good time, and I didn't want her with me, though the thought brought a pang of guilt. Mama'd say my little sister oughta come first, before any friend. Maybe Papa and Clemmie could keep Met with them that day.

"Well, now, if we wanta see the aeroplane, we gotta get up mighty early," Papa said. "Go south of town to a place called Lineberger Field. That's where this Curtiss Biplane'll be. Every John Brown and his brother'll be there. You can lay money on it."

The big day came sunny and hot. Independence Day, 1912, according to Papa, would be history-making for the city of Gastonia. "Folks'll be talking about this'n for years," he predicted.

Getting ready for the Piedmont's biggest parade ever started weeks ahead. Besides the parade and the biplane flight, there'd be a speech by Congressman E. Y. Webb of the Ninth District, then a sham battle and a baseball game in the afternoon. And something we'd waited for ever since we got to Boomtown—the running of the East/West trolley. It would cost a nickel no matter where you rode it to. But for the first runs on July 4th , rides would be *free*.

Mrs. Callaway said for something this big, Doreen's chores could wait. We grabbed each other and danced a jig while Mr. Gentry whistled "Yankee Doodle" and clapped his hands. He'd hung his flag, brought down from Rhode Island, on Mrs. Callaway's doorpost. It snapped in the wind like a whip, forcing boarders to dodge on their way up and down the steps.

"Damn Yankee and his flag," one of them complained.

Everybody at the boarding house was going to the celebration. With the mills closed they'd be off—happy to make their own beds and buy hotdogs and ice cream downtown.

It was still dark when Papa woke us up on the 4th. He wanted plenty of time so we could stop halfway to Lineberger Field and rest under some trees.

"Gonna be a scorcher," he warned. "But *Farmer's Almanac* says it'll be clear all day long. Couldn't of ordered better weather from Sears and Roebuck."

We put on straw hats and filled fruit jars with water.

Lineberger Field was marked off with ropes for folks to stand behind while the aviator got ready. His helpers checked the biplane's wings and tinkered with the engine. We could tell which one was the pilot. Hot as it was, he had on a leather jacket.

"That's him, Mr. Paul Studensky." Papa pointed to the group of men around the aeroplane. "Pilots always wear leather jackets and white scarves."

"Why, Papa?" I asked.

He didn't hesitate. "So's you'll know they're pilots."

Soon Paul Studensky strapped on his helmet and climbed to the pilot's seat where he stood and waved at us all.

"What in blazes is that funny-looking thing he's holding up?" Papa asked a man who seemed to know all about the flyer.

"It's a Japanese doll he takes on all his flights, his good luck charm," the man said.

"Well, I should say he needs one." Papa shook his head. "You'd never catch *me* in one of them contraptions."

Everybody cheered as the pilot held the doll high and kissed it. Then he strapped himself in. One of his helpers cranked the propeller to start the engine.

"That's a 75-horsepower gasoline engine," the man next to him told Papa. Papa shook his head like he couldn't believe it.

"What's that mean?" I asked.

"Same as it sounds," Papa said. "Powerful as *seventy-five horses.*"

I still didn't understand. Even with seventy-five horses pulling a wagon, it would never get off the ground. The engine sputtered and spit, then squalled like a pond full of bullfrogs. Blocks were kicked from beneath the wheels and the aeroplane started to roll. I grabbed Doreen and we clung together.

Papa held Met's hand till she pulled loose and slipped under the ropes. Before you could say *Jack Spratt* she was running down the field.

"Get that child!" a man yelled. "Somebody get her!"

"Met! Met!" I screamed. She was running toward the aeroplane. At the far end of the field the plane was circling, then headed straight at us.

Papa lifted the rope and sprinted toward Met.

"I wanta see the aeroplane," she hollered above the racket. "I wanta see! I wanta see!"

Papa grabbed her around the middle and brought her kicking and throwing a fit back to the roped area. Seconds later the sg machine approached.

"Oh God! Watch out!"

There were shouts and gasps and a few folks dropped to the ground. Others ducked as it went airborne just over our heads. The crowd, thousands now, yelled and waved.

Shaking, I covered my ears, afraid to look up. My stomach churned. Snot and hot tears squirted and ran down my face.

Doreen yanked my arm, squeezing till it hurt. "Look, S'lene, look!"

Her tangled hair streaked across her nose and mouth like strands of red licorice. She was laughing hysterically.

Folks started running the way the biplane went. Others coughed and gagged in blue smoke, strong

44 FLORA ANN SCEARCE

with the smell of burnt oil, billowing in the aeroplane's wake.

The pilot circled, dipping low, then roared back toward us.

"Look, it's a flag," somebody yelled above the commotion.

Behind the biplane streamers of red, white, and blue whipped wildly in the wind. The pilot tilted his wings like a soaring bird and waved, his white scarf flapping. The crowd clapped and cheered as he turned toward town.

Folks were scattering, bound for Main Street. It was almost parade time. Met jerked Papa's sleeve, trying to pull him ahead of the crowd. He was fit to be tied.

"Me and you won't be seeing no parade," he scolded through clenched teeth. "Me and you're heading straight home."

Met balked and started to squall, and he picked her up.

I felt sorry for Papa, but not one bit for Met. Papa'd looked forward to the big parade for weeks. Loray Mill's float would be "somethin' else," according to him.

When Mama was alive she never let Papa down. "Papa," I said. "Doreen and me'll take 'er to town. I'll hold one hand and Doreen can hold the other." It's what Mama would do. I glared at Met. "You'll be good, won't you? Promise now you'll be good."

Clemmie laughed like a hyena. She figured Met wouldn't behave.

"I'll be good," Met said. "Promise." She rubbed her tears away.

Other times Papa'd stick to what he said—take Met home and tan her hide. But I knew how much he wanted to see the parade. It wasn't right for him to miss it. Now I needed to prove Met could behave if she wanted to, just to show Clemmie.

The downtown streets were crawling with folks from Charlotte and other places. They came on the Southern, C & N-W, and the P & N trains, three or four extra coaches attached and packed to the very steps. People squeezed through windows in a hurry to get out like clowns at the fair, piling out of a car. Others were shoved from doors and just about trampled to death.

"How big would you say this crowd is?" somebody asked.

"I reckon 15, maybe 20,000."

"Oh yeah?" A man within earshot of the remark turned and faced the two. "Hey, y'all, I *live* in this town. We have 10,000 people in Gastonia alone. I guarantee they're all here today, meaning we got a good 25 to 30,000 crowd—at least."

The others just shook their heads.

Old Glory waved from every nook and cranny. Buntings, flags, and streamers draped from storefronts, and posters saying "Welcome to Gastonia, July 4th" were propped in every window.

On the sidewalks, huge blocks of ice were placed here and there to cool the concrete. Doreen, Met and me stopped at one to cool our bare feet when we caught a *rat-a-tat-tat* of drums in the distance. People surged, and a mounted policeman jerked his horse's reins.

"Stay back," he warned. "Stay back."

He guided his mount along the curb.

Papa'd told us the parade route was from Broad to Main, up Main to Loray, Loray to Franklin Avenue and on to South Street. Doreen found a spot between a lamppost and a garbage can.

"S'lene, S'lene, here's a good place."

We squeezed through to street's edge while I gripped Met's wrist like a vise. She didn't try to pull loose.

First came mounted police, clip-clopping on the paved street. Then parade marshals, waving their flags, a Battalion of North Carolina National Guards close behind. Loud bass drums gave a marching cadence as bands played martial music. I got all shivery.

"Lookee, lookee!" Met was jumping up and down so hard I could barely hold her hand. "It's Cinderella!"

A beautiful girl sat high atop a glittering gondola drawn by four seahorses each with emerald eyes. Her pale yellow hair hung to the ribboned waist of a white satin gown. A golden crown set with rubies and diamonds was on her head and she held a crimson parasol to shield her from the sun. On the gondola's bow Cupid held the red-ribboned reins of the seahorses.

On the gondola's side in bright red were the words, "TORRENCE-MORRIS CO.—DIAMONDS AND JEWELRY FOR THE SUMMER GIRL."

"She ain't Cinderella. She's the *summer girl*, Doreen said. "Ain't she prettiest thing you ever saw?"

"Almost pretty as Mary Pickford," I said, though Mary Pickford was forever while the girl in the gondola was only princess for today. Given a choice I'd rather be Mary Pickford.

Mutt and Jeff waved from a red, white, and blue float and threw sticks of candy to one side, then the other.

"I want candy. I want a piece," Met hollered, lurching.

I jerked her back and she scowled.

Gaston Loan and Trust Company's float drifted into view. Decorated like a plot of ground with a tall tree, the tree had a 'possum on a limb. The funny part was the fuzzy black dog beneath looking up, barking his head off. We laughed ourselves silly at the barking dog, wondering if he were real.

Woodmen of the World was next with a platform of giant logs. A woodman held his axe high, poised to split a log. Then came the Redman and Pocahontas Lodges in red, gold and green outfits, marching stiffly to the tune of "The Washington Post March."

Ahead the crowd started cheering wildly. Coming down the street was Loray Mill float. An artist's replica of the five-story red brick building, draped with buntings of the finest cloth made in the mill, loomed taller and bigger than any other float. Uncle Sam in a red-striped stovepipe hat sat at the very top waving the Stars and Stripes. Alongside on the street women in white aprons and men in blue shirts marched carrying wind-swept banners of red, white, and blue.

"Lo-ray, Lo-ray, Lo-ray, Lo-ray!" they shouted in unison.

It took my breath. I was hot and cold at the same time, goosebumps all over me.

"That's my favorite, that's my favorite," Met screamed into my ear.

For once we agreed. I was thrilled Papa'd seen it. It was everything he claimed. *It just had to win first place,* I thought, but next day *The Gastonia Gazette* said Modena Mill took that.

Loray Mill School got first place for school floats, so we had something to gloat about. That's where Doreen, Met, and me would be going.

Chapter 4

It was Saturday afternoon and, as usual, Papa was at Greasy Corner with his mill buddies. I didn't mind. Before leaving he'd paid me the ten cents I earned for two weeks of housework, and at The Ideal Theatre my idol, Mary Pickford, was playing in *Ramona*. That's where I planned to spend the afternoon and wasn't telling anybody, least of all my sister.

Met balanced on one foot inside the hopscotch grid she'd marked off in the soft dirt of our yard. She bent to pick up her token, a smooth piece of green glass from one of the squares. When she saw me she hesitated.

"Where you going, Sip?" She hopped to the end of the grid and landed on both feet.

She was keen as a mother fox. There was no slipping away from Marietta Wright.

"Don't call me 'Sip,'" I said.

"Where you going then, Miss High-Hat?" she came back. She blew dirt from her piece of glass and tossed it into the next square.

"I don't answer name calling," I said disgustedly.

"Where you going then, *Selena?*" She spat the words.

"If you must know, I'm going to Doreen's," though I knew Doreen couldn't leave the boardinghouse today. Saturdays were too busy; the day her mother changed all the beds and prepared the biggest meal of the week.

"Do-reen, Lo-reen, looks like a Mo-reen," Met chanted.

"You're jealous 'cause you don't even have a best friend."

"Do so."

"Don't."

"Do so!"

"Who?"

"Maggie."

"Maggie who?"

"I don't know 'er last name."

I laughed, knowing she'd made it up.

She smirked.

Today I planned to sit through the pianist's recital before the curtain went up, then stay for both movie showings. By then it would be getting late, so I'd use my second nickel to ride the trolley home. I couldn't get enough of Mary Pickford. With her big sausage curls and enormous, dark-lashed eyes, she was everything I wanted to be—beautiful, rich, famous. Men made fools of themselves vying for her attention, yet she pretended not to notice. I hoped that someday a handsome man who looked like Henry B. Walthall or

John Barrymore would notice me, so I could act like I didn't care. Of course, he would persist and I'd lower my eyes and sigh, "Well, if you must, yes, you may kiss my hand."

Between showings, *Tempus Fugit* flashed across the screen and I knew it had something to do with time passing. Still I couldn't bring myself to leave till the last show was over. When I walked outside, I was Mary Pickford, and those who saw me were thinking, *Isn't she gorgeous!* envious of my every gesture, the arch of an eye, the crook of my dainty hand.

I was shocked when I saw the streetlights were on. The sky was almost dark and a cold rain puddled on the sidewalk. I ran bareheaded to the trolley stop where passengers were scrambling to board. I gave the motorman my nickel and dropped into a seat, drying my wet arms on my skirt. The bell clanged a warning and away we went—going east. We were going the wrong way! I sat frozen for a minute, finally mustering the nerve to get up and face the motorman.

"I have to go home," I told him. "And we're going the wrong way."

"Young lady, didn't you read the card in my window? It says 'East.' When I get to the end of my run, I'll turn the card to 'West' and we'll head back your way."

"But I don't have another nickel."

"Don't worry. Just keep your seat till this car gets turned around."

I sat down wondering what Papa could be thinking with it getting so late. One and two at a time, all the passengers got off till no one was left except me and the motorman.

"Sit right there, young lady. I'll be back." The motorman opened the door and got out, disappearing into a dimly-lit diner. I waited and waited with no idea what time it was. Just as I thought he was never coming, I heard the door open. The motorman took his seat, turned the car around, clanged the bell, and headed back downtown. From there we went west toward Loray.

At the Loray stop he flung the doors open and said, "Well, little hobo, I guess this is where you and me part company."

I ran like a turkey all the way home. I could see Papa in the lighted doorway, his arms crossed over his chest. He was mad!

He sucked in air as I approached and blew it out hard. "Sip...er, *Selena Burzilla Wright,* where in hell's blazes have you been?"

"To town, Papa, to a movie show."

"That ain't where you said you'd be, meaning you lied to Clemmie and Met." He gripped his belt with both hands, but he wasn't taking it off. Not yet.

"I...I wanted to see Mary Pickford and I didn't have a nickel for Met." He knew it was a lie. I'd never been good at lying, least of all to Papa.

From his shirt pocket he pulled a folded piece of yellow paper edged in black. "Got this from John," he said. His voice caught in a choke. "Granny died."

He handed me the telegram.

⸻

Papa didn't stay mad long. Same as he used to depend on Mama, now it was me. I was the one he trusted. He'd be going to Waynesville for Granny's funeral. I wanted to go, but he couldn't afford three tickets. And Met would be a sight better off staying in Gastonia. Besides I needed to stay and keep house.

"Clemmie ain't no housekeeper," he reminded. "Place'd be a pigsty 'thout you here." His flattery always worked.

He knew how much I wanted to go and felt bad I couldn't. He knew I missed Waynesville, even if it wasn't the same without Mama and Granny. My cousins were there, and Aunt Mary and Uncle John.

I tried not to think how Granny looked last time I saw her; propped on feather pillows, limp as a rag doll. That wasn't the Granny I remembered. When I was five, we moved to a cabin on Utah Mountain less than a hundred yards from Granny's two-roomer where she raised my two cousins whose mother died. It was there she practiced her mountain medicine.

Utah folks came from miles around for Granny's help. She delivered babies, cured the grippe, and brewed herbal teas for pain. She measured doses of her potent blackberry wine for stomach ailments. Along with her "cu-ores," she dispensed advice free of charge and no one questioned her wisdom. The day a loosened log rolled down a mountain, knocking me unconscious and bruising my knee, Granny was the one who brought me to, placed poultices of plantain on my aching leg, and gave me poppyseed tea for pain.

'Tain't broke," she assured Mama. "Just bruised. She'll be all right."

Forever afterwards, I felt safe if Granny were near.

I was nine years old when Mama died, and Met barely six, but Granny was there. She helped me cope with losing the person I loved most. She taught me how to face a day, do what it took to carry on, like cooking a pot of beans to put food on the table.

"Now, Sippy," she said, showing me each step. "First thing you hafta do's pick over 'em, then wash 'em, then soak 'em overnight. If you don't *soak* them beans, you can cook 'em till the cows come home and they'll still be hard as cobblestones out on Main Street."

That was the Granny I'd miss, the one who ceased to exist on a cool October day when she went with my cousins and me to Haywood County Fair. She rode the merry-go-round and the Ferris wheel, same as us, till on the way home she fell and couldn't get up.

"What's the matter, Granny? What's the matter? Get up, Granny."

But Granny could not get up. It was a stroke, the doctor said. She never spoke again except with her dark piercing eyes. Sometimes those eyes were angry. After a life doing for others, she couldn't lift a hand. I wanted to hug her—tell her how much I loved her— but if I tried, she'd turn her head like a sulky child. Hugs and kisses had never been her way.

"Scat," she'd say. "Got no mind for such goings-on." Granny showed her love by the things she did.

After Papa left for Waynesville, I went to bed early so I could talk to Mama about Granny, settle things in my mind: *"Mama, is Granny there with you?"*

"Sure is, honey. And she's her old self, the way you remember."

I smiled into my pillow. *"I knew you loved Jesus and that's why you're with Him. But Granny never said she loved Him. So I didn't know."*

"How d'you think Granny did all them things? How d'you think she made her medicine, cured people? Jesus worked right alongside her, honey, else she couldn't of done a thing. Sure she loved Jesus. She was one of His the whole time."

"I'm so happy, Mama. Granny's with you same as old times in our cabin on Utah."

Falling asleep I felt safe and secure as when Mama warmed a soft quilt by the open fire, then wrapped it around Met and me in our feather-tick bed.

I snuggled close to Met and she stirred and mumbled, "What is it, Sip?"

"Nothing. Go back to sleep, sweet girl." I patted her cheek like Mama used to do.

Sunday dawned with sunshine flooding our window. I wanted to go out and find a place where people would care that my Granny was gone.

"Get up," I told Met. "We're going to church."

"I don't want to. I'm tired." She turned over and pulled the sheet over her head.

"Grandpa Spencer's preaching today at Loray Baptist."

"He's not my grandpa and he's not yours," came a muffled reply from beneath the covers.

"I still want to hear him, so get up."

She slid from the bed slowly and started to dress. I knew she'd rather go to church than stay home with Clemmie.

"*Ouch!*" she complained as I brushed knots from her wild, curly hair. I found a pink ribbon in our drawer and tied it around one lock.

We went to the kitchen, trying not to wake Clemmie, and ate cold biscuits spread with blackstrap molasses. Then we walked the three blocks, getting to Loray Missionary Baptist Church just as Sunday school was starting. Someone took Met's hand and led her to a class for ones her age. Doreen saw me and we found our way to a small room where ages nine through twelve met. Six of us, two boys and four girls, sat in chairs forming a semicircle in front of our teacher, Miss Glover.

"I believe we have a new person today," she told the group. "What's your name, young lady?"

"Selena, Selena Wright."

"We're happy to have you, Selena, and hope you'll come back each Sunday. Before we pray, is there someone you wish to pray for?"

"I don't know how to pray," I said. "But my Granny just died and went to be with Jesus." All eyes were on me and my voice began to shake. "I want her to know...how much I love her." I tried to hold back but tears came, hot and stinging.

Miss Glover got up and put her hand on my shoulder. "She knows, Selena. Your granny knows you love her."

She handed me a handkerchief, dainty and white, with lace around the edges. I sniffed hard, not wanting to blow my nose into something so pretty.

"Thank you," I said, dabbing my eyes and handing it back.

In church, Doreen, Met and I sat with Mrs. Callaway in the second pew from the front. That's where Mrs. Callaway always sat. Doreen was between her mother and me, and Met sat on my other side. Met kept fidgeting with a chain around her neck made of links of colored paper with Bible verses on them. All over the sanctuary, those her age were playing with their garlands, pulling them apart or trying to fix them. Met wore hers proudly, like a badge of honor.

"I made it myself," she said. "And I'm keeping it forever."

I thought of garlands of clover Mama made on Utah Mountain and placed around our necks. Met said then she'd keep hers forever. I knew she couldn't remember it—she was only three years old.

Grandpa was perched on a throne-like chair in the pulpit, till someone stood to introduce him.

"Today we're privileged to have Mr. Aaron Spencer bringing our message. Mr. Spencer's a lay preacher, a devout, dedicated man of God. Mr. Spencer, we're glad to have you preaching our sermon today."

The man held out his hand. Grandpa grabbed his hand and shook it firmly. He walked to the lectern and stood, not saying a word, just looking out at the congregation, as if waiting for something to happen. Children were fussing, especially the ones with paper chains who'd pulled them apart. Other people were coughing, whispering. Grandpa kept staring first one way, then the other. I could see his eyes above his half-glasses. They kept getting bigger. Soon children were muzzled or pulled back onto laps and pews. The coughing and whispering got quiet till it stopped altogether.

Grandpa cleared his throat loudly and opened the enormous Bible atop the lectern. He raised his right hand.

"Let us pray." His voice, deep with nasal resonance, was what God's voice must sound like.

When he got through praying, Grandpa asked everyone who had Bibles to turn to the scripture where his text was found–Romans, chapter three, verses 23 and 24.

"Everyone please stand in respect for God's Precious and Holy Word," he said. Then he read: "For all have sinned, and come short of the glory of God; being justified freely by his grace through the redemption that is in Christ Jesus."

"Please be seated." Grandpa looked from left to right and back again. "Every single one of you in this congregation today is a sinner, yes, a *sinner,* in the eyes of Almighty God." Grandpa thumped his finger on the big Bible. "That's what this scripture tells us. You think you're good? Don't matter one bit to God how good you think you are. You think you've done good things in your life? That don't make things right with Him. No, in God's eyes you're a sinner—same as that murderer sitting in his cell at Central Prison and same as that robber who broke into Nesbitt Grocery last night."

Grandpa walked from behind the lectern and stood near the edge of the high pulpit. His finger seemed to be pointing straight at me as he lowered his voice and spoke each word slowly and deliberately.

"Only the shed blood of Jesus covers sin and only trusting in Him can *you* be made right with God, and *you,* and *you,* and *you.*" He pointed his finger here and there in every direction.

When his sermon was over and the call came for those to go forward who wanted to trust Jesus, I felt pulled from my seat like a force was lifting me and guiding me to the front.

Grandpa took my hand, "Do you trust Jesus today as your Savior?" he asked.

"Yessir," I said.

"Are you asking Jesus to forgive your sins, and laying all of them at the foot of His cross?"

"Yes."

"Let's pray, child."

The following week at a service held at the creek, I was baptized along with six others.

That night when I went to bed, I told Mama all about it.

"It's all settled," I told her. *"I know I'll go to be with you when I die."*

I felt for Met's warm hand, limp and small beside my own. I squeezed it gently and held it close.

Chapter 5

Papa wasn't the old Papa anymore. And I didn't know exactly when it happened. I just knew I missed seeing my Papa laugh and have a good time the way he used to. Granny's death hurt him, but he'd known she was in bad shape.

"She'll be a heap better off going to her reward," was how he put it.

Our life in the Smokies had been hard. Fixed in memory was the morning we groped our way down a snowy mountainside, leaving everything we owned, never to see them again. Wrapped in blankets like Eskimos all we had to mark our trail was the ice-crusted rambling creek. But in the warm glow of an open fireplace at journey's end, Papa grabbed Met and me in an Irish jig to the tune of "Ole Joe Tucker." That's the Papa I missed, the one who could laugh and kick up his heels.

Papa spent more and more time at Greasy Corner. I supposed it was somehow connected to the nightly arguments he and Clemmie had. If I were awake when Clemmie got home, I strained my ears to hear what was said. All I ever caught was a word here and there—"Friggin' late," "*My own* business," "You *lousy* tramp." I didn't know what to make of it, but next morning Papa'd be gone to work as usual, and Clemmie'd get up cross as a caged 'coon dog, not saying a word to me or Met.

Clemmie wasn't one bit like Mama. I didn't expect her to be. That didn't bother me. After all, Met and I went anywhere we pleased, stayed as long as we pleased, did anything we pleased. The only exception was the time Met coaxed home two dogs of unknown breed.

We hadn't owned a dog since we left Old Blue with Granny when we moved to Greenville, South Carolina, and Mama was still alive. Met barely remembered Old Blue, but claimed she missed "her dog," and never ceased asking Papa to get her another one.

"When, Papa, when can I get a dog?"

"What'd we do with a dog, Met gal? Got no place for one. And who'd look after him?"

"I would, Papa, I would."

"*Huh.*" Papa'd drop the subject soon as he could.

Then one day in late summer Met came home carrying a puppy in her arms, with another nipping at her heels.

"Papa ain't letting you keep them dogs," I warned. "Take 'em right on back."

I was cooking a pot of navy beans for supper. It was five-thirty and Papa got off at six.

"You ain't got much time."

"They're my dogs and I'm keeping 'em."

I hated arguing with Met. She was all defiance. And she was almost big as me. Papa knew I couldn't handle her. He threatened her with his belt so many times her fear of it was gone.

"How'll you feed 'em? Where'll you keep 'em?"

"Under the house. I'll feed 'em slop same as we give the pigs." The puppies tumbled over each other and over Met's legs. "Oh, lookee, Sip. Lookee how sweet and pretty they are! C'mere, Queenie. This'n here's Queenie, and that'n's Bud."

When they saw me they perched on the back step like beggars waiting for a handout. Tiny ears went up and back, up and back, and stubby tails wagged fast as electric fans.

"They're somebody's dogs," I said, and slammed the screen door hard. But there they stood undaunted.

"They're *my* dogs," Met hollered through the door.

With that she marched in, found two hard biscuits stored in the oven, and gave one to each of the fuzzy black creatures. They gnawed and pawed till crumbs dotted the wooden steps. Then they scratched at the screen, whimpering till she went back out to play with them.

Papa'll never put up with this, I thought, and bided my time.

———

Papa ate his beans, mopping the tin plate clean with half a cold biscuit. The dogs were asleep under the house, the coolest spot to be found in late August.

Met was so quiet I wondered if Papa'd think some-thing was wrong from that alone.

He spread The *Gazette* on the table, devouring every line. The ads reminded him school was starting soon.

"Buying you each a new frock," he promised.

"Thank you, Papa," I said. Met didn't utter a word.

"See where Ole Fatty Arbuckle's playing at the Ideal," he went on, "with Mack Sennett and Alice Davenport. Love to see that'n myself."

A loud pounding at the door shook the front wall of the house. Papa's head jerked toward the racket.

"What the tarnation's that?" He got up, folded the paper, and threw it on the table. The rapping got louder. "All right! All right!"

A gravelly voice could be heard above Papa's. Someone was very angry and I caught the word *dogs*.

Papa was fuming. "What in blazes is going on?"

A frenzied yipping came from beneath the house, and Met started bawling like she'd been slapped across the face.

"They're mine!" she screamed. "Bud and Queenie are mine."

But they were not Bud and Queenie, and they were not hers. They belonged to the man who came for them. He tied each to a leash and led them down the street, while they yipped and yapped and peed here and there.

Met was fit to be tied. She threw herself on our bed and cried till she had the "snubs." Papa never threatened her with his belt. Instead he promised to get her a kitten.

"I just happen to know a fellow with a litter right ready to be weaned," he told her.

"I don't want no kitten," she screeched. "I want Bud and Queenie."

———

Loray School was located in one of the two-story mill houses with a rambling lower floor. All of us who attended walked from where we lived. Met was in second grade and I was in sixth. Fifth and sixth grades were together in the same large room where we sat three to a table facing the teacher's desk. Doreen Callaway was across the aisle from me, so we began a system of hand signals. Fingers to mouth meant lunchtime, or see you at lunchtime. Palms on our table meant wait for me, or wait for me after school. Hands clasped meant I did good, as on a test. It was fun communicating without notes the teacher could intercept. Not that I didn't like my teachers, Miss Lulu Whitesides and Miss Minnie Peeden. I liked them a lot. But if either caught you with a note, no matter what was going on, they'd stop and read it aloud to the class.

Second day of school a note signed "Nelda" was read. We all knew "Nelda" was Nelda Barkley, busybody and snitch.

"I saw Gertie kiss Billy Bradley behind a tree on the way to school," the note said. "She says he's her 'sweetheart.' Can you believe it?" Miss Whitesides arched her eyebrows as she read in a mocking falsetto.

Everyone roared with laughter and Nelda, Gertie, and Billy were teased for days. Doreen and I vowed right then we'd *never* be caught passing notes.

Miss Whitesides taught history and science, and Miss Peeden taught English and art. They were good friends and lived in Loray Hall for Single Women. All our assignments and tests were taken home where together they graded them. Soon they knew everything there was to know about each of us. Nothing was hidden from Miss Whitesides and Miss Peeden.

Doreen and I walked home on a chilly day in late October. Maple, oak and sycamore leaves sailed into our path in a walkway of gold, bright red and russet. Somewhere leaves were burning—pungent, crisp. Met lagged behind with her second-grade friends. She still "hated" Doreen and refused to walk with us. It suited me fine, since Met'd never been able to keep a secret. I could tell Doreen anything about anyone and she'd never tell. She could do the same with me. Doreen was my friend for life.

When we got to my house, Doreen said goodbye and I went inside. As always the house was quiet, but something wasn't right. Both Papa and Clemmie should've been at work. But Papa's tin cup and bowl hadn't been washed, and his and Clemmie's bedroom door was closed.

Met came in and threw her reader on the table.

"Hush," I said.

"Why?"

"I don't know. I think somebody's in the bedroom."

I tiptoed to the closed door and turned the knob slowly. Clemmie lay sprawled across the bed half-naked, her matted hair crusted with something. By the bed a pool of vomit smelled worse than hog slop. I turned away, my stomach queasy.

"What's the matter?" Met peeked through the door. "*Yeechh.*" She grabbed her nose.

Clemmie was breathing hard, wheezing sounds coming from her chest. I went to the bed and felt her forehead. It was hot and damp. Her eyes were glazed, half-open.

"What's the matter, Clemmie?" She didn't answer, just kept gasping and wheezing.

"We gotta help her," I told Met, who stood gaping just inside the door.

"What if she's got something catching?"

"We still gotta help her. Go get the mop." I got a bucket and headed to the pump to draw some water.

Clemmie seemed barely conscious as I washed her face and hair with a rag. I poured ammonia in the water bucket to mop up the puke. Together the smells were too much, and I heaved as I carried the bucket outside, retching as I dumped the vile water on the ground. I drew clean water and made a cool poultice for Clemmie's head, thinking all the while of Granny, how she always knew what to do. Granny never gagged, never got sick, no matter how messy the job. If only I could be like her, with her dried herbs and roots, her peach brandy and blackberry wine. Brandy! Yes, I thought, and opened Papa's dresser drawer for his bottle of scotch.

"Get a spoon," I told Met.

Clemmie stirred slightly and started to shake. Her teeth were chattering like a bag full of marbles.

"I'm cold...so cold." She writhed, her arms flailing about, her fingers clawing at the bedclothes.

"You'll be all right," I whispered in her ear like Granny always did. "Go get the quilt off our bed," I told Met. For the first time since we came to Gastonia, Met was doing what I said.

We wrapped the quilt around Clemmie's shoulders and she got still again. I poured a spoonful of whiskey and handed Met the bottle.

"Papa ain't gonna like this," she said.

Clemmie's mouth was open so I poured the spoonful in. She sputtered and spewed, but some of it went down.

When Papa got home he was surprised to find Met and me tending Clemmie. We'd forgotten all about supper. He felt Clemmie's forehead and pulled her eyelids back to take a look.

"I ain't no doctor, but my guess is it's typhoid," he said. "That's what's going around."

I told him about the whiskey. "It's what Granny used to do—for fevers and such."

Papa raised his eyebrows. "How much?"

"One big spoonful."

"You done alright, gal. Now you'ns go on, fix me something to eat whilst I see if I can't get a mill doctor to come, take a look at 'er." He grabbed his coat and was out the door.

By the time the doctor came, Met had set the table and I'd fried up some "streak o' lean" to eat with leftover hoecakes and molasses. It smelled so good Papa offered the doc some, but he said no, he'd already eaten. He listened to Clemmie's chest and looked in her mouth and ears, then reached in his bag and took out some big yellow pills.

"Make her take one of these three times a day soon's she starts keeping food down. It's quinine. Needs to be taken with food." He handed Papa the bottle. "Keep her in bed a week or so. Fever should be down by then. If not, let me know." He poured something over his hands that smelled like stuff they clean toilets with.

Met and I were peeking around the door frame and he spied us.

"Keep those children out of this room," he ordered. "And keep them home from school for two weeks. We don't need an epidemic in the schools."

He paused outside the door and wrote our house number in his book.

Next day before we were up a man was on our front porch nailing a sign to the post. QUARANTINE, it said in bold black letters. Beneath were the words, *Typhoid Fever,* and a warning not to enter.

Met was happy to stay home from school, but not me. I watched out the window for Doreen to come by in the afternoon.

When I saw her I tapped on the pane. "Doreen! Doreen!"

She stood in front of the steps, looking puzzled. "You sick?" I read her lips.

"No, it's Clemmie," I hollered. "Clemmie's the one that's sick." I motioned I was going to the door.

"Glad it ain't you," she said, as I opened it and peeked out.

"Tell Miss Peeden and Miss Whitesides I gotta stay home two whole weeks."

She made a face. "That's a long time."

"Can you bring my homework?"

"I'll try."

It would be a lonely two weeks without my best friend.

Chapter 6

Clemmie felt better, had started eating oatmeal and cream-of-wheat, sometimes part of a hoe-cake with cheese or apple butter. I still didn't know how to make biscuits like hers. Then ten days into the quarantine, with the warning still nailed to our front door, a man knocked, someone I'd never seen before.

"Where's Clemmie?"

"Still in the bed, she's been sick."

Clemmie hadn't dressed in real clothes, just moped around wearing the green satin kimono with shiny red fringe Papa bought her when they first got married. She lay across the bed reading pulp novels, or sat in Papa's easy chair holding our new kitten, Nelse II.

Clemmie heard the knock and was peeking around the corner. Her blonde hair was tangled and caught with a mother-of-pearl comb that used to be Mama's. I hated it Papa gave her that comb. I remembered how it looked in Mama's dark hair. Seeing it on Clemmie made me sad, like when Met tried to snitch the jade bracelet at Efird's and claim it was hers.

"Well, I do declare—look who's here, come on in, Ben!" Clemmie walked out pulling her kimono tight around her middle and retying the sash.

The man stepped inside our parlor and took his cap off. He shifted from foot to foot, pulling at the corners of his spiked moustache. He looked at Clemmie, then us, then back at her, like wondering why we all were there.

"Don't mind these here young'uns, Ben. They's my stepchildren, Selena and Marietta—home from school on account of me. Ain't that a snort?" She laughed for the first time since she got sick.

She looked at me. "Selena, this here's Ben. Ben McElroy. Works with me on the night shift." She fluffed a pillow on the settee. "Come on, Ben, sit down, sit down. How's things in the weave room?"

Met stood gawking, arms akimbo, till I grabbed her and pulled her to the kitchen. I could tell Clemmie didn't want us there. Nelse padded behind, meowing for a handout. Nelse was Met's pet, but he was afraid of her. He liked Clemmie about as much as he did me. Clemmie saved some of her oatmeal, let him eat it right out of the bowl. She'd spoiled him into thinking every trip to the kitchen meant a treat. I picked him up and put him out the back door. His ears flattened like, "How can you treat me this way?" but I closed the door anyway.

"Nelse ain't gonna like you no more, wait and see," Met said. "Already likes Clemmie best."

"I don't care," I said, and meant it. The cat wasn't mine like the first Nelse'd been. He was Papa's compromise to Met wanting a dog, yet every time she tried to pick him up, he scratched her.

"I hate that ole cat," she yelped each time. "I like dogs."

In the parlor the voices got low. I could barely make out a word here and there: "warpers...ole man Botkin...miss my honey."

"*Shhhh!*" Clemmie's kimono had fallen open and I could see one of her tits. I tried to catch her eye, signal her. But she was looking only at Ben McElroy. He moved closer, and she leaned against him, smiling like I hadn't seen her do since she came down with typhoid.

I walked back into the parlor and she scowled, grabbing her kimono top. "Selena, where's that girlfriend of yours...'Doreen,' ain't it? Where's Doreen today?"

"It's Thursday, Clemmie. Doreen's at school."

"So it is. *Heh, heh.* That old quarantine's been up a long time. How's about this, how'd you and Met like to go to Greasy Corner, or maybe Albion's, get yourself some candy?" She looked at Ben McElroy. "Got a nickel ain't you, Ben?"

He took his jacket off and felt in the pockets of his tight trousers. "Well hey, believe I got two of 'em. Yep, two whole nickels. One apiece." He held them out and Met grabbed them.

"Now one's for Selena," Clemmie said, laughing again.

I wondered why a stranger would be so generous. I had to earn every cent Papa gave me, sometimes waiting till he got paid, though I never let him forget. Now this friend of Clemmie's gives us money and we hadn't done a thing.

We got our coats and marched out, shooing Nelse to keep him from following.

"Go back, Nelse, go back." I picked the cat up and stuck him inside our front door. Clemmie and Ben were not in the parlor.

The grocery clerk was surprised to see us. "What you young'uns doing outta school?"

"We got quarantined," Met said, as if we'd won some kind of trophy. "Clemmie got typhoid and we have to stay home."

Met and I had a hard time figuring which pieces of candy we wanted with so many to choose from: peppermint sticks, suckers, licorice, horehound, caramels, gumdrops, taffy. We leaned on the glass counter, pointing first to one then another bright pile of goodies.

Met kept changing her mind. "I like cherry suckers best, no—licorice, no—purple gumdrops. How many purple gumdrops for a penny?"

Finally we made our selections and left with bulging brown sacks of candy, licking cherry suckers while window-shopping all of Greasy Corner. We saved our gumdrops and caramels and peppermint sticks to take home. Our loot would last all week.

At home the parlor was empty except for Nelse, curled in Papa's chair asleep. I figured Clemmie'd gone back to bed, so tiptoed to her bedroom to check. Ben McElroy was on the bed on his knees stark naked. Clemmie lay beneath him moaning. Before I knew what to think, Met ran to the bed.

"Get off, get off our Clemmie, get off!" She clawed at Ben McElroy.

Ben's face was sweaty and red.

"Get that *idiot* outta here!"

Clemmie's eyes were closed. She was whimpering like a puppy dog.

I ran and jerked Met away.

"Come on."

"That man's hurting Clemmie."

"He's *not* hurting her." My voice screeched through clenched teeth. "C'mon, let's get out."

I nearly dragged Met to the kitchen door, and onto the back steps.

"It's all right," I kept saying. "It's all right."

But I was shaking and couldn't stop. I sat down hard on the wooden step and started crying. A stiff wind blew at my skirt and I cradled my arms in my lap.

"What's the matter, Sippy?" Met dropped beside me on the cold step. "If it's all right, why're you crying?"

"I...I don't know. Why's Clemmie letting Ben McElroy do *that* to her."

Met put both arms around me. She hadn't hugged me that way in a long time, not since right after Mama died. Her breath on my neck was warm, felt good, like when she was a baby and I held her in my lap.

"Were they playing, Sip? Is that how grownups play?"

"Sometimes." I was thinking of Papa. Papa must *never* know about this. "Don't tell Papa, though. He wouldn't want Clemmie playing like that with another man."

"Why not? Because they're naked?"

"Yes. It's a game just for husbands and wives. That's why you must *never, never* tell Papa."

She squeezed my hand like old times when Mama was still alive, "I won't tell."

Met hadn't kept a secret since she learned to talk, but she didn't mention Clemmie and Ben McElroy again. I wondered how much she understood, though I wasn't about to ask.

Mama always knew what to explain and what not to, when it came to grownup things. What she left unsaid I mostly learned on my own—like the night Noble was born. My cousin and I were outside the door, hands cupped to our ears, while Granny midwifed for Mama. After that, no one could tell me babies were found in cabbage patches. My cousin thought Mama was dying, but I knew the baby inside her big belly couldn't come without lots of pain. When Granny finally let us in, baby Noble was all bundled up beside Mama, the sweetest, prettiest baby ever there was. Met was too young to remember any of that.

Soon's Met got to sleep that night I prayed: *"Mama, 'member how sweet baby Noble was?"*

"Honey, he's right here with me and Jesus."

"I know you and Papa were 'together.' That's how you got little Noble inside your stomach. But why would Clemmie do that with another man?"

"Lord, child, you seen too much. No woman should ever do that with someone that's not her husband. God made it one of his laws. It's in the Bible."

"Don't Clemmie know that?"

"I suppose, but Clemmie's 'loose.' She don't love your papa like she ought to. Don't worry yourself none about that. God'll work it out."

"Should I let Papa know? Should I tell him Clemmie was with Ben McElroy?"

"Your Papa knows, *honey. But don't let on you know a thing. It would hurt him to know you knew."*

Little Noble was on her lap, same as the night he died on our trip to Greenville, South Carolina—wrapped in the same white blanket, the one Aunt Ruanna knitted for him.

"Good night, Mama."

"Good night, Sippy-gal."

Chapter 7

On Monday Met and I went back to school. Miss Peeden and Miss Whitesides were happy to see us. Doreen had brought my homework assignments, so I had little catching up to do. But I started feeling puny, and by Tuesday my head was spinning like the time I smoked rabbit tobacco using one of Granny's old pipes. My stomach was upset. Before the bell rang that afternoon I knew what it was.

The quarantine was back on our door and for a week I didn't know if it were day or night. When I stopped throwing up I got shivery cold, then burning hot. I drifted in and out of sleep.

Someone was bathing my face and arms, so tender. "Mama?" She hovered like Mama, gentle and soft. Her hands were Mama's, her voice throaty and sweet. "Mama?"

"Hush," she said. "Go back to sleep." She smoothed the covers beneath my chin then kissed my cheek the way Mama did.

I tried to focus, but all I could see was dark hair pulled into a bun and the face I loved. When I woke, she cradled my head, feeding me spoonfuls of broth and I saw who it was: Mama's sister, Aunt Mary, from Waynesville. Clemmie was gone.

When the quarantine came down, Met went back to school, but my legs were skinny as sticks, too wobbly to stand on. Through my shift my ribs felt like a washboard. Papa told Aunt Mary I was "peaked as an albino 'coon."

"What time is it, Papa?"

"Why should you worry 'bout time, gal?"

"Why're you home, Papa?"

"Clemmie left us."

I wanted to ask where she'd gone and with whom, but Mama's words came clear to my mind. "God'll work that out," she'd said. I let it be.

"Is that why Aunt Mary came?" I asked Papa.

"I just couldn't handle it, gal," he said. "Mary came to help awhile, but she's got to git on back."

I remembered other times Papa couldn't handle it: the time our house burned down on Utah Mountain and we went to live with Granny, the day Mama died after childbirth and Granny took charge.

"Don't worry yourself, Jim," she told Papa. "Long as I live, these young'ns is got a place."

I remembered how Papa married Clemmie six months after Mama died. Papa always needed someone and Granny understood. Now Granny was gone, too.

"Mary's taking Met on back with her," Papa said.

"Back to Waynesville?"

"Yep. Mary's married again, living on a farm, too far from town for Met to get into trouble. You know how Met is, honey. I can't conquer her and you sure can't. Mary knows what to do with her.

I wondered. Met was almost nine. But in those nine years she'd seen more than most. What would Mama think if she were alive? Aunt Mary was more like her than anyone else on earth, so maybe it was the right thing. Aunt Mary had a hairbrush and threatened to use it when Met gave her backtalk. So far it worked. Met did what she said. Still I'd miss my little sister.

I raised my head to look at Papa. "Did Doreen bring my homework?"

"Sure did. I'd say you got a mighty good friend. That little gal came every day asking 'bout you." He laid my books, a tablet and pencil on the bed.

I blinked to clear my eyes. "Can you prop me up, Papa?"

He placed two pillows behind my back and I opened my history book. The words slithered across the pages as I strained to fetch them, then I read till my eyes refused to stay open.

⸺

As soon as I was able to get up and walk a little, Mary and Met were packed, ready to leave. Even Nelse II was in a cardboard box with airholes, ready for new life on the farm. Met didn't protest as she did with most things. She'd never liked school in Gastonia, nor her teachers. For Met and me, Waynesville had been our place of enchantment, and we'd talked of only the good times there.

Right up till Met and Aunt Mary left, Papa hadn't said much about Clemmie. But as soon as he got back from seeing them off, he was ripe to open up.

"Clemmie won't never happy here," he told me. "Didn't like her job, didn't like Gastonia." He winced. "Appears she didn't like me neither."

It hurt to hear Papa say such things. The mirror'd always been his friend and he'd stand there and preen. Women thought he was good-looking and he knew it. Now hard work and hard drinking showed on his face. His red curls were mixed with gray at the temples and he was thin as a rail. Papa was thirty-two years old. And Clemmie had left and wasn't coming back.

"Papa, I think it was mainly me and Met Clemmie didn't like."

"Nah, Selena, don't go blaming yourself. You'ns was more help to 'er than you was trouble."

"What we going to do?"

"I didn't want to bring it up whilst you was so sick, but now you're better, I got bad news. We'uns have got to get outta this house. They done sent for me at the mill office and told me so. This house is promised to a family with two workers. They give us three weeks, being you was ailing."

It was something I hadn't let myself think about. The mill had requirements for living in their houses and we no longer met them. Papa was the only one working, and he and I were not a family.

"I've thought a lot and come up with a plan. I'll move to Loray Hall for Men and you can go on over to Mrs. Callaway's Boarding House."

"You mean live there, Papa? How'll I pay?"

"I'm coming to that, and it's something you don't want to hear."

My wobbly legs gave way and I felt myself slipping to the hard kitchen floor. The linoleum was cold and gritty. My cheek rested on it and I started to bawl, harder and harder, till the wails fed on themselves and wracked my body. I couldn't stop.

Papa knelt beside me, patting my arm. "Go on, honey, cry all you need to. But, believe me, it ain't all that bad."

I felt helpless, like when Mama lay dying and I knew there was nothing I could do to keep it from happening. Maybe I should've gone with Aunt Mary, but what would I do there? Aunt Mary and Uncle Arthur had other mouths to feed. And Met was trouble enough. Soon the snubs set in, shaking me and robbing my breath.

"They'll go easy on you," Papa said, still patting my arm. "Somebody'll teach you everything you need to know. They know you ain't never worked in a cotton mill. But it ain't that bad."

Papa made it sound like something to be brave about, an adventure you go boldly into and soon have it mastered.

"And guess what," he said. "You get paid to boot! You'll have your *own money*. Won't that be nice?"

"I don't want my own money. I want to go to *school*."

Papa got quiet and drew up his long legs. His arms rested on his knees, cradling his forehead.

We stayed that way a long time. My snubs softened to hiccups, rhythmical, breaking our silence while neither of us spoke.

Finally Papa raised his head. "Sippy, you're the smartest young'n I ever did see, and I've seed lots. You won't never quit learning. You read. You write. You do numbers."

"You...you mean I know all I need to?"

"No. Nobody knows all they need to. I mean you'll *keep on* learning. You'll keep on reading, but most of all you'll keep *listening*. Ole Abe Lincoln never got proper schooling—taught himself, they say. If you can read good, ain't nobody in this world can stop you from learning."

I thought about Mama. Papa was doing the very thing she claimed he was best at—telling you what he believed and making you believe every word.

There was no use arguing. I must've seen this coming from the time we left Waynesville for Boomtown on the Charlotte line. I'd tucked it away in my mind, refusing to pull it out and look at it.

"There's a job to be had in Boomtown for every man, woman, and child," Papa had boasted about

Gastonia. Now the time had come for *this* child. And there was nothing I could do.

I sighed hard and pushed myself to a sitting position next to him. He handed me his handkerchief and I blew my nose. "Guess I'm a lot like Abe Lincoln," I said.

"Yeah?"

"Yeah. Both of us were born in log cabins."

Papa chuckled, nodding his head.

Next morning when I woke Papa was cooking fatback and eggs. He'd boiled some coffee and was drinking it black from a tin cup. A storm during the night left a large oak rain-soaked with wind-tossed branches sweeping our tin roof like tomcats on the prowl. But the eastern sky's pink glow promised the new day would be fair—a good sign, Mama always claimed. The sky told her things it told no one else, things "a body needs to take heed of."

Papa fixed me a plate. "Gotta clear out today," he said. "Best start with a rib-sticking breakfast."

I wasn't hungry, hadn't been since getting sick, but I forced myself to eat, knowing Papa was watching out the corner of his eye. He was moving into Loray Hall for Single Men and I was going to Callaway's. I loved the old boardinghouse, even dreamed of living there, but not this way—having to quit school and take a job in the mill.

We didn't need to worry about furniture. Papa owed the company store. They'd come and pick everything up soon's we got out. Papa said they couldn't wait to sell it to somebody else.

"Making money off'n us poor folks coming and going," he claimed about the mill owners. "Damn Yankees."

There was a knock at the door and Papa grunted. "Speaking o' Yankees, that'd be Mr. Winfred Gentry."

"Mr. Gentry?"

"Yep, promised he'd help get you over yonder to Mrs. Callaway's." Papa opened the door and in walked Doreen with Winfred Gentry right behind.

Mr. Gentry had on his Sunday suit: a three-piece pistol-legged pinstripe with a string necktie in a bow. He doffed his black bowler to me, then Papa, "G'morning."

Papa sized him up and down. "Well, now, loo-kee here! I didn't say we were *burying* her—er maybe you're Jewish, on your way to Beth Temple."

Papa'd met his match in Mr. Gentry, who never batted an eye. "Well, Jim, if *I'm* preaching, you're just the *sinner* I'm looking for."

Papa chuckled as he pulled an armed railback chair from the table and ordered me to sit in it.

"We're taking you for a little ride, Selena, same as how they take folks in 'Chiny.' He nudged Mr. Gentry. "Take a-holt of your side, Winfred," he told him, and they lifted my chair while I held on tight.

Doreen opened the door and out we went; down the steps, to the street, and around the corner. A few folks turned to stare at our little parade, but Papa and

Mr. Gentry stayed in lockstep, never stopping till we got to Callaway's where Doreen ran ahead to hold the door open.

Mrs. Callaway dashed from the kitchen, wiping her hands on her apron. "Come in, come right on in." Everybody was making such a fuss, I fought back tears.

"Sit 'er down anywhere." Mrs. Callaway motioned with her hands.

"They're...they're treating me like baby," I stammered. "I can walk, I'm all right." I stood up to prove it and my knees buckled. I sat back down.

Mrs. Callaway patted my arm. "Take her upstairs, let her rest awhile," she told Papa. I held on tight as they mounted the steps. Doreen pulled back the feather tick on her bed and took off my shoes. I was too exhausted to protest.

I slept three hours, they told me, before waking to piano music from the parlor. The wall-mounted clock was striking five o'clock as I slowly descended the stairs. No one was going to carry me down these familiar steps. The smell of Mrs. Callaway's corned beef and cabbage drifted throughout the house, leaving no doubt what was for supper. Mr. Gentry was "pleased as punch," where he sat at the player piano. Guided by the smells of supper, the roomers and boarders had gathered to sing along with the latest piano roll piece, Mr. Gentry's baritone and Grandpa's bass giving depth to "My Wild Irish Rose." From the kitchen Mrs. Callaway applauded loudly.

She'd spent all afternoon fixing Mr. Gentry's favorite, the once-a-week corned beef and cabbage, and no one complained at catering to her one Yankee boarder. Mr. Gentry was the perfect gentleman to her mostly female boarders and they ate it up. But his best manners, remarks, and gifts were for Mrs. Callaway. After all, she was a widow with her own business. At forty, she seemed old to me, but Papa called her "well-preserved."

My dream of living at Callaway's Boardinghouse had come true, though not the way I wanted. I'd have to pay my way by taking a job at the mill. But that was not the hard part. The mill needed workers, especially young females who were easily trained to handle the tedious work of spinning, spooling, and doffing. The hard part was leaving school. I loved Miss Whitesides and Miss Peeden. I loved reading and learning about people I'd never met and places I'd never been. Giving that up for the life I'd heard Papa and Clemmie complain about: long, hard hours, falling into bed only to get up and do the same the next day, and the next was staring me in the face.

My first night at Callaway's I waited till Doreen was breathing deeply, and beside us Etha, her younger sister, sleeping on a trundle. I couldn't pray out loud, like when lying next to Met. Doreen might rouse and hear me *talking in my sleep*. If I said I was talking to Mama, even my best friend might not understand.

"Mama, I can't go to school anymore," I whispered into my pillow.

"You'll go back someday, honey."

"But, Mama, I'll be working in the mill. I gotta work everyday and pay my own way."

"God knows how much you love learning, sweet girl. He'll find a way."

I never argued with Mama in my prayers. What she said I took for truth. In life, Mama never told me a lie. She might soften the edges of hard facts, but never outright lied, what she called "telling stories."

"Don't tell stories, Sip," she'd say. "Telling stories is a web you can get caught in, then you tell more to cover the first one and soon your word ain't worth two cents."

"Good night, Mama."

"I love you, Sippy-gal. Now go on, get yourself some sleep so's you'll get your strength back. You'll need all your strength."

Chapter 8

The following Monday I put on my best dress, one Clemmie gave me because it fit her too tight in the bodice, the one she wore when she married Papa. I thought it made me look grown-up. Navy blue dotted Swiss with white lace around the collar and sleeves, it was the longest dress I ever wore. I brushed my hair back and tied it with a ribbon so it hung in a ponytail. Papa'd warned that female workers never let their hair hang loose. It might get caught in a machine and scalp you.

I met Papa at the mill office where he introduced me to the man in charge of hiring.

"Selena's still a mite weak from a bout with typhoid," Papa told him, "but she's ready to learn. Learning don't take a whole lot out of a person."

The man eyed me suspiciously and I tried to act as if I were fine. "You able to come in tomorrow?"

"Yessir."

"Well, I'm putting you with Sudie Hailey in the spinning room. Mrs. Hailey's taught ones younger'n and smaller'n you to spin. If you do what she says you won't have a speck of trouble."

"Take her on up," he told Papa. "Show her where she'll be working. We'll expect her first thing in the morning." He wrote something in his ledger and we left.

The elevator stopped at the fifth floor. When the door opened the clatter vibrated the very boards beneath our feet. I reached for Papa's arm.

He laughed, cupping his hands to yell above the racket, "You'll get used to it."

I wondered. In the large open room row on row of machinery clattered and shook. Workers stood, walked, and reached, tending wheels and pulleys and spinning spools of thread. All I could see beyond the windows was sky and tops of trees. I'd never been up so high. I felt dizzy.

I looked where a woman stood in front of her spinning frame. Straight and tall, she wore a loose-fitting blue gingham dress. Her thick dark hair was pulled back from her face in a pompadour. She motioned us to come. When I hesitated, Papa gave me a little shove.

"Ain't gonna bite you," Mrs. Hailey hollered above the clatter of the machine. "I don't like to shut it off, not when it's running so smooth." She pointed with her toe to a pedal at the end of the machine. I understood she could stop it if need be. "Cain't never take your eyes off'n it, not for a minute. But I don't cut it off, not when it's going good." She had me reach for the very top row. "Go on, girl, see if you can reach them bobbins. I've had some that had to climb up to get to 'em."

"I might get hurt," I said, stretching toward the big white spools of thread.

She laughed. "Don't worry, girl. These machines is big, but they ain't never reached out and grabbed nobody."

"Yep, she can reach 'em," she yelled to Papa. "Now that there's half the job—keeping them bobbins in there, keeping 'em put up."

"Her name's Selena," Papa said, putting his hand on my shoulder. "You won't have a bit of trouble with Selena. She's a fast learner. She'll be here tomorrow bright and early."

"Selena'll do all right. I can tell."

I got in the elevator with Papa and he closed the door on the *clackety-clack* of machines. We didn't say anything all the way down. All I could think about was how noisy it was and how people said you got used to it.

Papa left me to go home by myself and I headed for the schoolhouse, as if a magnet had hold of me. With every step came sadness, like when Granny had her stroke and we figured she'd never walk again.

It was lunchtime and the lower grades were outdoors, clustered here and there eating, seesawing, and playing tag. Lunch pails and sacks were open on top of picnic tables. My eyes searched for Met till I remembered she was gone. I felt strange, like an intruder, yet compulsion pulled me to the open door.

Inside Miss Whitesides was entering the hallway. She looked surprised, then smiled, "Why, Selena, are you all right? We've missed you!"

I swallowed hard, words sticking in my throat. "I...I wanted to come and tell you and Miss Peeden. I...can't come back to school."

"Can't come?"

The dreaded words spewed from my mouth. "I have to go to work at the mill."

I knew she'd heard them before, many times. Loray schoolteachers understood most of us wouldn't graduate, yet they never gave up hope. And when one had to quit, they always protested.

"Oh, Selena, I hoped it would never be *you*. You're so bright, have such promise, such desire to learn. Wait here."

She went into the small room used for an office and library, and came out with two books. "I paid to have these printed," she said, handing me one of them. "It meant that much to see my work in print. There's only a few copies left and I want you to have one." *Dreamer*, it was titled, a book of poetry she'd written. "And this." She handed me the other one. "When I was your age I loved this book. We have two copies on our shelves, so I'm taking the liberty of giving you one." The book was titled, *When Knighthood Was In Flower* by Edwin Caskoden. "Like me, Selena, you're a dreamer. I think you'll enjoy this as much as I did."

"Thank you, Miss Whitesides. I'll keep them forever. I'll never forget you and Miss Peeden."

"Here, I shall autograph my poetry book." She took the thin volume and wrote inside, *To Selena: May your days be full of song, and your nights full of dreams. Lulu Whitesides.*

She added swirls and dots beneath her name.

"You're a poet as well, Selena," she went on. "I want you to always write down your thoughts. No matter where you are or what you're doing, stop and write a poem."

"Oh, I will. I promise."

She hugged me and said goodbye. Hot tears streamed down my cheeks as I hurried out. I'll never see her or Miss Peeden again, I thought. I couldn't bring myself to look back.

I walked the familiar path slowly, remembering happier times. My life had turned around. Instead of heading for the yellow clapboard house on Monroe Street, I was on my way to Callaway's Boardinghouse and a job in the mill.

It was still dark next morning when four blasts of the mill whistle jarred me awake. Sounds from the boardinghouse kitchen, the smell of bacon frying and coffee brewing, told me breakfast was well underway. Next to me Doreen was sleeping through it all.

I yanked the looped string hanging from our ceiling. Doreen turned over, squinting. In the light of the bald electric bulb, her copper-red hair frizzed around her head like a wild bird's nest. "What're you doing? It's still dark," she mumbled, one eye open.

"Have you forgot? It's my first day."

"Oh." She punched her feather pillow and plopped her head into it.

I stepped over Etha's low bed to get to our chifforobe. Etha sighed loudly and turned over. Dropping my nightgown I fastened a tight bodice around my small breasts. Over this and my cotton drawers I pulled on a muslin slip and the gingham dress Papa'd bought me for school. Even then he must've known it would be a mill dress. It was a small version of the one Mrs. Hailey wore.

Etha started to fuss. "What time is it?"

"Five o'clock."

She moaned.

"Don't worry, lazy bones. You get to sleep another two hours." She was so much like Met I wanted to cry, but no time to dwell on that. I had to get to work. The spoolers and spinning frames started promptly at 6:00 a.m., I'd been told, and if you weren't there, you got fired. I brushed my hair back and knotted it with string.

Mr. Gentry stood at the kitchen sideboard, dapper even in his blue work shirt and twill trousers. He poured himself a mug of Mrs. Callaway's strong boiled coffee along with warm milk from a pitcher, half-and-half, the way they do it in Rhode Island. Mrs. Callaway took pains Mr. Gentry's milk was always heated.

Mrs. Callaway raked scrambled eggs from a large iron skillet onto a blue willow platter. She placed the platter on the sideboard next to a stack of plates ready for those on first shift. Crisp fried side meat with milk gravy, sausage patties, grits, and hot-from-the-oven biscuits were there with homemade blackberry jam and the ever-present apple butter. I was too excited to eat. Still I had to or by ten I'd be shaky. Mama never let me leave the house without "something solid in my stomach." She'd seen me faint too many times. I spooned gravy on a half-biscuit.

"Selena Wright, you don't eat enough to keep a bird alive." Mrs. Callaway didn't miss a thing that went on at her table. "I'm fixing you two egg biscuits with some crispy-fried fatback to take with you."

"One's enough," I told her.

"Honey, I made these biscuits small." She shaped them by squeezing blobs of dough by hand and patting them into a pan, her breakfast biscuits smaller than her supper biscuits. "Two of 'em ain't that much."

No need to argue. She'd started treating me like a third daughter—may as well get used to it.

"Thank you, ma'am."

She made me take the red lunch pail left by a former boarder—a big eater, from the size of it. She scooped dried peaches from a box in the pie safe and dropped them in my bucket along with a blue checkered napkin.

The hall clock was chiming three-quarters of an hour when I waved goodbye and raced with other "first shifters" out the door. Toward the east the sun broke with shards of yellow in a sky of gray-pink. My heart raced and my knees were jelly. I wondered if I'd make it to Loray's fifth floor.

The smell of machine oil was strong when the elevator's cage swung open to the wide spinning room. Mrs. Hailey was already there, as if she'd spent the night. I wondered what time she got there. She nodded my way and beckoned me to come where she stood. Machines were starting up all over the room, vibrating the floor beneath our feet. I felt unsteady, like if I tried to walk I might fall. My throat was scratchy and I swallowed hard.

"What's the matter?" Mrs. Hailey yelled above the racket. She didn't sound the way she did when Papa was there the day before. She seemed mad about something or maybe somebody. I hoped it wasn't me.

"I'm...scared—scared I'll tear that thing up."

"How old are you, girl?"

"Thirteen."

It wasn't a *big* lie. I'd be thirteen November 10th, just six months away. Mama's voice echoed in my head: "A lie's a lie. Don't never 'tell stories.' Little stories lead to big ones."

Mrs. Hailey shook her head as if she didn't believe me. "I don't know," she said. "You might be thirteen, but I'll be John Brown if you don't look ten. I'm against children working in the mill. Got two little girls of my own and I don't want them here. No, ma'am, sure don't. Children working in the mill ain't right."

I hoped that was all she was mad about.

As the morning wore on I decided noise alone couldn't hurt me. And if I did everything the way Mrs. Hailey said, maybe I wouldn't break anything.

Besides, there were "fixers" on the floor, men whose job was to fix machines when they quit, and doffers to take off spools when they got full. Our job was to keep the threads going onto the spools. If a thread broke, it was up to us to tie the right kind of knot.

A man came by and stood watching. He motioned Mrs. Hailey over and talked directly into her ear. She nodded every now and then, and said things back in his ear.

"That's our straw-boss," she explained when he left. "He's goin' to be watching you, see when you've learned spinning good enough to start drawing wages. I 'spect it won't be long, not more'n a week or two. Whatever he thinks about your work he'll pass on to the overseer. So, keep your nose clean's my advice. You're goin' to work out all right."

The morning passed quickly and I was hungrier than I'd expected. The egg biscuits tasted good. But by mid-afternoon I was so give-out Mrs. Hailey noticed and told me to sit by the windows awhile, catch my breath where others were resting, a few hanging all the way out to grab some fresh air.

Two boys smaller than Met were sweeping floors, emptying piles into a cardboard box, dragging it along by a rope. Exhaust fans sucked air toward giant filters thick as flypaper with lint and cotton dust.

"They won't let you smoke in here," I heard a man tell another where they stood at a window. "That cotton dust'd catch fire, burn like the dickens."

The other one laughed, baring yellow gapped teeth. "I 'spect them big Yankee bosses'd be in a fix if that happened."

I wondered what he meant by "big Yankee bosses." And I wondered why some folks couldn't work much more'n an hour without needing to go where they could smoke a cigarette. Mama told me never to put one to my lips.

"Don't have nothing to do with them stinking weeds," she told Met and me, though she herself dipped snuff and I knew that was tobacco, too. Granny took her tobacco any way it came—smoked a pipe, dipped, even chewed when she could get hold of some good Bull Durham. Once Papa rolled her a cigarette and she smoked that, too.

When I got home my hair and clothes were full of lint. It was on my eyebrows, eyelashes, even in my ears! Doreen laughed at me. "Selena, you look *so* funny, like a gray-headed old lady."

I looked in the hall mirror and laughed, too. "Why do you think they call us *lintheads?*" I said. "Lots rather be a linthead than a *mountain hooger,* or a *damn Yankee.*"

She frowned at me. "Bite your tongue, Mr. Gentry'll hear!"

"Mr. Gentry's different," I said. "He's just a plain Yankee."

I was too tired to do anything except brush the lint from my hair and wash my face before suppertime. By nine I was in bed, long before Doreen or Etha. 5:00 a.m. would come too soon.

I couldn't talk to Mama out loud like I used to, not with Doreen around, so I whispered into my pillow. *"Mama, I was scared to death this morning when I got to the spinning room. But Mrs. Hailey said I did all right."* I didn't mention lying about my age.

"Sure you did, honey," Mama said. *"'Where there's a will there's a way,' and Sippy Wright'll find a way."*

"When I get paid I'll owe Mrs. Callaway three weeks' room and board, so every cent I draw goes to her."

"Mrs. Callaway's a real good woman. She'll treat you right, so don't worry none about that."

"I won't, Mama. I know she likes me." I didn't tell her Mrs. Callaway was treating me like a daughter.

"Goodnight, Sippy-gal. I love you."

"Goodnight, Mama."

Chapter 9

Three weeks later I drew my first pay. The time-keeper's book had me down making sixty cents a day. By then I was tending two spinning frames or "on two sides" we called it. My knees no longer got rubbery when I took Loray's elevator to the fifth floor. When the overseer came with our brown pay envelopes, he told me I was lucky to be making sixty cents a day. Some who'd been there longer than me were making fifty cents a day. The money in my pay envelope, $3.30, was for one week.

I took my pay to Mrs. Callaway soon as I got home. She handed me thirty cents back. "$3.00 is all you owe," she said. I didn't argue or ask her to explain. After that she charged me $2.50 a week.

Thirty cents would not only pay my way to The Ideal Theater's Saturday matinee where Mabel Normand was playing in *How Betty Won the School,* but there'd be twenty cents left toward a new dress I'd seen at Efird's. It was a "church dress," pink georgette with white ruffles in front and on the sleeves, and a sash of burgundy sateen. The price was $4.25. One dollar would "lay it away."

It felt good to have Mrs. Callaway paid up, and it felt good to have my own money to spend the way I wanted. I thought of Miss Whitesides, how she told me to write prose or poetry about everything that happened. But how could I put into words the feeling of working hard and earning my own money? Or how scared I'd been of the spinning machines?

Doreen planned to go with me to the movie-show. Mabel Normand was her absolute favorite. "She's beautiful and funny, both."

My favorite, Mary Pickford, wasn't funny, but handsome men were always madly in love with her. She teased them and kept them guessing. If I were beautiful and famous, I'd be mysterious and keep men guessing same as her.

Saturdays I worked a half-day, getting off at noon. Doreen got up early to get her chores done before the 2:00 p.m. movie time. Even so, her mother was not pleased about her leaving.

"Saturday's our biggest meal," she complained.

Mr. Gentry had spread word all over Loray, even into town, about Mrs. Callaway's topnotch cookery. Extra boarders were showing up for her famous corned beef and cabbage fare. She'd hired a woman, but needed Doreen to set tables and help with cleaning up.

"Etha knows how to set tables," Doreen argued. "I taught her myself. Selena and me'll wash dishes when we get home."

I nodded, holding my breath, glad we weren't asked to take Etha with us like I used to have to take Met.

"Guess what," Doreen said, as we headed out. "There's a new ice cream parlor on Main Street—only two doors from The Ideal—called Sweetland Ice Cream and Confectionery Parlor. Has every flavor of ice cream you can imagine."

"I'll only have twenty cents left and I'm saving that toward a new dress."

"Five cents is all it costs for a big ice cream cone."

I moaned. "How'll I ever get my dress?"

We laughed all through the movie as *Betty*, Mabel Normand, played tricks on her school's bumbling principal. When it was over we headed toward the trolley till Doreen turned blocking me, "Just a minute, S'lene, we're going to Sweetland, see what it's like."

"But you told your ma we'll do dishes."

"Hey, diddle-diddle, the dish won't run away with the spoon, not before we get home."

At Sweetland we ordered a ten cent Cherry-Berry ice cream soda with two straws. We checked out the potted palms to see if they were real, then giggled and sipped our soda at a bistro-style table lit with tiny gas lanterns. Doreen was Mabel Normand and I was Mary Pickford and, to us, this was Hollywood.

"Miss Normand, please turn this way." She posed, one hand behind her red curls, the other in the air.

Suddenly she stopped laughing. "Know what, Selena?"

It scared me when Doreen got serious. "What?"

"I'm quitting school."

"You're crazy as a bedbug! Why?"

"I don't like asking Mama for money. I want my own, like you."

"I'd rather go to school any day than have my own money."

"That's where me and you are different, Selena. I don't like school. Never have."

Dinner was underway when we got home so we slipped in the back door to the kitchen. Doreen fixed herself something to eat and we started cleaning up. Through the swinging door I glimpsed Mrs. Callaway's large oak table filled with diners. Papa was there, laughing, talking to Mr. Gentry. No one looked ready to leave, thanks to Mrs. Callaway.

"Have another biscuit," she said. "Etha, pour Mr. Gentry another cup of coffee. I just brewed a fresh pot." Etha brought plates in from the dining room sopped as clean as if they'd been washed.

One by one the guests filed to the parlor where Mr. Gentry got them singing with his latest piano roll, "By the Light of the Silvery Moon." When I walked in Papa was in a rare mood, the old papa I remembered from happier times. His tenor blended with Grandpa Spencer's bass while the female boarders sang melody.

At the end Mrs. Callaway clapped loudly. She was happiest when her guests were having a good time. She opened the chocolates Mr. Gentry had placed atop the piano's red velvet runner and passed them all around.

Papa looked well, best he had in months. Papa always seemed old because he was my papa, but at almost thirteen, I could see why women thought him attractive. Gray sideburns below his red wavy hair made him look distinguished and his blue eyes bluer. I wanted to ask about Clemmie, but hated to spoil his mood.

"Heard from Aunt Mary?" I asked.

"Just got a letter in fact," he said. "Mary's got her hands full with Met. Tangling with her 'bout going to school. Met ain't like you, honey, don't care one bit about book learning." When it dawned on him he'd hit a nerve, he looked away.

But the sting made me bold enough to ask, "Where's Clemmie now? Still at the mill?"

Papa flinched. "Nah, she quit. Gone back to Waynesville's what I hear. Had to pick that outen folks she worked with. Ain't seen hide nor hair of her, myself."

His jaw tightened. Talking about Clemmie got to him. He wasn't drinking like he had. I could tell it in his face. He'd put on weight, too. I expected Papa'd soon be all right. "Time heals all wounds," Granny would say.

I told Papa about the book Miss Whitesides gave me, *When Knighthood Was in Flower*, how I couldn't figure what she liked about it.

"It's about a princess who falls in love with a hand-some knight. Why would Miss Whitesides, old as she is, read about a princess who falls in love?"

Papa chuckled. "How old's Miss Whitesides?"

"I don't know. Older'n Mama woulda been."

Papa motioned me to a corner behind a large aspidistra plant where Mrs. Callaway had placed two stuffed chairs.

"I guess you're too young to understand, gal, but let me tell you a thing or two about women." His voice got low and he looked back over his shoulder. Women don't get too old for romance. Lookee over there."

"What?"

"Lib Callaway and Winfred Gentry. See how she's got eyes only for him? Like it ain't nobody else in the room right now but him."

Mr. Gentry was talking and Mrs. Callaway was laughing at everything he said. Papa nodded his head and smiled. "Women don't get too old to act that-away."

"Papa, something at my job's got me worried." I had Papa's ear and I needed advice. "It's Mrs. Hailey. She acts mad all the time. I try hard to please her, but I don't think she likes me."

He looked all around and narrowed his eyes. "Tain't you, honey." His words were clipped. "Tain't you Sudie's mad at. I can promise you that. Sudie Hailey's mad at the powers that be." He leaned forward as if somebody might be trying to listen. "Sudie had her heart set on a job in the weave room where I work. Most of us is men. Weaving's hard work, a sight harder'n spinning, but pays better. You know Sudie. That woman ain't afraid of work—make a damn good weaver." He struck a match and lit his pipe, puffing till it caught. "Well, Sudie marched right in and asked for that job soon's word got out, but they give it to a younger woman. Sudie's been at Loray a lot longer'n that woman."

"Why didn't they give it to Mrs. Hailey?"

"*Huh!*" Papa paused like thinking how to explain. "Well, you might call it politics," he said. "Or you might call it...well, something a man don't like to discuss with his daughter, or admit happens." He puffed hard, shifting in his seat.

"You...you mean the woman was 'good' to somebody, somebody important?"

"You might say that; 'be good to me, I'll be good to you' sorta thing."

My face flushed. I thought of the day Met and I caught Clemmie in bed with a man, a "co-worker," she claimed. I felt bad for Sudie Hailey. She was a widow with two little girls she hoped would never have to work in the mill. She needed the extra pay weavers earned.

"It ain't right," I told Papa. "Ain't right Mrs. Hailey didn't get that job." Now I was mad, too, and I didn't know who with.

"Oh, Sudie didn't just take it on the chin. No, siree. She ain't the type. Pranced right in and asked to see the big boss, the superintendent. But he let her know right off the bat he don't get involved with such stuff. Lets his overseers handle job assignments, says they 'know their workers.' I don't blame Sudie one bit, but she cain't seem to get over it, cain't leave it alone. So that's what you're up against. Like I said, honey, she's got no quarrel with you."

On Monday I tried being extra nice to Mrs. Hailey, and she seemed more cheerful, especially when she talked to the straw boss. I couldn't hear what they said, but he patted her arm and she smiled, as though something was settled and they both agreed. All day I wondered what it could be.

Next morning I got to work same time as always, but something was wrong. The spinning room was quiet except for a row of frames at the far side. Mrs. Hailey wasn't there. I looked everywhere till I spotted a fixer I knew by name.

"Hey, Freddie! Where is everybody?" Seemed funny I didn't need to yell.

"Y'mean you ain't heard?" He laughed and shook his head.

"Heard what?"

"There's a *strike* on."

"Nobody told me."

He smirked. "That's 'cause me and you ain't important. If me and you quit today it wouldn't shut nothing down."

"Mrs. Hailey ain't never missed a day of work. She's a widow, needs the money."

He cackled like I was crazy as a bedbug. "Way I hear it she's a ring leader."

———

Doreen worked third shift in the card room. She worked while I slept and I worked while she slept. We saw each other a few hours at night before she went to work. She hadn't mentioned a strike either, and I wondered if she knew. I wondered, too, if our time-keeper was striking. How'd we get paid?

I walked around wondering what to do when a bossman came, one I didn't know.

"Go on home," he said. "Ain't nothing to do right now. Come back tomorrow and we'll see if we can't get some of these frames going."

Outside picketers were carrying signs: "UNFAIR." "LONG HOURS, SHORT PAY."

One caught my eye: "MEETING TONIGHT, ALL MILLWORKERS INVITED."

"Where's that meeting at?" I asked.

"Why should you wanta know?" the man holding the sign said. "We don't want nobody there that's not with us. Scabs ain't welcome."

"I work with Sudie Hailey."

"Yeah? What does that make you?"

"A friend."

"If you're really a friend, you're welcome. Meeting's at her house, 819 Lee Street."

I wondered how much Papa knew about this. Was that why he was whispering last Saturday night?

Chapter 10

Doreen and I decided to go to the meeting on Lee Street. We'd been cooped up all day and were fit to be tied.

"I'm itching to go somewhere, anywhere." Doreen combed her frizzy hair over a rat and pulled on a black knit cloche. We got our coats and headed downstairs till Grandpa loomed in front.

"Just where're we headed?" he asked.

I looked at Doreen and she looked at me. We dared not say.

"To see a friend," Doreen said, better at lying than me. She'd never had her mouth washed out with soap. "May be a tad late getting home."

Grandpa raised his eyebrows. "*How* late?"

"'Bout ten."

He pulled out his watch and took a look. "I'll be waiting up," he said. "Don't catch cold."

We lit out in near darkness, shivering in November's early frost. Ahead a bonfire blazed in the middle of Lee Street in front of Sudie Hailey's. Sparks popped and cracked, flying skyward. People hovered around, warming their hands, laughing and chanting, "*Tyler,*

Lyler, Bootsling, Pepperwood, and Sienksing—Mills, and Ryals, and Terry—Leatherwood, and Berry."

"Hey, what's that mean?" Doreen asked one of them.

"Names of all them dirty rotten scabs." He kept chanting, "*Tyler, Lyler, Bootsling, Pepperwood, and Sienksing.*"

It was more exciting than a tent revival. We joined in. Wood was thrown on the fire and flames leaped. My face got hot and I backed away.

A crowd gathered—the fire casting shadows— ghostly, mysterious. Sudie Hailey's frame house took on an aura, like the castle in *When Knighthood Was In Flower.* Any moment Sir Charles Brandon in silver breastplate might come charging up on his white horse. "Where's Judson, the Walking Death?" he'd ask, his sword drawn, ready to lop off a head.

"*Tyler, Lyler, Bootsling, Pepperwood, and Sienksing.*"

I tugged at the sleeve of the loudest chanter, his billed cap low on his face, "Where's Mrs. Hailey?"

"You cain't go in. The house is full."

The door of the house stood open in spite of the cold. People milled around on the porch, smoking, talking loudly.

Doreen grabbed my arm. "Betcha I can get in. C'mon."

We climbed the wood steps to the banistered porch. Through the door we saw Mrs. Hailey talking to men in dark suits, like ones Grandpa wore when he preached. The spinning section boss was there, dressed in his best Sunday-go-to-meeting. I wondered where Mrs. Hailey's daughters, Ada and Kizzie, were.

Doreen pushed her way through while I clung to her coat sleeve.

"Selena!" Mrs. Hailey was making her way toward us. "I didn't expect you!"

"Me and Doreen, we...we wondered if we could help." I tried to sound as if we really cared and weren't just curious. Mama would've fussed me out. "Where's Ada and Kizzie? Doreen and me got little sisters, you know. We like keeping young'ns."

"In the bedroom, go on back." She seemed relieved somebody would check on them.

We squeezed past the men in dark suits and through an inside door. Ada and Kizzie were on their bed playing with dolls. They seemed happy to see us.

Ada was eight and Kizzie six. Both went to Loray School. We talked about Miss Whitesides and Miss Peeden, what good teachers they were.

"Miss Whitesides says I'm the best reader in the whole third grade," Ada bragged. "Want to hear me?"

"Sure," I said.

She read *Jack and the Beanstalk* from her Third Reader till Kizzie fell asleep. We pulled the covers up and tucked her in. Voices in the next room got quieter.

"*Shhhh,* stay here," I told Doreen, and cracked the door to peek.

The mantel clock showed close to ten. Mrs. Hailey, the section boss, and two men in dark suits were the only ones left. The air was heavy with cigar smoke.

"All of you have pay coming," the cigar smoker said. "After that you'll start getting food, within weeks. You can count on that—everybody who signed cards."

"What about my house? I got nowhere else to go," Mrs. Hailey said.

"They'd *never* put you out of this house," the loudest one said. "Mark my words. They know you been wronged—every one of you. They wouldn't *dare* put you out. *Hah! The Gazette*'d spread you all over their front page. We'd have 'em for sure then, right where we want 'em." He laughed.

They all laughed except Mrs. Hailey. She looked worried.

"Yes, Mrs. Hailey, you're our champion in this fight. All you gotta do's sit tight and let us do our job." He checked his clipboard and shook her hand.

Mrs. Hailey spied me. "Selena, come on in."

I went in, closing the door behind me.

"This is Selena, Selena Wright," Mrs. Hailey told the group. Each nodded. "She works with me in the spinning room, or *did*." She gave a nervous titter.

"This here's Mr. Karpov and Mr. Fremlin," she told me. You know our section boss, Mr. Kyle. Mr. Karpov and Mr. Fremlin are union organizers all the way from Massachusetts."

I didn't know what it all meant, except that something big was happening. I'd heard Papa talk about unions, how mills up north had them but mills in the south didn't, how some folks were for them and some were hot against. I figured Mrs. Hailey had the meeting because the mill bosses did her wrong.

"Doreen and me gotta go," I said when the men were gone. "It's after ten and Grandpa's waiting up. He won't go to bed till we're home."

"Thank you for staying with Ada and Kizzie," Mrs. Hailey said. "It helped me a lot."

The fire out front had dwindled to glowing ashes. Two men raked road dirt over them. "Watch out, young lady," one of them warned. "Them coals is hot as hell, burn your socks right off."

We hurried past and on home, saying little. What happened could affect us and we knew it.

"What you gonna do?" Doreen asked as we turned the corner to the boardinghouse.

"Going to work same as always," I said. "I need my job. How else can I pay my room and board?"

"Know what that makes you?"

"What?"

"A rotten scab, just like they said. Well, I'm staying home. I'm joining Mrs. Hailey. I think she's right."

With less than five hours sleep I got up next morning and ate with the ones crossing picket lines. Etha and Doreen were still asleep when I crept down to the kitchen.

Winfred Gentry was sitting in front of a plate of biscuits and white gravy. He looked surprised to see me.

"Good girl," he said. He poured warm milk into his coffee cup and added two lumps of sugar. "We'll brave the storm together. There's safety in numbers, you know."

Was he being funny? It was hard to tell. Papa said Mr. Gentry had a wry sense of humor, was wittier and funnier himself than all his "Pat and Mike" jokes put together.

Mrs. Callaway dumped a skillet of scrambled eggs onto her Blue Willow platter. Without a word she placed it on the table in front of Mr. Gentry. She didn't tell me I needed to eat, or that I ate like a bird. There were no ham or egg biscuits ready for my lunch pail. Was she sick? I'd heard the grippe was going around. Only Mr. Gentry seemed jovial as we ate.

Weeks passed and Doreen didn't go back to work. She went to Mrs. Hailey's every day, meeting Ada and Kizzie after school and walking them home. I saw her so little, it was as if I no longer had a best friend, just a person I shared a bed with. At night she stuffed cotton in her ears so I wouldn't wake her when I got up at five.

Then one Friday after a supper of salmon cakes, mashed potatoes, and turnip greens, followed by apple turnovers topped with whipped cream, Doreen came in the parlor where I was sitting.

"Guess what, Selena."

"What?"

"Sudie Hailey's going back to work."

"What are you talking about? She's a striker, a ring leader."

"She's *got* to go back. That's what she told me. First she ran out of coal and couldn't get credit. Then she ran out of food. Her pantry's empty, S'lene, I saw it. Remember the men who promised her food?"

"Yeah. I heard 'em."

"Well, they never delivered a thing. She's not putting up with it anymore. That's what she said. She's got to think about Ada and Kizzie. They have to eat."

"I cain't believe it."

"It's true. The section boss is madder'n a wet hen. Calls her a 'coward, a liar, and a fool.' Last night some of 'em stood out front of her house chanting—like they did at the meeting. Only this time it was: 'Sudie Hailey's a brown-nose clown, laughingstock all over town.'"

"But the mill bosses—they won't take her back."

"Well, they *did*. She begged 'em for her old job back. They said she could come back with the same wages as before. She'll be there Monday."

I didn't know what to think. How could she go back after all that happened? Still it was just like Sudie Hailey, putting Ada and Kizzie first. She always wanted what was best for them.

"Hey!" Doreen rattled the newspaper, jarring me from my thoughts. "*America's Sweetheart*'s playing at The Ideal tomorrow. Says so here in *The Gazette*."

"Mary Pickford?"

"Yep, in *Oh, Uncle,* with Billy Quirk and James Kirkwood."

"Who else?"

"Okay. Mabel Normand *and* Henry B. Walthall. Promise not to swoon. Henry's *mine.* Wanta go?"

"Sure."

"Sweetland after?" Doreen was back helping her mother in the boardinghouse, while I had to work a real job.

"If you can afford it, I can," I said. Trolley fare, a movie, and a trip to Sweetland was *not* something I could afford every week.

Saturday we left early to window-shop Love's, Efird's, and Belk's before movie-time. We bought our tickets and settled in our seats as the pianist played "Peg O' My Heart." Doreen looked back and elbowed me.

"What?"

"Don't let on, but sneak a look back."

"Where?"

"Three rows behind us."

Winfred Gentry was holding Miss Lulu Whitesides by the arm, helping her into a seat. He took a seat beside her.

I slumped low. "I cain't believe it," I whispered.

"Why?"

"I don't know. She's an...old maid."

"Maybe not for long."

We kept whispering, the scene behind us as interesting as the one on the screen.

"*Shhhh!*" someone warned. We piped down till the movie was over, then waited for Miss Whitesides and Mr. Gentry to leave.

"I don't think they saw us," I said.

"Well, what difference does it make?"

"But your mama, what'll *she* think?"

Doreen gave a blank look and shrugged. Either she hadn't noticed the attention her mother lavished on Winfred Gentry, or didn't know what it meant. Oh, well.

At Sweetland we got our usual Cherry-Berry ice cream soda with two straws. It was 5:30 p.m., nearly dark. A siren wailed, followed by the *clang-clang* of a fire engine as it left Main Street station. We joined others at the window as a team of horses pulled the engine, heading west. Firemen in asbestos suits stood on running boards. A smaller engine followed, with several firemen.

"A two-alarmer," someone commented. "Must be a nasty one."

We slurped our soda and ran for the trolley. "Fire's in Loray," the motorman told us as he rang his bell.

"Loray? That's where we live." I grabbed Doreen's hand. It was icy cold. I stuck both our hands in my coat pocket while neither of us said a word.

At Greasy Corner the smell was strong, like burning rags. Ahead an orange glow was ominous and smoke billowed into the night sky.

"Oh, my God! It's the boardinghouse!" Doreen panicked and lit out running.

"No!" I yelled. "Wait up! It ain't the boarding-house. It's on past."

She slowed, turning around. "How can you tell?"

"Nighttime fires look closer. In the mountains our house burnt to the ground. Miles away at Granny's, the fire looked like it was right on us."

"God, I hope you're right."

We sprinted to the boardinghouse. The fire was blocks beyond.

"Thank you, Lord Jesus." Doreen was panting, her breath misting in the cold air. "My knees, my knees are mush." We slowed down.

People streamed from the opposite direction. "Where is it?" I asked a man passing. "Where's the fire?"

Saliva glistened on his gray beard. He shook his head like it was over. "Mill house on Lee Street, wom-an name of *Sudie Hailey*."

Chapter 11

Men were shouting. Water sloshed from their buckets and ran into gullies in the street. Smoke, burning rubble, the stench of it all was too much. My stomach was churning.

"Stop, wait—I gotta sit down." I grabbed Doreen's arm as I fell to my knees.

"Selena! What's the matter?"

"I'm sick. I need to puke. Have mercy! Find out... find out if...they're okay." I cried and retched till I threw up. I couldn't quit.

Doreen ran to a group of men. One shoved her out of the way. "Get back, get back." She stood her ground and he shoved her again. "I said get the hell back or you're gonna get hurt bad!"

Doreen cursed a blue streak. "Just tell me where they are—the Haileys—where are they?"

I'd never heard Doreen use curse words before. But I knew she wouldn't leave them alone till she found out.

"Got 'er young'ns out, but that woman, she's pure crazy. Ran back in."

"*Oh, no!*" Doreen screamed the words.

"Hey, we pulled 'er out, but she's bad, *real bad*."

I stood up, my legs wobbling. Torchlights, stuck in the mud here and there, lit a path down the street. Women huddled, talking.

Doreen went where they stood. "Where's Ada and Kizzie Hailey? Y'all know where they are?"

"Mrs. Bradley took 'em, honey. You know them young'ns?"

"Yeah. They're good friends, like my sisters."

"You can go on in; the Bradleys'll be happy for you to. Them little gals lost everything they owned in this world. Ain't got nothing 'cept their dolls. Hung onto them dolls like they was real."

"Mrs. Hailey, where's she?" Doreen asked.

"Don't tell her gals but their ma's on her way to Charlotte. Doc Bennett wrapped her up hisself, sent her in his own motorcar." She shook her head. "Said she couldn't get what she needed here, so he sent her to Charlotte."

I felt too sick to talk. Mrs. Bradley made us come inside and brought me a glass of water. "Just sit awhile, child, till you get all right."

When I tried to stand up my knees buckled. Ada and Kizzie were fine—braver than me. They didn't know all that was going on, but they knew their house was burnt up and their mama hurt.

"Stay here," Doreen told me. "I'll be back."

She went to the boardinghouse and came back with Mr. Gentry. He and Doreen held me up while I stumbled home. I was embarrassed as the day I moved in, when Papa and Mr. Gentry carried me there on Papa's railback chair.

Mrs. Callaway fixed me a cup of chamomile tea, made me drink it and go straight to bed. She pulled her softest quilt around my shoulders and I thought of Mama, how she used to tuck me in.

When I was alone I talked to Mama: *"It's terrible, Mama, what happened to poor Mrs. Hailey. So awful it made me plumb sick."*

"It's evil people what did that but they'll pay, honey. God said, 'Vengeance is mine, I will repay.' Come Judgment Day they'll pay for sure."

"Mrs. Hailey's hurt bad and her little girls is got no home."

"You're too tender-hearted for your own good, Sippy-gal. Don't let all this get you down. Just learn what God wants you to learn from it. He'll take care of them young'ns same as He takes care of you. Go to sleep now, get your rest, so's you can work and pay your keep. Goodnight, sweet gal, I love you."

"I love you, Mama."

———

Mrs. Callaway asked all her friends and neighbors with children to donate clothes for Ada and Kizzie. She sent two coats Etha had outgrown to Mrs. Bradley's along with a big bowl of cooked snap-beans and half a ham.

"That poor soul ain't had nothing but bad luck," she said about Mrs. Hailey. "Pa's got the whole church praying for 'em."

On Sunday Grandpa promised damnation on those who set fires, quoting from the book of Matthew: "The angels shall come forth, and sever the wicked from among the just. And shall cast them into the furnace of fire: there shall be wailing and gnashing of teeth."

I could barely keep food down when Papa came on Saturday, Corned Beef and Cabbage Night. Mrs. Callaway fixed me a bowl of pot liquor with cornbread crumbled in it before supper and I ate it in the kitchen.

Miss Whitesides came. She was a "regular" now, Mr. Gentry's guest. Afterwards in the parlor Mr. Gentry played "By My Side," his favorite piano roll while Miss Whitesides sat close to him on the piano bench. Mrs. Callaway stayed in the kitchen. When Mr. Gentry began singing and Grandpa joined in harmonizing, Mrs. Callaway's pots and pans got noisier than ever, like a drummer gone berserk.

Papa motioned me to the alcove by the aspidistra. His voice was low, like the time he told about Mrs. Hailey complaining to the mill superintendent.

"I'm leaving Loray," he whispered, the piano all but drowning him out.

"Why?"

"I've had it with 'em, Sippy, had it up to here." He motioned like his throat was cut, the piano so loud I was reading his lips. "Damn Yankees, the lot of 'em, damn Yankee mill owners. Don't give a hoot about us workers. We ain't nothing. *Huh!* Nothing but a bunch of greenhorns and lintheads they can get rich off'n."

"Where you going?"

"Hendersonville. I'll give Loray notice all right, they won't have no complaints about me. Bosses in Hendersonville treat people right. What I hear. They're looking for workers. Reckon I'll take my chances."

Clemmie was gone, Met was gone, now Papa was leaving for Hendersonville. Where would I be without Doreen, Mrs. Callaway, and Grandpa? They meant more to me now than ever.

A week later Papa took the train for Hendersonville. The same day it was official between Mr. Gentry and Miss Whitesides. They set a date of Saturday, May 17, 1913, at 10:00 a.m. for their wedding in Gastonia's Presbyterian Church. Grandpa felt a little cheated not being asked to perform the ceremony for his roommate of two years, but Mr. Gentry's bride-to-be was a Presbyterian.

Miss Whitesides looked different than she did when I was at Loray School. Her hair was tangled into a pouf, with a curl in front of each ear. Sometimes she wore a pearl headband like Mabel Normand's in *The Fatal Chocolate*, with Mack Sennett. Was Winfred Gentry her Sir Charles Brandon, coming to whisk her away to a castle like Princess Mary in *When Knighthood Was In Flower?*

That night I read from the book of poetry Miss Whitesides had written:

Farewell My Love

The setting sun dripped blood red
Into the shining sea
And, flying by, the seagulls screamed
As if they wept for me.
It was our last farewell, my love,
The day we had to part.
Now all I have left of you
Is buried in my heart.

Had she written this for a lover she once had? If so, now she could write a happier one.

———

Early in April, a short plump woman with a thick German accent checked into the Armington Hotel near the train station. The desk clerk told Grandpa she'd come in on the P & N Railway. Said his eyes like to've popped out when she registered as Mrs. Winfred Gentry.

The woman calling herself Mrs. Winfred Gentry claimed she and Mr. Gentry lived together for twelve years before he came to work at Loray Mill. Since then she'd waited, expecting he'd send for her.

Two days after the strange news came out, Miss Whitesides called off her engagement to Mr. Gentry and canceled their wedding plans.

Mr. Gentry made no explanation, but Grandpa informed all curious to know that, in Rhode Island, common law marriage was treated same as the regular kind. Mr. Gentry gave three days' notice at the mill, checked out of Callaway's Boardinghouse, and he and his common law wife left for Rhode Island on the B & O before we could properly say goodbye.

Losing Mr. Gentry was the furthest thing from the minds of us boardinghouse girls. Saturday nights wouldn't be the same. Harmonizing at the player piano with Grandpa, telling Pat and Mike jokes in his clipped Yankee accent were things that made after-work hours something to look forward to. I felt sad, not sad as when Granny died or Clemmie left, but sad like if Doreen were no longer my best friend or I'd never see another Mary Pickford movie.

Mrs. Callaway's eyes stayed red-rimmed for days. She claimed she had a touch of pink-eye, but most of us knew better. Mr. Gentry was her perfect gentleman boarder, the sole reason for Corned Beef and Cabbage Night.

No one was privy to how Miss Whitesides took it. I could only imagine. I pure ached to go to her, but what would I say?

The night Mr. Gentry left I sat in bed with the book of poetry Miss Whitesides wrote propped on my knees. "Write, Selena," she'd said when she gave me the volume, "write about things you see, things that happen to you." Did "Farewell My Love" happen to her? It seemed prophetic:

> It was our last farewell, my love,
> The day we had to part.
> Now all I have left of you
> Is buried in my heart.

Would she write another poem, more poignant than "Farewell My Love?" Or would she never write again?

I closed the book and turned out the light. Tears came hot on my pillow: *"Mama."* (Not aloud since Doreen was still stirring.) *"Mama, Miss Whitesides is hurting. What can I do?"*

"Cain't nobody do nothing, Sippy-gal. That kinda hurt takes lots of time."

"But why?" Why would Mr. Gentry do such a thing? He was a good man and I liked him so much."

"Men don't think same as women, honey, you'll find that out soon enough. I reckon he loved Miss Whitesides, but it's best she found him out before the vows. Now go on, get your sleep."

Two weeks after Mr. Gentry left, Miss Whitesides was back at Loray School. Etha said it was as though nothing had ever happened. The ring and the make-up were gone. Her hair was back in a bun. She never mentioned what happened or spoke the name *Winfred Gentry* to anyone.

Chapter 12

On Saturday Grandpa rushed around, puffing his pipe like a full-throttle steam engine, his self-appointed task of keeping tabs at a high. All day it was: "Where you going, Alma? When'll you be back?" and "Lucille, you'll be here for Corned Beef and Cabbage, won't you? Don't forget now."

He bought a box of chocolates and opened it atop the piano, like Mr. Gentry used to do. Nobody could bring themselves to eat the sad reminders. Doreen and I waited till Grandpa was down at Greasy Corner on an errand, and we sneaked out the back door to catch the trolley.

"I got a feeling we better be back for supper," Doreen said as we rumbled along. "Something's up."

America's Sweetheart was at The Ideal in *Ramona* with Henry B. Walthall and Kate Bruce. We cried when *Alessandro* took *Ramona* in his arms and stole away with her during the night. We cried harder when *Alessandro* got killed, till Doreen gave me a sidelong look.

"Selena, honey, it's *only* a movie." She got out a hankie and blew her nose hard.

Something about the way she blew it made me snicker, and she laughed at me snickering. Once we got started we couldn't quit. People were staring at us. "*Shhhh*," one of them hissed. Another gave us a sign. When an usher came down the aisle, we stifled ourselves into hiccups.

"*Ramona*—all that really happened, didn't it?" I said when it was over and we were heading out the door. "I mean it's a true story, ain't it?"

"I don't know," she said. "But, for sure it didn't happen to *Mary Pickford*. She's only a movie star, S'lene." Her favorite was Mabel Normand and she never let me forget it.

"Mary Pickford's not just *any* movie star. She makes it all seem real. There's a book about *Ramona*. I want to get it and read the whole story."

"Well, you can't today. Got no time for the library." She pulled me toward the trolley stop. "Grandpa'll kill us if we're not home for Corned Beef and Cabbage."

Ramona and *Alessandro* hung on us like a pall till we clanged into Greasy Corner. From a block away we saw people crowded on our porch.

Doreen squealed. "It's Ada, Ada and Kizzie Hailey. She started running. "Ada, Ada!"

We ran and hugged Ada, then Kizzie.

"Mama's here, Mama's here!" Kizzie was jumping up and down. "She's in the house! Come on!"

We went to the parlor where others were sitting, talking excitedly. I barely recognized Mrs. Hailey. She had on glasses and her hair was streaked with gray. She was skinny as Granny before she died.

Mrs. Hailey wrapped us both in her arms. "Oh, Selena, Doreen! I do declare!" When she patted my face I caught sight of her hands. Parts of fingers were missing, her hands and forearms scarred. I tried not to stare.

"It's...it's so good you're back," I stuttered.

"Oh honey, you don't *know* how glad I am to be back. I've missed my girls something awful."

Kizzie hugged her mama tight as if nobody would ever take her away again.

"Lord knows I cain't thank everybody enough for all you've done for me and them." Mrs. Hailey's eyes were rimmed with tears. "My girls has been looked after so good." She wiped her eyes with finger stubs.

"I hate to see big girls cry," Grandpa bellowed, opening the piano. He put in a brand new roll and sat down. "Time we all learned a new one. Gather 'round, now don't be shy!" His bass voice picked out the words from the sheet music. The rest of us joined in:

NEW WIFE

She was only three weeks from Ireland,
Ignorant as she could be.
She seemed good-natured and willing,
And I thought we could agree.
So I took her into the kitchen,
To her everything was strange.

She didn't know how the pump worked,
And she'd never seen a range.

Grandpa knew how to get folks laughing. We sang till Mrs. Callaway rang the dinner bell.

When all were seated Grandpa cleared his throat to get attention, "Today we're not only praying for God's blessings on this food and the hands that prepared it, but we're earnestly thanking Him for healing Sudie Hailey and watching over her two little girls." He told us all to hold hands around the table, forming a *circle of love*. "There's spiritual power when we're all 'of one accord.'" He prayed twice as long as usual.

I was thankful for Mrs. Hailey and Ada and Kizzie, but the smell of corned beef and cabbage brought memories of Mr. Gentry—how he helped Papa carry me to Callaway's Boardinghouse when I was too sick to walk, how he loved the Fourth of July and flying the flag, his perfect table manners. He was dashing, yet gentle, like *Alessandro* in *Ramona*. He treated all women with respect like Sir Charles Brandon in *When Knighthood Was In Flower*—only Sir Charles was not real and Winfred Gentry was. Next to Papa and Grandpa Spencer, the man I admired most in life was Winfred Gentry. While Grandpa was praying over the food, I prayed Mr. Gentry would be happy in Rhode Island with his common law wife.

After the meal a loud rapping at the front door made Grandpa scratch his balding gray head. "Now, who could that be?" He got up and shuffled through the parlor. "Come in, come in, Shorty, come in, boys," he shouted loud enough to be heard all the way into the dining room.

It was Shorty Lowe and his "Fiddlin' Fools," as they called themselves: two fiddlers, one bass, a banjo player, and Shorty himself on the guitar. Grandpa pretended they happened to be in the neighborhood. Most of us knew they went where they got paid.

They started with "Cripple Creek." Grandpa stomped his foot and clapped his hands, and motioned for the rest of us to do the same.

"Libby, let's see if we can get the parlor rug rolled back," he told Mrs. Callaway. "If somebody's got the urge to dance I ain't about to stand in their way."

Grandpa was a Baptist lay preacher and *never before* had I heard him mention dancing.

Doreen grabbed Ada. "Come on, Ada, let's show 'em how."

I pulled Kizzie from her mama's lap. "Let's you and me do a jig." She clapped her hands while I did one of Papa's Irish jigs around her.

Grandpa's curfew came and went and nobody said a word. This was *his* party and we were having lots of fun. Near midnight Etha, Ada and Kizzie and a few adults had gone to bed when Grandpa told Shorty to play a final number. "Y'all wanta hear more of the Fiddlin' Fools?"

"Yeah," everybody shouted.

"Then come to Loray Baptist Church tomorrow at eleven o'clock. They're playing my favorite, "Shall

We Gather At The River," and a whole bunch more. I want you all to be there. If this old gray head can make it, you can, too."

We figured Grandpa wasn't through with us. And when he expected something, we usually did it. Except for Doreen. His own granddaughter got a kick out of challenging his authority.

"Maybe I will, maybe I won't," she whispered as we climbed the stairs.

Soon as Doreen was asleep, I shared it all with Mama, *"Grandpa helped me forget Mr. Gentry, but I know he misses him too."*

"Grandpa Spencer's got a mighty big heart," she said from heaven.

"Poor Mrs. Hailey, her hands are so scarred. She won't never be able to work in the mill. She can't spool or spin. Can't weave, can't even sweep."

"Sudie Hailey'll be all right. God saved her from a fiery death. He'll take care of her and them gals."

"How do you know?"

"Jesus told me. He's right here, honey."

"I love you, Mama."

What Grandpa failed to say was that *he* was filling the pulpit on Sunday morning at Loray Missionary Baptist Church. Yet somehow word had spread over town that Sudie Hailey was back and would be Sunday's sermon topic. The grapevine began as it often did at Greasy Corner, and fanned to the fashionable Armington Hotel where the elite gathered to eat pie *a la mode* and plan social moves.

Grandpa was known for speaking his mind and stepping on toes and there were those who ate that up. Others showed up when he preached to make sure their toes weren't the ones that got stomped. But the Fiddlin' Fools' *Free Appearance* handbills tacked to miles of telephone poles got the attention of saints and sinners alike, and by ten-thirty there was standing room only at Loray Missionary Baptist Church.

Members from First Presbyterian Church on Marietta Street, curious enough to trade padded pews for wooden benches for one Sunday only, crept in. A few Episcopalians jammed against Holy Trinity Lutherans on folding chairs hastily set up in back.

Mrs. Callaway sat three rows from the front, her usual pew, white straw hat masking her eyes as she craned to survey the crowd.

"Look there." She punched Doreen, who'd changed her mind about coming when boarders all came down to breakfast in their Sunday go-to-meeting clothes.

"What?"

"I declare if it ain't Mayor Armstrong. What's going on? Now don't stare!"

The sanctuary bustled like a train depot as the Fiddlin' Fools tuned up. "On Jordan's Stormy Banks" got things going followed by what Shorty introduced as Robert E. Lee's favorite, "How Firm A Foundation."

Hand-clapping busted out all over the congregation, and swaying, but no foot stomping. Grandpa and the preacher didn't stand for foot stomping in church—dancing could be next. I wondered what the Presbyterians and Episcopalians were thinking about clapping hands and swaying.

"Shall We Gather At The River," Grandpa's choice, was followed by the Fools' finale—"Church In The Wildwood," Papa's favorite. My eyes smarted with tears. Since he'd moved to Hendersonville, I missed my papa more than I'd expected.

The mayor and an alderman sat stiffly. This was obviously not their cup of tea, nor why they came.

The preacher sprang from his ornate chair to thank the Fiddlin' Fools.

"Folks, let's give the Lord a big clap offering."

Shorty and his group took bows to hearty applause and seemed ready for an encore till the preacher lifted his hand heavenward.

"Almighty God..." he began.

I sneaked a peak at the mayor who never bowed his head, just looked around during the prayer.

"Amen and amen!" the preacher shouted at the end as if God might be hard of hearing. Amens echoed here and there as he turned to Grandpa. "Mr. Aaron Spencer, revered lay minister of the Gospel, a man you all know well, will bring today's message...Mr. Aaron Spencer."

Grandpa stood, shook the preacher's hand, and approached the lectern. His white beard and thin gray hair were combed to perfection. He looked like the picture of God I'd seen on memory verse cards, except

God wore white robes and Grandpa had on his brand new, three-piece black pinstripe suit.

Grandpa scanned the congregation, something he always did, as if searching for some special person, making sure they were present before opening his mouth. Hymnbooks fell into racks. There was coughing, throat clearing. Grandpa waited, like he didn't care how long it took. A final hymnbook plopped and one last cough was stifled. Then, silence.

"Let's bow again for prayer." Grandpa intoned the words as if everything that followed would hinge on this one petition. "Great God of all life..." he began.

I sneaked another look at the mayor. His head was bowed this time.

The deacons and a few brethren echoed Grandpa's "Amen." He cleared his throat and opened his worn black leather Bible. "In case some of you forgot your Bibles," he said indulgently, "you'll find one in your pew rack. Turn in God's Word to the book of Daniel, chapter three."

He waited patiently for the final shuffling and fluttering of pages.

"I don't preach on this text often, but you'll soon see why it's in God's Word, why it begs to be preached on today." He laid his open Bible on the lectern and walked to the front of the pulpit.

"First I want to talk about a lady going all over our country today, telling her story—how she was delivered from a watery grave in the depths of the ocean—a woman, the name of Molly Brown. Molly Brown, by her own words, was 'unsinkable' when that mighty ship, the *Titanic,* sank in the icy deep. Yes, beloved brothers and sisters, Molly Brown was tried in those murky waters and spared. Though a thousand people died, *she* was spared, spared to help others. Now Molly Brown is hailed as a hero."

Grandpa went back and picked up his Bible. "Let's take a look at what God's word says about heroes."

He read from Daniel, chapter three, about how King Nebuchadnezzar fashioned a golden image of himself and commanded everybody to bow down to it.

"Verse eleven says, 'And whoso falleth not down and worshippeth, he should be cast into the midst of a burning fiery furnace.'"

Grandpa stopped and looked up as if expecting the congregation to respond to the words. Neither a cough nor a shuffle was heard.

"We'll see what happens...verse twelve. Nebuchanezzar's men come back and report to him: 'There are certain Jews whom thou hast set over the affairs of the province of Babylon—Shadrach, Meshach, and Abednego; these men, O king, have not regarded thee: they serve not thy gods, nor worship the golden image, which thou has set up.'

"These three young men would not kneel down to an idol. Why? Because they trusted and worshiped the one *true* God. This troubled old Nebuchadnezzar and he warned them, but verse seventeen says they answered: 'Our God is able to deliver us from the burning fiery furnace, and will deliver us out of thine hand, O king.'

"God's word says Nebuchadnezzar's men got that flaming fire so hot the ones who stoked it got burned alive. Yes, burned alive by *their own hand*. Nebuchadnezzar was 'astonished,' the Word says, had to go take a look for himself. 'Did not we cast three men bound into the midst of the fire?' he asked.

"'They answered, True, O King.' Then verse twenty-five, 'He answered, Lo I see four men loose, walking in the midst of the fire and they have no hurt; and the form of the fourth is like the Son of God.'

"What does the king do? He shouts, 'Shadrach, Meshach and Abednego, ye servants of the most high God, come forth,' and the three of them walked right out of that fire! The king decreed that they and their nation would be 'forever spared.' God was that fourth man Nebuchadnezzar saw walking with them in the fire. God spared them to tell their story for all time.

"Molly Brown was spared from the mighty *Titanic's* watery grave, spared to tell her story to the world. But, beloved friends, listen to me: there's a woman right here in our midst today who's been tried in a *fiery furnace stoked by cowards*, yet God spared her! Like Shadrach, Meshach, and Abednego, God *was right there with her* as she saved her little ones from a fiery death, spared her so her story could be told today. Sudie Hailey, come on up here. Come up where everybody can see you."

Sudie Hailey whispered something to Ada and Kizzie. Then she got up from the pew in front of us and made her way up the steps to the pulpit. People were whispering, stretching, craning necks.

Grandpa took one of her scarred hands in his, looked at it, then held it up for everybody to see.

"Cowards did this," he said, gently patting her hand.

He stared at the congregation, from one end to the other. "Friends, I believe those cowards are here today. Yes, I'm talking about *you* who set Sudie Hailey's house on fire. I believe you're sitting in our midst, and I'm asking you to come on down right here and now and confess. I'm giving you a chance to beg this brave woman's forgiveness, make things right before God and before her."

He waited. No one moved, as if hypnosis had set in on the entire congregation.

Grandpa kept looking this way and that. "If you're still as cowardly as you were that night, then, mark my words, God will take care of you. Sin must be dealt with—His Word promises that. Justice will come, if not in this life, then surely in the next."

He motioned for Mrs. Hailey to go back to her seat.

A commotion erupted in back.

"That's all right, that's all right," Grandpa said as ushers escorted someone out.

Grandpa's voice got friendly-like, "As I look out amongst you, I see familiar faces and some that ain't.

I see Mr. R. B. Babington, alderman, and our distinguished mayor, Colonel C. B. Armstrong. Welcome, gentlemen. I hope y'all will come back next Sunday."

There was muffled laughter and a few near-hisses. Grandpa got a kick out of keeping the flock in the palm of his hand.

Those named stood briefly in turn, nodding this way and that, but neither said a word about why they'd come to Loray Missionary Baptist Church on this particular day.

———

"What was that all about, Papa?" Mrs. Callaway asked at supper that evening.

Grandpa chuckled. "All about timing, my dear, all about candidate-filing time. They think I might run for alderman."

"Well?"

"Can't rightly say, Libby. The Lord'll let me know when and if He wants me to quit trying to please Him and start trying to please the populace. Don't think that time's come yet."

After supper on Tuesday, Grandpa sat reading *The Gastonia Gazette* when he cleared his throat loudly. "Listen to this:

AN ATTEMPTED SUICIDE.

J.D. Newell, a young White Man drinks contents of ounce bottle of laudanum here Sunday night. He was rushed to City Hospital where medical aid was given. At last accounts he is on a fair road to recovery."

No one said anything, waiting to see what Grandpa made of it.

"I'm thinking the time might be right for a certain young fellow to get a thing or two off his chest." He nodded his head. "Yep, I'll be making a hospital visit tonight."

Chapter 13

Mrs. Callaway paced the parlor floor. "Papa ain't been out this late in years." She kept parting the lace curtains to take a look.

"What could happen?" Doreen said. "Everybody knows Grandpa. Nobody's going to bother him."

"Papa's got enemies. He talks too much—always has. Won't stay outta things." She pulled back a lace panel. "Lord help!"

"What?" Doreen and I ran to the window.

The porch light reflected on white letters of a police wagon. Grandpa got out, talked briefly to the driver and came up the steps.

Inside he flopped into his favorite chair and pulled out his pipe.

"Where've you been?" Mrs. Callaway stood over him like a mother fussing at a willful child.

"Stay calm, stay calm now, Libby. Let me sit here and rest a while, gather my wits."

He lit his pipe, sucking it like a peppermint stick, and settled back. His breathing got easier as bit by bit he told how he persuaded J.D. Newell to confess to setting Sudie Hailey's house on fire, how he got him to repent and ask God's forgiveness.

"Called the police to him, Libby. Had no choice. Arson's a felony. That troubled young man'll do time. No doubt about it. There's others involved. J.D.'s co-operating. That'll help." Cherry-scented smoke ringed his head.

"Who else, Grandpa?" Doreen was heating up.

"Well, it won't be secret, not for long. *Gazette* reporter was already there at the station. The spinning section boss, for one, Mr. Finley Kyle. J.D. said Kyle gave him money for kerosene and cans to use. I expect there'll be others."

"Mr. Kyle talked to Mrs. Hailey in the mill before the striker's met," I said. "I saw him at her house with union organizers. Oh my goodness, Doreen, so were we."

"We never signed," Doreen said. "Never put our names on nothing."

Still I felt like a criminal, like somehow we were involved.

"Poor Mrs. Hailey," I said. "It all started when the mill bosses wouldn't give her that weave room job. All goes back to them."

Grandpa shook his head, sucking his pipe all the while like priming a pump, "Nah, Selena, uh-uh. Started way 'fore that. Started when Loray Mill was bought and paid for with Yankee money and—mark my words—worse things than this'll happen 'fore it's over."

Three weeks after Sudie Hailey went back to Charlotte with Ada and Kizzie, Mrs. Callaway got a letter from her and passed it around for everyone to read.

We're living with relatives, the letter said, *but hope not for long. The girls are in school, and I'm working as an aide in the hospital where I spent all those weeks recuperating. These people know me well. My hands may be scarred, but they trust me to work with the sick and dying.*

I cried when I read it. "They can depend on Mrs. Hailey," I told Mrs. Callaway. "She'll give them her best. It's the way she is. She taught me that at the mill."

That night I could hardly wait to talk with Mama, *"Mama, Mrs. Hailey don't need to work in no mill. She's got a job helping people hurting same as her."*

"You done learned the best lesson in the world, Sippy-Gal. No amount of schooling could teach you what you learned from Sudie Hailey. Life's hard, but God's on His throne. He takes the broken pieces and puts 'em back together so they're better'n ever."

"God's right there, Mama, on His throne?"

"I'm sitting here right now looking up at Him."

"What does He look like?"

"Member how the evening sun looked in the mountains when we saw the rays from our cabin, how it just

about took our breath away till it fell beyond the gorge?
God's like that, only his light don't never set."

⎯⎯⎯⎯⎯

The boardinghouse parlor was the best place in Loray
for a meeting. Mrs. Callaway made sure there were
treats to be served: lemonade or cider, Jeff Davis tarts
and Black Walnut fudge. Grandpa claimed Baptists
weren't about to meet without something to eat. He
and the preacher had a plan and needed our help.

"We need a playground behind the church," he
said, "but it takes money. That's where you girls come
in." He looked at Doreen and me, then at the other
female roomers. "Thought we'd have a box supper."

Doreen screwed up her face. "You mean *sell boxes*.
Who'd buy what I fix? I cain't cook."

"That's where your mama comes in. Libby's the
best cook in Loray. She'll help fix boxes."

The boxes would not be sold, but *auctioned* to the
highest bidder, and the girl whose box was sold would
share the meal with the bidder. We looked at each
other. It was like paying to spend time with someone
of the opposite sex, but if Grandpa didn't see it that
way, it must be all right.

A date was set for Saturday, October 10th at Loray School since the church "should not be used for
buying and selling." We had time to talk it up, get as
many girls as possible involved and let as many *boys*
as possible know, so they could save up their money.

Getting the chance to spend time with the girl they admired most was the key.

When word got to the Loray Mill bosses, they donated $100 and printed up flyers. It was getting bigger than we ever imagined.

"The prettiest girls'll make all the money," Doreen complained. "I'm not exactly Mabel Normand and you're not Mary Pickford."

"So? We can work on it."

"What d'you mean?"

"I mean we got time."

"My hair's red and curly and ain't a thing can be done about it." She tucked in straggles of red hair that strayed from her bun and frizzed over her ears.

"Get a bob, a 'Mabel Normand' bob. She's your idol. You always wanted to look like 'er."

She glared like I was a nut case. "Easy for you to say, S'lene. You don't have a mama telling you what you can do and not do." She knew it stung soon as she said it. "I mean, what'll Mama say?"

"Don't ask. Just do it."

"Can you cut it?"

"Get Lucille, she's real good. Wants to be a beautician. Lucille cuts hair all the time, does it for nothing, just for practice."

Haircuts were the first step of our make-ourselves-beautiful-in-four-weeks plan. Doreen spent a week's wages for a beaded headband for her bob. The headband pressed her red frizz tightly against her temples. She plucked her straggly brows and penciled them into long thin arches, then outlined her dark eyes so they looked enormous.

"You're *her*," I said. "You're Mabel, I swear it."

"You look like a harlot," her mother said, but didn't act too mad, just irked she wasn't asked about it.

Mrs. Callaway hardly noticed the changes in me. If so, she didn't say anything.

My hair stayed in a bun all day, required for women millhands. But when I got home I took out the pins and let it fall to my shoulders. I combed out the lint with a fine-toothed comb and finger-waved the top. The ends I twisted into ringlets, and tied them in place with rags. Sunday mornings I shaped them into sausage curls like Mary Pickford's, powdered my face white and outlined my green eyes with brown. We were getting noticed.

"Looking mighty growed-up," the straw boss commented. "Just keep your mind on your work's what I say. This ain't no social club."

The doffers and fixers smiled when they caught my penciled eye.

Freddie yelled, "Hey, S'lene, got a fella? If you ain't, hows 'bout me?"

I ignored him. Freddie was the last person I'd go out with. *Henry B. Walthall* he was *not*.

Saturday night at Sweetland, Doreen and I had just ordered our Cherry-Berry ice cream soda with two straws, when in came two men, fancy-dressed, olive-skinned, one with a dark mustache. They sat at the table next to ours. We tried to ignore them, but they kept staring.

The clean-shaven one finally spoke up, "You regular customers here?" His clipped accent made me think of Winfred Gentry.

Doreen smiled, "Yeah–every Saturday night since they opened."

I kicked her ankle. "*Ow*," she said, keeping the smile on her face.

I slurped, glaring at her, but she didn't take the hint.

"This is Selena, Selena Wright. I'm Doreen Callaway," Doreen said, as if they might want our autographs next.

"We're new in town," one said. "I'm Sol Green and this is Abe Goldman. We rented a store across the street. Maybe you'd like to go over, take a look."

"Sure," Doreen said. "Sure we would. What do you say, S'lene?"

I was slurping bubbles at the bottom of the glass, not believing what I heard. "We gotta get home," I said. "Remember we promised Grandpa we'd be home early."

"I don't remember that."

I scowled at her. She was acting like the harlot her mother claimed she looked like.

"*Doreen*." My teeth were clenched. "We got to get home. We got chores to do for your mother."

"If you say so. Sorry, fellas," she said to the two.

"Well, ladies, maybe some other time," the mustachioed Abe was saying. "We're painting right now, putting up shelves, getting the place ready for a shipment of shoes. Grand opening'll be Saturday, October 10."

"*Oh, oh!*" Doreen squealed. "Same day as our Loray Box Supper Auction."

I shifted from foot to foot while she explained the rules of our box supper to total strangers.

They smiled, nodding all the while I eased Doreen out the door.

"I was *so* embarrassed," I told her as we headed for the trolley. "How could you carry on that way with perfect strangers?"

"Selena, look at me, look at you—a couple of lintheads. Those fellas got money, their own *store!*"

"We don't know beans about 'em, Doreen. Don't know where they came from, if they got wives way off somewhere like Mr. Gentry."

"So? Did I say we'd go out with them?"

"You came awful close, *Miss Mabel Normand.*"

If we needed proof our beautiful-in-four-weeks-plan was working, I suppose that was it. But it left me downright scared—of my best friend, Doreen.

———

Sunday after dinner Doreen said little as she washed and I dried her mother's primrose-patterned china.

"Mad about last night?" I asked her.

"No, why?"

"Ain't like you to be so quiet."

Etha stacked plates in the cabinet, listening as always. "What ya'll talking about?"

"None of your business, Miss Priss." Doreen never confided in her sister, never invited her to go with us anywhere.

Sometimes I felt sorry for Etha. She reminded me of Met and I missed my little sister. "We're hiking to the cemetery to take pictures. Wanta go?"

"Yeah! Yeah!"

"Well, *I'm* not going," Doreen piped up.

"You mean 'cause *she's* going?"

"No, I...got something else to do."

Was she trying to get at me? She never gave me the run-around before. She was mad, had to be.

"There's a bunch of us going," I told Etha.

Alma had a brand-new Kodak she'd saved for months to buy. She'd studied the instructions and put in a roll of film that would take twelve pictures. We'd be her first subjects. All the boardinghouse girls except Doreen were going.

"You'll miss a gay old time," I told Doreen.

She gave a smug look. "I got a job," she whispered like she didn't want Etha to hear.

"You mean...at the new shoe store?"

She nodded.

I untied the bib apron from the black faille dress I wore to church. With my black stockings and pumps, and eyes lined with charcoal, I felt glamorous as Mary Pickford. I ought to look good in a photograph.

Alma had on a new middy outfit with navy tie. "She's the spitting image of Pearl White in *Perils of Pauline*," I told Lucille who was wearing a brown crushed velvet jacket and matching hat. Marvelee looked pure sassy in her blue stovepipe hat.

"Go on, put that crazy hat on," Lucille teased her as we headed out the door.

"Makes me look too tall–taller'n everybody."

"Well, why're you carrying it?"

"Matches my new dress," Marvelee explained.

When we got to the cemetery we all took seats on the stone retaining wall, long and short legs dangling. Marvelee put her hat on while Alma took our picture.

"C'mon, S'lene, get one of me." Alma brought me the Kodak.

"Lordee, Alma, ask somebody else. I'm scared to death of new-fangled gadgets."

"Aw, c'mon, it's easier'n grits."

I jumped from the wall and she showed me how you look in the little window on top to make sure it's aimed right, then press the lever.

"Don't cut our heads off now," she warned, taking my place on the wall.

"What d'you mean?"

"Keep it steady when you click." After I snapped it, she jumped down. "Now, take one of me by myself. Got a special person I want to give it to."

She walked around looking for the tallest tombstone till she found a marble monument to one of Gastonia's deceased founders. She hugged it with both arms, then smiled like she was embracing Henry B. Walthall. "He's the best I can do," she said, laughing.

"Well, honey, don't waste no kisses on him," Lucille yelled. We laughed so hard I could hardly aim the Kodak.

"I'm gettin' tired of this old codger," Alma said.

"Wait, wait," I squealed. "Ain't got it yet."

"He's too cold for me," she admitted when I finally got her picture. She stuck both hands in her wide sleeves.

Going home Alma taught us the words to her latest piece of sheet music, "In the Shade Of The Old Apple Tree."

Grandpa was listening from the porch as we walked down the middle of the street. *I could hear the dull buzz of the bee in the blossoms, as you said to me with a heart that is true, I'll be waiting for you, in the shade of the old apple tree.*

"All right, girls, I'll be expecting you all in the choir on Sunday." He laughed. "Where's Doreen?" he asked as I came up the steps.

"She didn't go."

"But she left when y'all did."

"Said she had something else to do."

"I think I know. Come on, Selena. I want you to go with me." He took my arm.

"Where?"

"I believe you know *where*," he said out of earshot of the others. "Doreen's fifteen, too young to be going off by herself."

The others stayed on the porch, puzzled, as we walked toward Greasy Corner's trolley stop.

We'd both figured out Doreen was at the new shoe store.

"What's wrong with that?" I asked Grandpa. "If they gave her a job? They need help getting ready for the opening."

"Did they offer *you* a job?"

"No. I guess they only needed one."

At the store we peered through the glass front, no sign of anybody. Stacks of shoeboxes and fake feet were strewn here and there. A stenciled sign read, "GRAND OPENING, Saturday, October 10, 10:00 a.m., Door Prizes, Bargains Galore."

Grandpa grabbed my arm. "Come on."

We rounded the corner to the alley where crude doors bore the shopkeepers' names. Grandpa stopped in front of one that read, "The Shoe Hub, *Sol Green, Proprietor*." He pounded hard on the door, waited a few seconds, then pounded louder.

Sol Green opened the door. "Yes, can I help you?"

"Where's my girl?"

"Beg pardon?"

"Doreen, Doreen Callaway. Where's Doreen?"

Sol looked at me. I wanted to run, hide. I looked away.

"Oh, yes, Doreen. She's here, come on in. And who are you?"

"I ain't coming in. I want her to come out."

"I don't think you understand, sir."

"I understand enough–too much."

With Grandpa's voice getting louder, Doreen must've heard. She came and stood beside Sol.

"What're you doing here, Grandpa?"

"It's Sunday. You realize that? *Christians* don't work on Sunday. You're coming with me."

"You can't tell me what to do. All my life you've told me what to do and how to do it. Just leave me alone! I'm old enough to make my own decisions."

She acted as if I were not there, her best friend. I wanted to die right on the spot.

"It's all right," Sol told her. "Do what your grand-father wants. Go on home with him."

Finally Doreen looked at me. "You know, Selena Wright, you're lucky. You got no one to tell you what to do."

My heart felt torn to pieces. What could I say? Doreen was like my sister, and Grandpa like my grandfather. He was the only man at the boarding-house now. He was being protective. Why couldn't she see it that way?

The three of us took the trolley back without a word being said.

I talked to Mama that night, *Mama, why cain't Doreen see Grandpa loves her and wants the best for her.*

"Doreen's a rebel—wants things her way. It's part of getting growed-up."

"What can I do? I don't want to take sides."

"Bide your time, honey. Things got a way of changing you ain't never thought of. It's how God works. His time and yours ain't the same. Just bide your time."

I hugged the pillow beneath my chin, "Goodnight, Mama."

"Love you, Sippy-gal."

Chapter 14

Monday when I got home from work Mrs. Callaway came to our room. "Beulah's off tonight," she told me and Doreen. "I'll be needing help in the kitchen."

I could tell something was up.

When everybody got through eating and headed for the parlor, Doreen and I started scraping dishes, stacking them by the dishpan.

"Leave 'em be for now," Mrs. Callaway said, fidgety as I'd ever seen her. "I'll heat up the coffee and we'll talk."

She turned the gas on under the pot and got four cups, motioning us to sit down.

Doreen sat glum as a pond frog. Did she know something I didn't? Straggles of damp hair flanked her ears like corkscrews. Mabel Normand, she was not, and apparently didn't give a hoot.

I was trying to think of something cheerful to say when in walked Grandpa from the parlor, closing the door behind him. His briar pipe was clean and stuck in his vest pocket, a bad sign. When Mrs. Callaway poured his coffee, Doreen turned her cup upside-down. Her mother ignored it, pouring mine and her own.

Grandpa added one sugar lump to his coffee and stirred, watching the spoon's wide circles. He looked at me, then Doreen, and cleared his throat loudly.

"We need to get a few things straight. We need an *understanding*. First off—this family's a *Christian* family. We're Baptists. There're things we do and things we don't do. One thing we *don't do* is work on Sunday."

Doreen pounced like a cornered cat. "What about *Mama?*" She hissed the words. "Mama don't knock off a thing for Sunday, works hard as any other day."

"Don't get smart with me, young lady. You and I know running a boardinghouse is a seven day a week proposition. We ain't talking about necessary work."

"I cain't see a speck of difference. *She* works Sundays and gets paid for it."

"There *is* a difference whether you see it or not. I'm not here to argue or to educate you about jobs. We don't do business with gospel-haters. The Lord Himself said, '...Whoever disowns me before men, I'll disown him before my Father in heaven.' You know what I'm saying. We—your mama and me—agree you will *not* work for Sol Green and his shoe store another day. *That's final.*" He punctuated the pronouncement by downing the last of his coffee in a single gulp. "Well, that's all I've got to say on the subject." He banged his palms on the table and stood.

Without a word Doreen burst from her chair and ran up the stairs. Above the parlor sounds we heard her door slam shut.

I went to the parlor where Alma and Marvelee were singing with the piano roll, "By My Side." Before I walked away, Marvelee grabbed hold of me.

"Wait, S'lene, wait." She motioned with her head toward the kitchen. "What's going on?"

"Oh...nothing," I lied.

What could I say? Telling Marvelee would be same as announcing it to the whole boardinghouse as well as Loray spinning room. "We're ironing out some details about the box supper." What had taken place was a family thing. The thought frightened me. If I were family, and Doreen my sister, did it mean I was my sister's keeper?

I trudged up the stairs, racking my brain for what Mama would say. Always the peacemaker, the words came, "Don't say nothing you might be sorry about."

The door squeaked its familiar warning as I opened it gently. Doreen looked like she was sleeping. I knew better.

"Doreen."

She didn't move a hair. One arm lay stretched across her face, but from the hall light I could make out an eye. It quivered when I switched on the light.

"You might not think so, Do', but Grandpa really does love you." I waited, no response. "My own grandpapa, 'fore he died, used to claim we were, 'All for one and one for all.' That's what the Three Musketeers said, and it's how a family oughta be.' My grandpapa used to say that."

The eye kept twitching like it was trying hard to stay shut.

"Grandpapa couldn't read, so he never read *The Three Musketeers*, but somebody who did told him that's what they said and he liked the way it sounded. So he went around saying, 'All for one and one for all.'"

Doreen never moved a muscle, but started breathing in short spurts, like any minute she might sneeze or something.

I looked around and grabbed the stick we used for propping our window. I held it straight in front of me and lunged like a sword fighter.

"All for one and one for all," I yelled above the racket of the parlor piano's "Alexander's Ragtime Band."

It was too much. The bed commenced shaking and I knew I had her. Doreen tried stifling but couldn't hold it in. She busted out laughing, laughing so hard tears squirted and ran down her face.

"Selena, you crazy nut!"

I got to giggling and couldn't quit, and dropped to the bed beside her. We laughed till the cackles turned to sobs. We locked arms and cried till no tears were left, drying our eyes on the muslin sheet, then we lay for a long time.

Finally Doreen said, "What am I gonna do?"

The answer came clear as if Mama were making up words and putting 'em in my mouth.

"You gotta do what Grandpa wants. You *got* to, Do', till someday when you leave home or marry." *Or when he dies,* I was thinking, but didn't say it. I knew she was thinking that, too.

"Guess you're right. Selena *Wright's* usually *right.*" She was her old self.

"I'm *always* 'Wright,'" I said. Mama would've been proud how it went.

The door squeaked open. Etha was coming to bed. "I heard y'all laughing," she said. "What's so funny?"

"Nothing, Miss Priss."

Little sisters want to know everything, but some things are beyond explanation. This time I sided with Doreen. I thought of Met, what she might be asking, and if Aunt Mary had the answers.

When Etha settled in her trundle bed and her breathing told us she was asleep, Doreen and I talked for hours.

"We're getting shoe boxes delivered tomorrow," she said.

"Shoe boxes?"

"Yeah, for the box supper, one for every girl in the boardinghouse, courtesy of Sol Green. And tissue paper to wrap them with."

"What'll Grandpa think? Won't he send 'em back?"

"Mercy, no. What you don't know cain't hurt you and he'll never know. Unless you tell."

"You know I won't."

"Sol's man is bringing 'em to the back door, leaving 'em with Beulah. All he'll say is somebody sent 'em for the box supper. Our boxes'll be the prettiest ones. And I'll just bet we get the highest bids."

———

The day of the box supper was chilly and overcast, but spirits were high and the number of boxes up for bid surprised even Grandpa.

The auctioneer picked up a lavender box, turned it slowly, showing off hand-painted books and scrolls on its sides, when he noticed a poem in purple calligraphy.

"What have we here?"

A book of verses underneath the bough,
A jug of wine, a loaf of bread, and thou beside me.

"Ah, paradise in a lovely box," he said. "How much am I bid, gentlemen, for box number one?"

"Thirty-five cents," came the automatic bid from one who couldn't know or didn't care that someone put heart and soul into decorating this box.

I *knew* whose it was. When I looked them over, a hundred or more, arranged so prettily on a red-checkered tablecloth—I *knew*. Miss Lulu Whitesides' box was poetry itself, distinctive, delicate, like her. How could the meal inside be anything but delicious?

The auctioneer hadn't noticed the poem on the other side, written in red and decorated with seagulls in flight, one that tore my heart everytime I read it from my autographed copy:

The setting sun dripped blood red
Into the shining sea.
And, flying by, the seagulls screamed
As if they wept for me.

Grandpa and the preacher had agreed thirty-five cents would be the starting bid. I'd have bid my dollar right then and there, all the money I had in the world. But only men and boys could bid.

To build a proper playground the committee agreed three hundred dollars needed to be raised. The mill bosses gave one hundred dollars and word had it they also promised to match the amount brought in by the box supper. Some railed against tainted money, earned by the sweat of mill workers' brows, but Grandpa said the cause was worth it.

"Fifty cents," a second bidder yelled. I was glad. Miss Whitesides deserved at least that.

"Ten dollars!" came loud and clear from the back of the room. That voice, that familiar accent, made my heart jump. Could it be? Yes! *Mr. Winfred Gentry*—tall, pale, sporting a short beard, but there was no mistaking. He was back from Rhode Island, standing near the last row of seats.

"Who'll make it eleven dollars?" The box was held high. "Do I hear eleven? Ten dollars once, ten dollars twice, sold to the gentleman for ten dollars."

Miss Whitesides rose from her seat and looked around. It was electric. Their eyes met, like on the silver screen when Mary Pickford as *Ramona* saw Henry B. Walthall as *Alessandro*. For a moment no one moved. Then Winfred Gentry strode down the aisle and took the box from the auctioneer's hands. He carried it to where Miss Whitesides stood and handed it to her. Everyone broke into applause.

I reached for Doreen's hand. We started to bawl.

"What's wrong?" Etha asked, pulling my sleeve.

"Nothing. Nothing's wrong," I said, blowing my nose.

Etha scowled and tossed her braid over a shoulder. She was already mad because Grandpa told her she was too young to fix a box.

"Who wants supper with a twelve-year-old?" he asked her.

"How would they know I'm twelve?"

Grandpa just shook his head.

The auctioneer held up a second box, one from the boardinghouse. Alma's. We knew it by the red satin bow. We also knew inside was the best fried chicken ever to come out of Lib Callaway's kitchen, buttered corn on the cob, spiced apples, biscuits, and either two large slices of seven-layered chocolate cake or fried peach pies. For an "Armington Hotel" touch, we each had added four homemade heart-shaped mints tinted pink.

The auctioneer touched the satin bow. "What am I bid for this box with its pretty red bow?"

Mine was next. Doreen took hold of my arm.

"Here's a box with goodies inside and out," the auctioneer said, pointing to Bartlett pears and Bing cherries I'd painstakingly cut from seed catalogs and pasted on.

"Fifty cents," someone bid, guessing it was a "boardinghouse box," fixed with Mrs. Callaway's help.

"Sixty," said another.

"Sixty-five."

Oh, Lord, no. It was Freddie, the spinning room fixer.

"Somebody told him!" I said to Doreen. "Please, God, I don't want to eat with Freddie."

"Do I have a seventy? Sixty-five once, sixty-five twice, sold to the young man for sixty-five cents."

"He *knew,*" I said, gritting my teeth. "Somebody told him and it had to be Marvelee. She's the only one in the spinning room who knew. I'll get her, so help me, I'll *get* her for this."

Up front Freddie scooped up my box and came smiling to where we sat. "I'm waiting for Doreen," I said icily. "We'll eat with her and whoever buys her box."

Doreen's was the only boardinghouse box wrapped in pale blue tissue. Yellow roses from the seed catalog were pasted around the sides. Pulled into a bow on top was one of her "Mabel Normand" headbands—white linen, the edges tatted with ecru silk. She'd done the tatting herself.

"A lovely blue box and with yellow roses," the auctioneer observed. "What am I bid for this lovely blue box?"

"Fifty cents."

"Who'll make it sixty?"

"Sixty."

"Who'll make it sixty-five?"

I squeezed Doreen's hand. It was warm, damp, like when she got excited. She squeezed mine back and turned as if searching for somebody.

From way in back came the bid of all bids, *"Twenty dollars!"*

Some in the crowd gasped and a few whistled. Others were laughing like it had to be a joke.

The auctioneer was unruffled. "We have twenty dollars! Who'll make it twenty-one? Twenty dollars once. Twenty dollars twice, sold to the gentleman for *twenty dollars.*"

Sol Green came grinning like the Cheshire Cat all the way down the aisle.

Grandpa never flinched, just handed the next box to the auctioneer.

We took our boxes outside where Japanese lanterns hung from tree limbs and tables were spread with checkered oilcloth. Shorty and the Fiddlin' Fools stood on a wooden platform swagged with red, white, and blue bunting.

As soon as Miss Whitesides and Mr. Gentry found a table and sat down, Shorty tapped his stick for attention and picked up his megaphone.

"Mr. Winfred Gentry, this'uns for you."

The band struck up "I'm A Yankee Doodle Dandy."

Mr. Gentry stood and clapped his hands in time with the music. The rest of us did the same. "Thank you all, thank you," he said at the end when everybody quieted down. "By the way, Shorty, I want to point out, the chap who wrote that song, Mr. George M. Cohan, is a flag-waving Yankee like me from my home state of Rhode Island, the smallest state but with a big heart for this great land of ours." Everybody applauded and a few shouted "Hooray for Rhode Island."

Pinned to Miss Whitesides' blouse was a white chrysanthemum with ribbons of red, white and blue. Her face beamed, the happiest I'd ever seen her, certainly happier than since Mr. Gentry left months before with that short fat German woman.

Freddie said little and I was glad. Maybe he'd gained some gumption since turning sixteen. He didn't look half bad in his Sunday-go-to-meeting clothes. His hair, parted and combed free of spinning-room lint, was dark brown and wavy, a fact I'd never noticed. Still I planned to get Marvelee Davis. It had to be her that told him which box was mine. She had no right!

Sol Green did most of the talking at our table and kept us laughing. Doreen giggled till she got hiccups.

I leaned over and whispered, "Drink two swallows of water without breathing."

Sol'd been all kinds of places, mostly in New York, where his father came to from Austria as a young man and where Sol was born. New York had restaurants and delicatessens on every corner that sold lox and bagels and all kinds of food we never heard of. Sol told about Coney Island's *roller coaster* that gave you the ride of your life, and how the Statue of Liberty held her torch high for incoming ships. Doreen and I swore we'd go to New York someday and see those magical places.

The box supper brought close to seventy dollars. If the mill company matched that, along with the hundred they'd already given, the goal of three hundred was just around the corner. *The Gazette* gave the affair front-page coverage:

> ". . . The Fiddlin' Fools outdid themselves with a wide range of numbers - from "Cripple Creek" to "The Star-Spangled Banner." A good time was had by all..."

Grandpa puffed hard on his pipe and grunted his approval after reading the article.

"Money's still coming in," he said. "This'll get more."

He was pleased how things turned out, though he still hadn't uttered a word about Sol Green's generous bid.

Surprisingly Doreen, too, said little. If getting Grandpa's goat was her intent, the thrill was over.

I pressed my face to my pillow that night and imagined Mama's reaction. *"Nobody wins in mind games,"* she said. *"Don't never fall into that."*

"But Sol gave twenty whole dollars."

"Honey, what's twenty dollars compared to hurting an old man?"

Chapter 15

Mr. Gentry was back at the mill, but not back at Mrs. Callaway's. He'd taken a room at Loray Hall for Single Men. No one seemed to know what happened with his common law wife. I hoped she'd never come back.

Mr. Gentry deserved someone like Lillian Gish in *An Indian's Loyalty*—sensitive and refined, someone like Lulu Whitesides. She was Princess Mary in *When Knighthood Was In Flower*, trying to find a way to be with her lover forever. No one could deny they were destined for that. I got chills thinking how much she must love Mr. Gentry, her Sir Charles Brandon, pouring out her soul to him in poems. No one must come between them, least of all that *fat German woman from Rhode Island*.

Marvelee was on second shift now and I still hadn't confronted her about blabbing to Freddie which box supper box was mine. It was a dirty trick, one I'd never play on a friend. Sooner or later I'd have it out with her. Alma claimed changing shifts was bad for Marvelee—she didn't get enough sleep, had even lost weight. I felt bad, but that was no excuse for what she did and I'd never forgive her.

A few days later about 7:00 p.m. someone pounded on the front door. Etha ran to answer and opened the door to a stranger who barged in and came close to knocking her down.

"Marvelee Davis," he ranted loudly. "Is this where Marvelee Davis lives? Who can I talk to about Marvelee?"

"What is it?" Mrs. Callaway heard the racket and rushed from the kitchen wiping her hands on her apron.

"Are you Mrs. Davis?"

"No, this is my boardinghouse. Marvelee lives here. What's going on?"

"Sit down, Ma'am."

"Oh, my goodness! What? What?"

"Ma'am, Marvelee's long hair. You know how she keeps it put up, well, that hank of hair pulled loose, got caught in a warper." His voice started to break. "Pulled the scalp clean off her head. I seen it! Oh, I *seen it.*" He was sobbing.

"No, no! God have mercy on us!"

"Yes'm. Blood all over the place. They done took her to the hospital, sent me to tell you. They stopped that machine, got her scalp out, that long blonde hair out. But what can they do? She's bad, ma'am, real bad." He was bawling like a baby.

Etha started screaming, holding her head. "Is she gonna die, is she gonna die?"

Mrs. Callaway was wringing her hands.

"I'm going to her. Where's Papa? Where is he? Papa! Papa!" she hollered.

Grandpa was on his way down the stairs. "What's wrong, Libby? What is it?"

"Marvelee. She's hurt, hurt *bad*. I'm going to her, Papa. Come with me."

Grandpa dumped his pipe in a bowl and snatched his hat and coat from the hall tree. Mrs. Callaway threw off her apron and put on her everyday hat.

"Poor Marvelee." Doreen grabbed me and we hugged and cried.

"Can they put it back on?" Etha asked. "Is it same as when Indians scalp people?"

"Stop asking silly questions," Doreen scolded.

"What's silly?"

"All we know is Marvelee's bad off," I explained. "Come on. We need to pray.

It's what Grandpa would do."

Alma came downstairs. When we told her, she started shaking, "Marv *hated* second shift!" she screeched. "Couldn't get no sleep. That's when things happen."

All of us locked arms, swaying back and forth, crying, begging God to help her.

Grandpa talked to the doctor who tended Marvelee. "She lost a lot of blood," the doctor told him, "but she's young. I think she'll make it. Be a long hard road ahead."

Grandpa sent a telegram to the Davises in Besse-mer City asking them to come to their daughter's side. He hoped to hear back in a day or two.

The mill company was footing the hospital bill, but Grandpa wasn't satisfied with how they handled things. "Cold as Russian river rats," he said.

Grandpa'd never been out of the country, though he camped at Morehead City during war with Spain. Still, same as Papa, he kept up on things. War had started in Europe, he told us.

"I pray to God we never have to tangle with Rus-sia. You'd never beat them Siberians—toughened by the worst weather on God's green earth."

I was at our chifforobe getting ready for work, carefully wrapping my head with a turban, when I no-ticed Etha asleep on her trundle. Blood was all over her sheet. I touched her shoulder.

"Etha. Etha, honey, wake up."

Etha looked dazed, half-asleep. "What?"

"There's blood."

She jumped up, screaming. Blood was matted on her shift and trickling down one leg.

The commotion woke Doreen. "What in heaven's name?"

"Etha's got 'the pip,' Do'. Ain't you ever told her?"

"No! I..." She crawled to the end of the bed. "Oh, my gracious. What a *mess!*"

Etha was shaking from cold and fright. I put my arms around her. "It's all right, honey, it's all right. You're a big girl, now. That's what all this means."

"You mean you and 'Do' bleed like this?"

"Every month, four or five days of it."

"*Every* month? Every single month? What're you supposed to do?"

"You tie on padded rags. And you need to wear two pairs of bloomers, old ones, "pip pants" we call 'em, and two underskirts—to make sure nothing comes through."

Etha couldn't believe she'd do this the rest of her life till middle age.

Doreen pulled off Etha's shift, took it and her sheet downstairs to soak in warm water. I got soft cloths from our special rag drawer and folded them into a bandage for her.

"If this means I'm grown-up," Etha grumbled, "maybe Grandpa'll let me fix a box at the next box supper."

We laughed. When I hugged her she pulled away.

"S'lene." Her voice got whiny. "Maybe God sent *the plague* on me for...a reason. There's something I need to tell you. Hope it don't make you mad."

"What?"

"It was *me* that told Freddie."

"*You!* You told Freddie which box was mine?"

"Uh-huh."

I groaned. "Oh, Etha, I just thank the Lord I never got the chance to accuse Marvelee." The way things happened, how could I get mad at anybody?

Marvelee was in the hospital a long time, her head swathed in gauze. Doreen and I went to see her several times a week. We chatted about everything—except the accident and how it happened. We brought the pictures we took with Alma's Kodak camera that Sunday at the cemetery. It seemed so long ago.

"Look at my silly old stovepipe hat," Marvelee said staring at one.

"It matched your new dress real good. That's why you wore it, remember?" Doreen handed her another.

Laughing made her head hurt, she said, but she could smile and she smiled a lot about our afternoon at the cemetery, "Will you just look at me in this one! I 'clare if I don't look like Abe Lincoln in that hat, taller'n anybody."

"Honey, you're a darn sight prettier'n Abe Lincoln," I said. We didn't dare voice what all three were thinking—Marvelee would be wearing hats a lot. Thank goodness I never accused her of telling Freddie which supper box was mine. It had become so unimportant.

When Grandpa called for a meeting after supper one night, Doreen raised her eyebrows and screwed up her mouth. Same as the rest of us, she had no idea what it was about. It was December already and the Davises of Bessemer City were coming with mule and wagon next day to fetch home their oldest, Marvelee. We'd stacked her belongings, ready for pickup just inside the front door. Was our meeting about that? I doubted it.

Doreen and I perched on the piano bench. Others flopped to settees, careful to leave Grandpa's favorite wingback with its ash-burnt holes, for him. He settled down, propped his favorite pipe by the humidor, and cleared his throat loudly. We knew the signal. It meant "quiet."

"We...that is, Libby and me, don't want none of you getting upset. Most of all, we don't want y'all doing something you don't want to."

I glanced at Doreen. She shrugged and made another face. Alma looked worried.

Mrs. Callaway sat wooden, staring straight ahead, hands pressed deep inside the pockets of her apron. The hall clock hammered its deafening tocks.

Grandpa sensed the apprehension. "*Ahem!* I don't mean to scare nobody. No, what this is all about is, well, Libby, that is Mrs. Callaway, and me are leaving Loray."

His words stretched taut as frayed threads on a warper. Breaths were sucked in and a few "Oh, no's."

"Wait, now. Hear me out. This's been in the works awhile. Had to wait till it was a sure thing 'fore I could say anything. We're going to *Maysworth*, to a brand-new boardinghouse. Mr. J. H. Mays built a spinning mill over there near the Catawba, east of here, coupla years back. Call it Maysworth. He added on, built houses, and a nice school. Things got even better when the Good Lord sent a Mr. Stewart Cramer. Mr. Cramer bought that mill and he's running it like a mill *oughta be run*—fair to workers—something Loray bosses ain't never understood.

"Well, I went over there, talked to Mr. Cramer and he offered us a boardinghouse. Got everything Libby ever wanted or needed: electricity, indoor plumbing, big parlor, six bedrooms, and would you believe it—a *washing machine!*"

Etha perked up. "A *real* washing machine? I saw one in *The Saturday Evening Post.*"

"Well, there's one there. Best of all, there's a six-burner gas range with *two* ovens." He picked up his pipe, blew into it and knocked it against his knee.

Doreen spoke what all of us were thinking. "What about *us?*"

"I'm coming to that. Good news! There's a job to be had over there for anybody that wants one. It's all up to you. We're not twisting no arms. Two women done spoke for this place here. I'm sure they'll be happy if you stay on, if it's what you rather do."

He leaned back, filled his pipe from the humidor, tamped it down and lit up. Apple-scented Bull Durham smoke filled the air. Breathing its fragrance eased the tension.

"Papa, they need to know how much time they got," Mrs. Callaway said. She got up, ready to head back to the kitchen.

"Oh, plenty. Plenty of time. Be after Christmas. You got time to think on it. If you wanta go, got time

to give Loray two weeks' notice. Cain't have this looking like some kinda strike. No need getting folk's dan-
der up."

Everybody sat there. This was totally out of the
blue.

Doreen would go. I was sure of that, though she'd
no doubt act as if they'd staged some kind of betrayal.

"Ain't like Mama to keep secrets," she told me
afterwards as we emptied Grandpa's ashtray and
straightened the parlor. "I knew she'd been acting
funny."

I wanted to laugh, remembering her mother's in-
fatuation with Mr. Gentry; or was it only great admi-
ration? Whichever, it stuck out like a sore thumb to
everybody at the boardinghouse except Doreen. She
never even noticed. I decided I could read her mother
better than she could.

That night in reverie I talked it over, *"What should
I do, Mama? I got a good job here, but I love Mrs. Callaway." Like a mother,* I was thinking, but banished the
thought. *"I love Grandpa, too. He reminds me of Papa.
He's Republican and he keeps up with all that's going on
in the world. 'Course Papa likes to take a drink and likes
to dance, and Grandpa's a teetotaler and one of them Baptists that thinks dancing's a sin."*

If Mama were really there, she'd be laughing out
loud at such talk. She always looked the other way at
Papa's drinking, but when he rolled back the rug, she'd
kick up her heels right along with him.

"Do what you will, Sippy-gal." Her words came clear and expected. *"But remember—Doreen and Libby Callaway and Grandpa Spencer have made you same as family."*

"Etha, too, Mama. She's like a little sister." I thought of Met and choked up. I hadn't heard a word in months.

I went to sleep knowing I'd make the move to Maysworth. I'd miss Gastonia; Main Street, the movie theaters, Sweetland Ice Cream Parlor, folks at Loray, even Freddie and my straw boss. But then all of it was just a trolley ride away.

One Saturday Doreen and I decided to go see Alma following the movie show at Gastonia's Ideal Theater. Alma was married now, the only one who stayed put when the rest of us moved to Maysworth. We figured, too, she'd have news from Marvelee. They'd been roommates and good friends.

Doreen's idol, Mabel Normand, was showing at the Ideal in *A Little Hero* followed by Fatty Arbuckle's comedy *Passions, He Had Three*. We laughed till we cried at Fatty Arbuckle's antics, but Doreen, as always, was fixed on Mabel Normand.

"She's not only beautiful," she bragged as we left, blinking in bright sunlight, "she's a comedian, funnier'n Ole Fatty Arbuckle. *Directs* movies too. She's gotta be smart, smarter'n most men."

"Mary Pickford's my type."

"Yeah?"

"Yeah. *America's Sweetheart*'s not just beautiful—she always gets her man. Another thing, you won't catch Mary Pickford bobbing off her curls." Soon as it left my lips I knew it was the wrong thing to say to your best friend.

Doreen twisted a stray wisp of hair and worked it into her red bun. The inch of growth since her daring Mabel Normand bob was still too short to updo. To look fuller she brushed the frizzy ends over a rat and fastened it with every hairpin we owned.

The trolley stopped and we boarded, plopping glumly to a front seat facing the motorman. It *clang-clanged* all the way to Loray, neither of us speaking a word.

Alma had been at Loray since she was sixteen, and boarded at Callaway's the last three years. She kept her engagement to Gus Keeter, a weaver at the mill, secret while they saved for a honeymoon. None of us guessed till Grandpa broke the news of the move to Maysworth, upsetting her plans. She and Gus married within a year and got their own millhouse, a one bedroom duplex.

Alma fixed us glasses of sweet tea while Doreen and I looked at photos of their Raleigh honeymoon pasted neatly in an album titled "Memories." The Governor's Mansion, The Capitol, she'd written in white ink on black pages. Several were labeled State College, two were Central Prison, where she added, "Now *we're* shackled, too. Ha!"

We laughed.

"Hey," I said, "'member our Sunday afternoon at the cemetery when your Kodak was new? Very first time you used it."

"Uh-huh."

"Well, I still got the one of you hugging that big old tombstone. You wrote on it, 'This is the best I can do.'" Seemed ages ago.

She laughed. "What I remember's Marvelee's stovepipe hat she brought but wouldn't wear, claimed it made her look tall as Abe Lincoln."

We stopped laughing. "Have you heard from 'er?" I asked.

Alma reached in her pocket, pulled out a letter and handed it to me. Doreen leaned over my shoulder and read aloud:

Dear Alma:

Will you please quit worrying about me. Yes, I'm happy. And yes, I met somebody. His name's Jonah. Him and me plan to get married. He's a sharecropper, but he's a good man, hardworking and saving. Jonah treats me like I'm Queen May herself. We're getting married soon's he sells his tobacco crop. Don't know when that'll be but I'll write and let you know. Maybe you can come and stand up with me.

Hope you and Gus are both fine.

As ever, Marvelee

I refolded the letter and handed it back. I couldn't keep the tears from coming.

"For God's sake, S'lene, what's wrong with you?" Doreen asked. "She says she's happy. Ain't that enough?"

"I don't believe it. Does she really love this, this Jonah? She never said so."

"Does it matter that much? What's a poor girl's chances in *Bessemer City?* She says he's good to 'er."

"It *matters,* Do'. It matters a lot. Think about *Ramona,* how crazy she was for *Alessandro,* how she waited long years for him. All that time their love never changed one bit. That's how it oughta be. That's what I'm looking for."

"Selena, you're way too romantic. You think every girl in the world oughta be swept off her feet like Mary Pickford in that silly old show. For Christ's sake, *Ramona* ain't nothing but a story!"

I dabbed my eyes with my handkerchief. "Alma, tell us how y'all fell in love. Did Gus 'sweep you off your feet?'"

She forced a laugh. "Not exactly. We went to Sweetland one Saturday night for ice cream cones—two scoops, one chocolate, one vanilla. We got the trolley home to the boardinghouse and sat on the porch. 'Member our old swing, how it used to creak every little move? It was creaking away when Gus sneaked his arm around me and asked if I liked him. 'Sure,' I said. He said he liked me a whole lot and would I marry him."

"Did he give you a ring?"

"Not right then, said he was saving up for one. I told him all I wanted was a little gold band when we tied the knot." She showed us her wedding ring. That's when her shoulders commenced shaking and she covered her face.

"Alma, honey—what's wrong?" Doreen set her glass down and leaned toward her.

"Ain't nothing. I declare. Don't mind me." She pulled a handkerchief from her sleeve, started dabbing her eyes. "I...I just wish..."

"Wish what?"

"Nothing. Really. Just...both y'all...wait. I mean... be sure and wait a long time. Have...lots of fun first."

I didn't know what to make of it. I'd never seen Alma cry, not even when Marvelee got scalped in that awful accident. Alma was oldest of us boardinghouse girls. She was always calm and collected, always in control.

She patted her eyes dry and her face brightened. "Hey, y'all, guess what?"

"What?"

"I'm...'in the family way'—about three months. Ain't told a single soul but you two, 'cept of course Gus."

We hugged her. "You're the very first one, honey," I said. "The first one to get your own family."

"Yeah." She smiled and sniffed hard.

———

"What d'you make of her?" Doreen asked on our way to the trolley. "Crying and all?"

"I can't figure it out. If she really loves Gus, wouldn't she be happy about having his baby?"

"Gotta be something she ain't telling."

"Gus Keeter seems sorta hick to me. I mean, he's not exactly Sir Charles Brandon."

"Not by a country mile. But Alma's no Princess Mary, either. Or Mary Pickford. But let me tell you something, Selena Burzilla Wright. If you're looking for a knight in shining armor, you'll be looking a *long* time."

I laughed.

"We're heading back downtown," Doreen announced when we boarded.

"Why? It's getting late. Won't your mama...?"

"We're going to The Shoe Hub."

"Do', I thought that Sol Green thing was over with."

"This is strictly 'tween you and me. What Mama and Grandpa don't know won't hurt 'em." She stared out the window, pensive-like. "Know what, S'lene, the main thing I like about Sol? He's the only person that treats me like a woman."

"You just turned sixteen, Do'. Does that make you a woman?"

She turned, glaring. "I *am* a woman! So are you. I work six days a week. Earn my own money. I'm old enough to leave home if I want to, and there ain't a thing nobody can do about it."

"What about folks who love you—your mama, Grandpa, Etha, your friends? What about *me?*"

"Did I say I was leaving? I said I *could,* for Christ's sake."

"You keep saying 'for Christ's sake,' 'for Christ's sake.' Grandpa says that's taking the Lord's name in vain."

"Grandpa ain't here. So don't tell me what I can say!"

It hurt me when we argued, though it didn't seem to bother Doreen. Do' was the way she was. No one was going to change Doreen Callaway. I figured if I wanted to keep her for my best friend, I'd best take the bad with the good.

She yanked the bell in front of The Shoe Hub. Abe was there, looking every bit the successful businessman: pistol-legged trousers, tweed jacket, stiff white collar with black silk tie. He bustled about, helping customers. He nodded our way but seemed to have no time to talk. We dawdled, inspecting shoes and pocketbooks a half-hour or so till I suggested we leave.

"Wait a minute." Doreen walked to where Abe was ringing up a sale. "Where's Sol?"

"Oh, didn't he tell you?" He's gone to New York." His expression was pained. "Sol's...getting married, a girl he's known since his *bar-mitzvah.*"

Doreen looked stunned. I grabbed her arm and led her out the door. What could I say?

"Sol...shoulda told you," I said.

Her face took on a fierce look, her mouth tight. She jerked her arm from my grasp. I followed her into the street where we dodged, narrowly missing a honking motorcar.

"Come on," she screeched.

"Where we going?" We made it across and headed toward Sweetland.

"I'm getting the tallest Cherry-Berry ice cream soda they make and *you can get your own.*"

Chapter 16

At Maysworth people were happier than at Loray. They made me think of folks back home in the mountains. My Mays Mill job was better than the one in Loray's spinning room. Doreen and I worked in the large "winding and twisting" section where thread was wound onto bobbins and stacked in wooden boxes for the weave room.

At night I shared it with Mama:

"Maysworth's the best place in the whole world to work, Mama."

"Your Father in heaven's the one you oughta thank, Sippy. Since I ain't there, He's looking out for you."

"I know and I'm so blessed. Mrs. Callaway and Grandpa Spencer treat me same as family."

"Praise God, he's give you another family. I love you, sweet girl."

"Night-night, Mama."

———

Grandpa was happier than I'd ever seen him. If he wasn't one of those "dancing's a sin" Baptists, I believe he'd pull back the rug and do an Irish jig like Papa used to do.

Mr. Stuart W. Cramer had given Maysworth Baptists a frame house in Mays Company village for an interdenominational Sunday school and meeting-house. Grandpa would assist the pastor, a job made in heaven for him. With its membership growing fast, Mr. Cramer authorized the building of a large brick Baptist church, the bricks to come from Charlotte by rail. The church's roof would be shingled with wooden shingles to match the houses. The village was already a model—pride of the entire Piedmont area.

"I've lived a long time," Grandpa declared, "and Mr. Stuart Cramer's the most generous man I ever did meet. He believes religion, not laws, should shape the way a town oughta be. He believes in education. This mill village is like a big happy family. We got *him* to thank for all of it." Grandpa admired few people. If he admired a man it was for good reason.

It pleased us boardinghouse residents that Grandpa was involved in Maysworth's civic doings. Since the box supper for Loray's playground, he was known as one who got things done. Following the playground's groundbreaking his picture appeared on the *The Gazette*'s front page. Respect for him directly affected Callaway's and a waiting list of roomers and boarders formed. Good cooking kept them coming back.

The boardinghouse itself, with a wide wrap-around porch set with rockers and two swings, made me proud I lived there. Friends met on the porch or gathered in our parlor to sing, party, or just sit and talk. Fellows weren't shy about coming around. It was like a clubhouse. They brought roasted peanuts to toss up and catch in their mouths. They told Pat and Mike jokes and regaled us barbershop style with the latest songs. They mimicked Charlie Chaplin and Fatty Arbuckle, and fell all over themselves imitating the Keystone Kops.

Across the street a Lover's Lane rambled over the railroad tracks, through some woods, and by a shallow creek filled with stones you could walk across. It was perfect for after church picnics, or slipping off two by two for intimate walks.

The engagement announcement of Miss Lulu Whitesides and Mr. Winfred Gentry was in the Friday afternoon, February 26, 1915, *Gastonia Gazette*. The wedding ceremony, to be conducted by Dr. Henderlite, minister, would take place at First Presbyterian Church, Gastonia, on Saturday, May 15, a reception to follow at the Armington Hotel.

The write-up on the society page gave me goosebumps and I showed it to Doreen.

"Do', here's a real life Princess Mary and Sir Charles Brandon. So there—it *can* happen."

"You looking for another Winfred Gentry? Is that what you want?"

"Sure."

"Well, forget it. He's one of a kind."

Doreen and I were in the parlor viewing brand new stereoscope pictures of Claude Monet's *Cathedral at Rouen.* Mrs. Callaway ordered the tinted set from Sears and Roebuck.

"Ever seen anything so pretty?" Doreen handed me the scope. "They say Monet made a water garden just so's he can paint the lilies."

"Wish I could paint. I could give Miss Whitesides something really pretty, something different."

"She likes poetry, don't she? Write her a poem."

"But Miss Whitesides is a *real* poet. She wrote a whole book of poems. I'm not good like her."

I remembered her words when I quit school and went to work: *Keep writing, Selena. Write poetry. Take note of all around you and write it down.* Now she and Mr. Gentry were getting married and I wanted desperately to give her something to treasure, to let her know how much it meant knowing she cared.

"You're a poet, too, Selena. You notice things other people don't. I know Miss Whitesides. A poem would please her more'n anything."

I was flattered Doreen thought this about me. She never said so before. Maybe there was a side to her I hadn't discovered.

That night the lines of Miss Whitesides' poem, "Farewell My Love" echoed and re-echoed in my head. I'd never been to the seashore much less watched the sun drip blood red into it. Yet the scene came clear as if I were on that sandy beach. How could I write something like that? What would I write about? Not about working in the mill, though that's where I spent most of my waking hours. No, it had to be something *beautiful* like "Farewell My Love," inspiring like Miss Whitesides' love for Mr. Gentry, her knight in shining armor.

The prettiest spot I'd seen since leaving Utah Mountain was across the tracks near the creek on our "Lover's Lane." Once, after a hard rain, I discovered a small pool of water with wildflowers circling it. I stood enchanted, knowing the pool would be gone next day, receding into the creek. In a lined book Miss Whitesides gave me I wrote—"Yesterday when I was alone walking in the woods, I saw purple flowers bending over as if taking a sip of water." The picture had stayed in my mind ever since. I could still see them plain as on that day. Words fell over themselves in my head as I went to sleep.

Next morning, Saturday, was half-day at the mill. Before leaving for work, I scribbled a verse that haunted me all night long:

> Yesterday I walked alone
> Beside a fragrant wood,
> Where dark against an azure sky
> The somber pine trees stood.

As bobbins flew on the winders, the sound made a cadence of unfinished lines:

> *Dark* against an azure sky,
> The somber pine trees stood.

No—

Green against an azure sky,
Stately pine trees stood.

I saw the tall pencil grass
Bend its yellow head.

No—

Bowed its *bushy* head.

Doreen shouted over the roar of the winders, "Have you seen *him?*"

"Seen who?"

"Stuart Cramer, *Jr.*"

"Who?"

"Stuart Cramer, *Jr.*, Stuart Cramer's son, the best looking man I ever saw. Better looking than Henry B. Walthall will ever hope to be."

"I don't believe you."

"Just wait, honey, wait till you see him."

A thread broke. I stopped the winder and reached for the bobbin. My "wooded vale of somber pines" was lost in a maze of winders, twisters, and news of a good-looking son. I had no time to bring it back.

When I got home I hastily combed lint from my hair, grabbed three pencils and ran to the kitchen to sharpen them with a paring knife. In a corner of the parlor hidden by a potted aspidistra I scribbled, erased, and scribbled again till the supper bell rang:

THE SHRINE

Today I walked a leafy path
Down to a fragrant wood,
Where green against an azure sky
The stately pine trees stood.

There the yellow pencil grass
Bowed its bushy head
To sow a million tiny seeds
In a brown and russet bed.

And hidden in a sheltered spot
Where the earth lay dark and cool,
I saw a band of purple flowers
Drinking from a pool.

I bowed my head in reverence there
'Neath a softly whispering pine
And thanked the God of Nature
For such a lovely shrine.

I wish for you and Mr. Gentry a long and happy
marriage,
    Selena Wright

———

After supper I showed Doreen the poem.
    "Oh, S'lene, that's pretty, *real* pretty. Get Naomi

to do it up in pen and ink. Naomi does that fancy writing."

Naomi was our newest boarder at Callaway's—what Doreen and I called an "old maid." How old, we didn't know but, at sixteen, anyone over twenty-five was old to us.

Naomi liked the poem. "Need vellum," she said. "You can buy it in town at John Love's. Get me two or three sheets, in case."

The rest of my pay, after board, I spent on the paper and brought it to Naomi. She took everything off the corner secretary and sat down to copy the poem. After dusting it with sand and waiting for it to dry completely, she decorated the margins with trailing ivy, rosebuds and curlicues.

I showed the completed piece to Mrs. Callaway. Her eyes grew misty and, without a word, she went straight to the pantry and brought out a framed print of a shipwreck. "I hate this picture," she said, blowing the dust off.

The face of the man in the picture was grotesque, contorted, as if desperately screaming for help while clinging to a piece of wreckage. Beneath were the words: *Rescue the Perishing*.

"I'll see if Papa cain't use this to frame your poem," she said. "It's ebony, carved by my dear departed brother, John, God rest his soul."

I was so moved a knot formed in my throat, but I swallowed hard and blinked back tears. Mrs. Callaway didn't like to see big girls cry.

Mr. Gentry and Miss Whitesides were invited the following Saturday evening for Mrs. Callaway's special Corned Beef and Cabbage dinner planned specially for them since the dish was Mr. Gentry's favorite. There'd be spring peas and pickled artichokes on the menu with Jeff Davis pie and chocolate layer cake for dessert.

I decided that would be the best time to present my gift.

———

On Wednesday before Saturday's big supper, Mrs. Callaway called me to the telephone. We'd had the telephone for weeks, but I'd never answered it or had anyone call me. *Oh, my goodness,* I thought, *somebody's died.* What else could it be? I was scared silly.

"Hello. Hello," I said, not sure which part to speak into and which to listen with. "Who's there?"

"That you, Sippy?" Sounded like Papa all right, only off somewhere in a box.

He was calling to say he was back at Loray with a job that paid better than the one in Hendersonville. Typical Papa, trying something new-fangled. He'd never liked writing letters.

"Speak up," he kept saying. "Speak into your mouthpiece."

When I raised my voice, he laughed. "No need to knock my ear off. Y'all still have that Corned Beef and Cabbage Night?"

Papa loved the dish almost as much as Winfred Gentry.

I told him Mrs. Callaway's plans.

"All right if I come?"

"Sure, I'll tell her to set another plate."

I hadn't seen Papa in a long time. Maybe he'd have news from Waynesville.

On Saturday Beulah and Grandpa put extra leaves in the dining table and Mrs. Callaway laid out her best damask tablecloth with matching napkins. When Doreen and I got home we combed out lint, tied up our heads with mill ends, and put on cobbler aprons. We got out her mother's primrose-patterned china with matching tureen and platters.

All day long smells from the kitchen where Mrs. Callaway and Beulah were cooking spread through downstairs and up to our rooms. "*Mm-mm*" was the hallway greeting. Not a boardinghouse roomer would miss this meal.

Guests came early finding places to sit in the parlor where checkers and Parcheesi boards were set. Only the brave or unsuspecting accepted Grandpa's checker challenges. Doreen and I knew better. Papa didn't, and in no time he got trounced.

My gift for Miss Whitesides, wrapped in white tissue with purple flowers cut from seed catalogs and carefully pasted on, was stashed in the hall closet. At just the right time I'd bring it out.

At quarter past six the honored couple arrived and promptly at 6:30 p.m. Mrs. Callaway rang the supper bell. Everyone filed to the dining table and stood behind their designated chairs while Grandpa returned thanks, "Our Gracious Father, for what we're about to receive we give thanks, careful always to give you the honor and glory and praise due your Holy Name. Amen."

Immediately talk of war in Europe dominated the conversation.

"Mark my words. We'll be in that fray before long," Grandpa said, head bobbing all the while like nobody would disagree. "Things ain't going good for the Allies. They need our help. This old world's getting mighty small while our teacher-president, Mr. Woodrow Wilson's, a pipe-dreaming pacifist."

Papa slathered a biscuit with Mrs. Callaway's home-churned butter, "Wait, now, Aaron, wait a cotton-picking minute. Question is: is it in our *interest* to get in? What do we stand to gain? And do Americans really have the stomach for war?"

Mr. Gentry kept nodding or shaking his head, agreeing or disagreeing. He appeared biding his time for the right place to inject his down-to-earth Yankee wisdom. At Mrs. Callaway's insistence, he took generous second helpings then peered at Papa from the tops of his eyes. "Mr. Wilson takes credit for keeping us out of the war thus far, so he'll be running for re-election on that."

Mr. Gentry picked his knife up with his left hand and his fork with the right, holding them poised above his plate. Etha always snickered at that, but tonight she knew better. "We'll see, Jim," he went on. "We'll see, come election time, if that's what the people want. I'm afraid it's all politically driven. Too bad when you think about it. But war's are fought, thousands killed and maimed, on which way the political winds are blowing. Then down the road we look back and wonder what it was all about."

Grandpa glared at him, stabbing the air with his fork, "Winfred, I take it you're against war in general."

"I'm not for nor against," Mr. Gentry said, "But the case needs to made, the costs reckoned."

"Who can know?" Grandpa countered loudly. "Only God knows the costs. Only *time* will tell the effects."

Beulah was hastily frisking away empty plates while Mrs. Callaway looked worried. Things weren't going her way. To her mind conversation should be only pleasantries at mealtime. It "made for good digestion."

"Ya'll will be wanting dessert," she reminded. "There's chocolate layer cake and Jeff Davis Pie. Tell Beulah which you want, or maybe you'd like a small piece of each." She gave a nervous twitter. "This is such a special time. We're honored our bride and groom-to-be are here. I think it calls for toasts. Pa, will you do one?"

"I will indeed." Grandpa raised his iced tea glass. "To the happy couple: good health, long life, and may the Good Lord bless you all of your days." He took a sip.

Papa stood to give the next one while Beulah came with dessert trays and more toasts were offered. No one noticed as I sneaked to the hall, got my gift, and laid it next to Miss Whitesides' iced tea glass.

"Oh! What's this, Selena?"

"Something for you and Mr. Gentry," I said. "Open it."

She tore off the paper and held up my framed poem. I started back to my chair when she took hold of my arm.

"Wait, wait, Selena! I want to read this for all to hear." She tapped her glass with a spoon, like she would at school. "Listen, everyone. I want you to hear the poem Miss Selena Wright wrote for Winfred and me."

Everyone got quiet while my cheeks burned so hot I could only stare at my folded hands. Talk of war in Europe was forgotten as Miss Whitesides' sweet voice read my lines about purple flowers and peace.

At the end, Doreen started clapping, then Etha. Soon everybody joined in.

A great sob burst from my throat racking my shoulders. I ran to the parlor to an ottoman hidden by the aspidistra and tried to collect myself. Miss Whitesides was right behind.

"Selena, Selena, it's all right." she said. "Let it out. You're a true poet—with all the emotions. We poets are moved by our own words because they're straight

from our hearts. They say who we are. I shall treasure your poem forever. I mean it sincerely. So will
Winfred."

"Thank you, ma'am," I could only whisper. At last
the sobs were under control.

Papa came and stood next to her. "You're good,
gal. Didn't I always know it? Didn't I say you'd keep
on learning? Rachel'd be proud."

With mention of Mama came another wave of
sobs. Papa handed me his handkerchief and I blew
my nose.

Others drifted to the parlor and Doreen got out
the latest piano roll, "Molly Malone." Soon Winfred
Gentry's smooth baritone dominated a sing-along.
Grandpa challenged Papa to another game of checkers, and ever the optimist, Papa accepted.

Chapter 17

I had to agree with Doreen. Stuart Cramer, Jr., was the best looking fellow I'd ever seen. "Where's he been hiding?" I asked my straw boss.

"Oh, that one. He's a cadet, at the Military Academy, West Point."

"Where's that?"

"Gal, you *are* a hick! New York State. But don't think Stuart Cramer, Jr.,'d pass the time of day with the likes of you. *Hah!* Ain't no winding room linthead got a Chinaman's chance catching *his* eye."

"Who says I want to?"

"I seen you looking."

"No law 'gainst looking!"

I couldn't wait to tell Doreen. "Best forget him, be easier to get a date with Henry B. Walthall."

"So," she smirked. "Handsome don't mean fun to be with. Take Douglas Fairbanks. Now there's a fella a girl could have fun with. Does his own stunts, they say. Ain't nothing that fella can't do."

A week before the big May wedding of Lulu Whitesides and Winfred Gentry, news came that a German submarine had sunk a large British liner named *Lusitania* off the coast of Ireland. Nearly 1200 people died, more than a hundred of them Americans. President Wilson sent Germany a strong message demanding "reparation so far as reparation is possible."

Grandpa sneered. "The man don't believe cow horns'll hook! Asking 'reparations' is like asking Cain to produce his brother. Huns ain't a bit sorry. Mark my words—this won't be the last."

He was right. German U-boat sinkings began dominating *The Gastonia Gazette*'s front page. All conversation stopped at the breakfast table as Grandpa read the latest news aloud, shaking his head.

"What we need's a president with guts enough to stand up for American rights on the high seas," he griped.

Grandpa aimed most of his presidential faultfinding toward our over twenty-one male boarders, especially those who'd never voted. Yet all of us were left with impressions of a weak president unwilling to stand up to German bullies.

After their wedding and honeymoon, the Winfred Gentrys bought a home in Gastonia but came twice a month to Maysworth for Mrs. Callaway's Corned Beef and Cabbage Night. No hint had been given at the previous week's dinner when one Saturday afternoon in July a dray pulled up in front of the boardinghouse, followed by a loud rapping at our door. Mrs. Callaway hurriedly wiped her hands and ran to answer.

"Y'all got a freight delivery from Baltimore sent by a Mr. and Mrs. Gentry," the driver said, studying his clipboard.

"Oh, my goodness, my goodness, me." Mrs. Callaway crowed like a barnyard rooster all the while two men unloaded and pried open a wooden crate stenciled VICTOR TALKING MACHINE COMPANY. The first real phonograph I'd ever seen was taken out and its legs attached.

The men lifted the mahogany cabinet and carried it inside, setting it carefully in the middle of the parlor floor.

"Where you want it, ma'am?"

Mrs. Callaway was having a conniption. "Lordy me, I do declare, where?" She scanned her parlor jammed with sofas, tables, a player piano, lamps, chairs, Grandpa's smoking stand, and the large aspidistra.

Doreen pointed to the aspidistra. "How 'bout getting rid of that ugly old plant. All it does is catch dust."

"I love my plant. I've had that aspidistra since before you were born. I'd sooner get rid of you. Come on, you and Selena roll it to the dining room, that corner by the sideboard, where it'll get some light."

Next a large sofa in front of the bay window was inched to one side and the talking machine placed next to it. The men opened the Victrola's lid and attached the horn. On the outside they fitted the handle to its rod. Four disc records with paper jackets were stacked in the record compartment and spare needles dumped into a pocket.

"All set," one of them announced. They stood grinning, arms akimbo, like it was party time and they were guests.

Doreen placed a record on the turntable, cranked the handle, and put the needle in the groove. Strains of "In the Good Old Summertime" rose from the horn, and life in Callaway's Boardinghouse parlor was never the same.

———

Long summer days meant more time to sit on the porch or go for walks beyond the railroad tracks to the creek. Saturday and Sunday afternoons we bought round-trip trolley rides to Belmont, taking pictures of the Abbey, or to Dallas or McAdenville where Doreen had cousins.

On a humid July night word came that Alma'd had her baby, a little boy, and that something awful was wrong with him.

"I have to go to her," Mrs. Callaway said.

She pinned her Sunday hat on and gave Beulah instructions for fixing a cold supper. Doreen and I went with her to Gastonia Hospital where Alma lay flat of her back on a narrow steel bed. Her face was puffed out, her hair scraggly as hay on a scarecrow. Only her eyes told us it was Alma and that something was terribly wrong.

"Alma honey, we came soon's we heard." Mrs. Callaway bent over, looking into her eyes.

Alma shook her head and turned away, "He's dying." Her voice was raspy like she had the croup. "My little baby's dying."

Mrs. Callaway clasped Alma's hand in both of hers, "I'm so sorry, honey. I wish there was something we could do."

"Ain't nothing *nobody* can do." She turned to us, her mouth quivering. "His little spine's got a hole in it and they can't close it up. My little boy's dying and ain't no doctor in the world can do nothing."

Moans came from deep inside her like the cooing of a mourning dove.

Mrs. Callaway squeezed her hand and kissed it, "I'm so sorry."

We stayed till a nurse came with a sleeping potion and Alma drank it. We waited till she was drowsy before tiptoeing out.

In the hallway stood Gus Keeter, his eyes swollen and red-rimmed.

"Doctors say little Augustus won't live 'cept maybe a day or two. For *her* sake I hope it ain't long."

Loray Mill was taking care of the bills, he told us, and they'd pay for the baby's burial.

"Will you be home Sunday?" Mrs. Callaway asked.

"Yes ma'am, till time to come back here 'bout one."

"We'll come, pack the baby's things away," she said. "Alma don't need to see such after her little one's gone."

On Sunday we folded the legs of a wicker bassinet for Gus to take back to the owner. We made sure the bedroom furniture sat like it did before. We took folded diapers and tiny handmade kimonos from a bureau drawer, wrapped them in tissue and packed them away in the back of a wardrobe.

Three weeks after Alma got home from the hospital, she packed all her clothes and left to visit Marvelee. We heard she'd never go back to Gus.

———

1916 came with a heavy blanket of snow and news of Woodrow Wilson's re-election bid. Predictions were he'd be reelected come November. "He's kept us out of the war" was the Democrats' campaign theme.

"Nobody wants a war," Grandpa declared. "But it's coming. You can take that to the bank. Handwriting's on the wall. Need to send somebody to the White House that'll stand up to the Kaiser."

According to him the French were ready to throw in the towel, and the British were losing one in four ships to German torpedoes.

"And, God bless him, Mr. Wilson thinks it *ain't our fight. Hah!* Thinks women oughta have the vote. Know why? He knows women don't want their sons going off to war."

Doreen loved to pounce on points of disagreement with Grandpa.

"Women oughta have the vote! We're good as men, if you ask me, and a whole lot smarter. If I could join the National Women's Party I would, and I'd go with them to Washington. If they ever come to Maysworth, you can bet I'll be marching with 'em right up front."

Grandpa shook *The Gazette's* pages and cleared his throat loudly. "Women marching in the streets, *hah!* Where're their children while they're making spectacles of themselves? If women want to change the world, let 'em do it by staying home and raising their children like the Good Lord intended."

Mrs. Callaway was exasperated. "Papa, no need getting our boarders hot and bothered. Election ain't till November."

She poured Grandpa a second cup of coffee. "As for that awful fray, there's a wide ocean 'twixt us and them."

"Not so, Libby. The world's gettin' smaller and smaller. U-boats are prowling right off our North Carolina coast. Who knows when or where they'll strike."

When Charles Evans Hughes resigned from the Supreme Court in order to run for president on the Republican ticket, Grandpa was tickled pink.

"Hughes is the man we need in the White House," he declared. "Anybody who can govern New York, then sit on the bench making all the right decisions is the man we need to lead this country. With the world at war we got no need of a namby-pamby, wishy-washy *compromiser*."

Come November not only would Grandpa cast his vote for Charles Evans Hughes, he felt duty-bound to persuade every over twenty-one male boarder to do the same.

He didn't need to convince Papa. Papa'd been a Republican since I could remember. On Corned Beef and Cabbage nights he and Grandpa kept us all up-to-date on the campaign, with not a doubt in their minds Hughes would "trounce the professor handily."

But Winfred Gentry's prediction, that the people's wishes to stay out of a European war would be the determining factor, proved the sage of Corned Beef and Cabbage night was right again. On Tuesday, November 7, Woodrow Wilson was reelected with 277 electoral votes to Charles Evans Hughes' 254. Grandpa was flabbergasted.

All he could say was, "We Easterners got trumped by the West and Midwest. Well, *hah*, they voted themselves a losing proposition."

Like thumbing her nose at his bad political news, Doreen changed the subject. "Hey, Gramp, what's on at the Ideal Friday night?"

Grandpa sucked his empty pipe disgustedly and shoved section two her way.

"Guess what's playing on your birthday, S'lene! *The Butcher Boy*. Fatty Arbuckle *and* Buster Keaton! Both in one movie. We gotta go! Buster Keaton's the fella with that 'stone face.' Funniest man alive, funnier'n Chaplin, they say."

"What about my new dress on layaway at Belk's? And my new hat? Both due for a payment. Two installments and they're mine in time for Christmas."

"Your silly old dress can wait."

Friday, November 10, my sixteenth birthday, Mrs. Callaway fixed my favorite dessert: stacked applesauce cake like my granny used to make. She stuck a big candle in the center and told me to make a wish, then blow it out.

"Don't tell your wish now, Selena," she warned. "If you tell, it won't come true."

I wished what I always wished when the chance came: to go back to Waynesville and visit Met and Aunt Mary.

While we were at the movies, a telephone call came for me at the boardinghouse and Mrs. Callaway took the message. It was Papa. He was going to Waynesville when the mills closed for Christmas and figured I might want to go. We'd take the local to Charlotte and connect there for Waynesville. He left a telephone number for me to call.

"Oh, my goodness, Mrs. Callaway, I cain't use that thing. I don't know how," I said.

"Honey, ain't nothing simpler in the world than making a telephone call. Just take it off the hook, crank the bell, and the operator answers. All you do is tell her what number you want. She does all the work."

When the operator rang the number I gave her, somebody on the other end said, "Loray Hall for Single Men." I waited.

"Go ahead, ma'am," the operator said. "You've reached your party."

"Papa?"

The man chuckled. "Lady, I ain't nobody's papa."

"I thought you were Mr. Jim Wright."

"Jim Wright lives here. I'll see if I can get him."

There was a long pause. I didn't know if should hang up or hold on. Finally somebody said, "Hello, hello, who's there?" I recognized Papa's voice.

"Papa, it's me, your daughter, Selena Wright."

"You got my message then?"

"Yeah, and I *do*. I wanta go with you to Waynesville. When're you going?"

"Soon's the mill lets out for Christmas. Now you'll need to buy your own ticket. And you'll need to ask off two extra days."

"They don't pay for days off."

"Well, do you wanta go or not?"

"Yeah, sure. I wanta go real bad."

"You'll be needing to pack your BVD's. 'Member them cold mountain winters?"

"I remember."

I was in a fix. I wanted my new dress. But how could I take it out of layaway, pay Mrs. Callaway, and buy my train fare? I went to Mrs. Callaway.

"You'll have your dress, Selena honey," she said. "And you'll make that trip to Waynesville if I have to pass the hat. I don't think we'll need to though. I got my *rainy day fund*. We'll dip into that."

"I'll pay you back," I promised, "every cent. It might take awhile, but I'll pay you back."

"Don't worry yourself none about it. Life's too short. Just go, see that little sister you ain't laid eyes on in nigh onto two years. How old's Met now?"

"Thirteen, be fourteen in May. I can't believe Met'll be fourteen!"

Mrs. Callaway arranged with Beulah for me to start helping with kitchen cleanup after supper Fridays and Saturdays—something I could do to pay back what I owed.

After an hour of kitchen duty the first night following a full day at the mill, I went to bed worn-out. Still I had to share it with Mama:

"Mrs. Callaway does me same as her own daughter," I said.

"Since I ain't there, the Good Lord sent you this woman. Don't never forget how good she is to you."

"I won't, Mama. But no one, not even her, could take your place."

"That's mighty sweet, Sippy-gal. But life goes on. And God opens doors for them that trust Him."

"I do trust Him. And I'm trusting someday He'll take me to heaven where you and little Noble Garrett are."

"Oh, He will, honey, I promise that. Now go on, get your rest."

"Goodnight, Mama."

It took a full week's pay to get my dress and hat off lay-away. The dress was coffee brown serge with collar and trim of ecru silk. The wide-brimmed hat was brown felt.

"Look, Do'." I tried them on in front of our bureau mirror, turning this way and that.

Etha gawked, hands on her hips. I declare, S'lene, if your hair was fixed in curls you'd look *just like* Mary Pickford."

"Think so?" I pulled the pins out and let my hair fall around my shoulders.

"*Hah,*" Doreen mocked Etha. "You wouldn't know Mary Pickford if she walked in that door right this minute."

"Would so. I saw pictures of 'er in a magazine."

"Mary Pickford's hair's lighter'n S'lene's and it hangs in sausage curls."

"So!" Etha persisted. "Naomi can fix it like that. Fixed mine for the school play and everybody said I looked like a movie star. She can, S'lene. Naomi can fix it real pretty."

I gave Doreen a twisted-mouth look.

She shrugged, "Hey, why not?"

The night before Papa and I were to leave on Saturday, December 23, Naomi had me cover my shoulders with a terry mill-end. She got a glass of water, her big-toothed comb, and a box of assorted hairpins. Dipping her comb in the water, she pulled it through the length of my hair and parted it into sections.

Beginning at the top of my head she fingered deep waves, pressing them hard against my scalp and clasping them with clips. She took the lower sections, one on each side and four in back, and curled them around her forefinger, tying each with strips of cloth.

"Let it dry like this," she said. "In the morning after you get dressed, I'll take all these out and fix it."

Before I went to bed she pulled her own satin sleep bonnet over my head, stretching it below my ears.

Etha laughed. "Look like a 'haint' if I ever saw one."

I stuck my tongue out at her.

I didn't sleep a wink that night, partly from excitement, but mostly my head hurt and no amount of feather tick would soften the metal clips.

———

Beulah fixed sacks with fried chicken, buttermilk biscuits with blackberry jam, and apples. We'd eat in Charlotte depot or on our way to Waynesville. Doreen rode with me to the depot where Papa was waiting and I checked the large carpetbag Naomi loaned me. They tied on a tag that read in bold letters, *Waynesville, N.C.* I was really going!

"All aboard!" The conductor stood beside the steel steps as Papa and I mounted. We went inside our coach and took seats by a window. I waved to Doreen. Her fingers brushed one eye, but I knew she wasn't crying. Doreen never cried.

Chapter 18

The *whoosh* of steam and *clickity-clack* of wheels took me back to the trip Papa, Met, and I made years earlier to what Papa called "Boomtown."

"Still think Gastonia's Boomtown?" I asked him.

"That I do. Look what all's happened since we got here. Loray's bigger and better. More stores, more houses, more churches. Trolley line. And your mill at Maysworth with new jobs, new houses. I swear, Sippy, you and me's come a long way from scratching out a living on the side of Utah Mountain. Just wish your ma coulda lived to see it."

I didn't remind him I hated the nickname Sippy, like I did on that train ride from Waynesville years before. I was sixteen now and by Doreen's definition a woman. A woman doesn't quibble over small things. Mama never did, and neither did Mrs. Callaway. I didn't remind him, either, that Clemmie was with him in Gastonia all those years ago, and now she was gone who knows where. I'd stopped asking if he heard from her. A woman doesn't pick at old wounds. Papa wasn't drinking like he had and for that I was grateful. Maybe he'd met somebody. I didn't ask that either.

Pulling into Waynesville Depot I couldn't help it. Hot tears stung my eyes and it was all I could do to keep back open sobs.

Papa grinned. "S'matter, gal?"

"Nothing. Just thinking how it used to be."

Outside the station many of the horse-drawn coaches were gone, replaced by motorized versions. But when we walked through the wide station doors— the sounds, the smells, the excitement—we were back in time. Peddlers hawking wares.

"Shine, mister? How about a shine?" Papa shook his head.

"*Waynesville Citizen, Waynesville Citizen*, get your newspaper right here." Papa bought a paper while our bags were unloaded.

Arthur, Aunt Mary's husband, was waiting outside with his mule and wagon. Their twelve-year-old daughter, Nancy Burzilla, called "Bur," was with him.

"Whoa, Sara, whoa," he hollered when the mule lurched. "Hold it, gal."

He tied the reins to the seat and jumped down to find space for our bags. "Mary ain't talked about nothing but you'ns for days," he said.

"And Met? What about Met?" Papa asked.

"Yeah, yeah. Met, too."

"Surprised that little gal didn't come with you'ns to town, much as she loves this depot." Papa pulled himself up front with Arthur, while I settled in back to share a folded-up quilt with Bur.

Arthur glanced back. "Well, you'ns may as well know—Met's been feeling poorly. But I'll let Mary fill you in there. Giddy-yap, Sara. Let's git on back, gal."

We were mostly quiet the slow bumpy ride past Water Street where Aunt Mary used to live when Mama was alive, and up a rocky incline toward their Hazelwood farm.

A cold wind picked up as we creaked along the red clay road. Bur leaned hard against me and I pulled a second quilt around our shoulders. Bur was big for twelve with a wide ruddy face like her papa. Her breath smelled of onions and I thought of the wild leeks Mama used to gather on Utah.

We lumbered into a shady creek bed where wet rocks jutted from the rippling stream. Bur and I grabbed the side of the wagon as it quaked and the wheels dug in. The mule stopped.

Arthur hacked, spewing brown spittle from his plug. "Giddap, Sara," he yelled, wiping his mouth with a sleeve. "Dang stubborn female."

Papa laughed. "Watch out!" He twisted his head toward us. "Got two of 'em back there."

"*Huh!*" Arthur yanked Sara's reins.

The mule shuddered, straining against her harness. The wagon pulled from the hole, bumping and clattering through stones to dry road.

Arthur bellowed above the grinding wheels, "Jim, this side o' the creek's where my spread starts. Come spring, I'll be a'planting this here fallow with corn. See them rows o' trees straight off. That's my orchard—Jonathan's, Delicious, all pruned and ready."

On a hill stark limbs stretched skyward like eerie figures pleading to God for mercy. I shivered.

We rounded a bend and the log house emerged on a crest squat to the ground in front like a brown mushroom nestled in a bed of green. Stacked pillars of rock supported the cabin's rear. Smoke trailed above a stone chimney. Dogs came running, barking alongside.

"Them hounds is my pride," Arthur yelled to Papa. "We'uns'll get a little hunting in whilst you're here."

Two women stood on the front porch. I made out it was Met and Aunt Mary, both in pinafores, arms akimbo. Nelse II was brushing against their legs.

"Whoa, Sara, whoa, gal!" Arthur jumped down and tied the reins to a tree trunk, then reached up to help us.

Met came running. "Sippy! Sippy!"

She sounded like the Met of old times. The setting was same as Utah Mountain. Aunt Mary could be Mama.

"Met!" I felt a roundness when we hugged. Met had plumped up. I hugged Aunt Mary.

"Come in, come on in." Aunt Mary took my hand. "Too cold to stand out here."

Inside the warmth was heavy with smells of spiced apples, cornbread, and fried smoke-cured ham. I was famished.

"Go on," Mary said. "Get yourselves freshed up whilst Met and me dish up some supper in less time

than you can say 'jack rabbit.' Good ole mountain vit-
tles, Jim, like I reckon you ain't put your mouth to in
a coon's age."

I stared at Met. Her roundness was all in front.
Oh, dear Lord. Please no. It can't be.

Met helped take up food while Bur showed me
the room I'd stay in, Met and me sharing a featherbed
while Bur slept on a quilt pallet.

I was in a daze about Met. How could this happen
and where, who? I needed to talk to Aunt Mary—
alone. Had Papa noticed? I doubted it. Men see only
what they want to. He and Arthur's thoughts were on
dogs and hunting. Well, he'd know sooner or later. I
felt dizzy, my appetite gone, the smells now all but
nauseous.

Through the meal till an early bedtime, we talked
about our train trip, about Gastonia and Maysworth,
about the mills, how all of it was booming.

"Well, you'll never get me off the farm," Uncle
Arthur said. Before retiring, he unlocked his gun case
and showed Papa his rifles, cleaned and ready. "More
deer out there than you can shake a stick at, Jim. A
few bear, too, just waiting for Mutt and Jeff to sniff
'em out. Them dogs d'ruther hit that woodsy trail
than eat."

They'd get up before dawn, get an early start.

Papa was as excited as a boy, certainly not ready to
hear he'd be a grandfather. All hell might break loose
when that happened.

Undressing for bed, Met's muslin shift plainly outlined her pregnant form. I wanted to cry. Maybe God knew best, that Mama didn't live to see this. Or maybe if she'd lived...

We got into bed and I cleared my throat to whisper, "Met, honey, what happened? Did...did somebody make you...I mean...who got you 'that way?'"

She started sobbing quiet-like. "I...I cain't tell. Ain't telling nobody 'cause ain't nothing nobody can do about it."

"But, Aunt Mary, what does she think?"

"Them's *her* words: 'Nobody cain't do nothing about it.' Says her and Uncle Arthur'll look after me. They'll raise the baby like it's theirs, like it's in place of their own little Peggy, the one that died when she won't but two."

She kept sniffling till I put my arms around her.

"I'm so sorry, sweet girl," I said. "I wish you could've stayed in Gastonia with me. Maybe it wouldn't have happened."

I thought about the time she caught Clemmie in bed with Ben McElroy and thought he was hurting her. She was so innocent then. Maybe she still was and somebody took advantage of it. I gritted my teeth. But who? She wasn't telling.

I lay awake while Met and Bur's gentle snores mixed with log cabin creaks and the winds of the wild mountain. *"Mama,"* I whispered in prayer, *"Met's in the family way and she ain't fourteen yet."*

"*I know, gal, but tain't your fault. Don't never blame yourself.*"

"*I thought she'd be safe with Aunt Mary.*"

"*Orter been. We don't know Mary's husband, honey. So I say, Stay away from him.*"

"*What're you saying, Mama?*"

"*Ain't saying nothing. Just don't git yourself alone with Arthur Hinson.*"

Papa and Uncle Arthur were already gone next morning when we got up. Aunt Mary was wiping skillets where she'd fixed fried eggs and streak-o-lean with wheat hoecakes.

I sat down to leftover hoecake drenched with fresh-churned butter and wildwood honey. She poured me a cup of boiled coffee.

"Met won't tell me who bigged her," I confided.

She turned, glaring at me, "Just as well. What's done's done. Ain't no boy alive goin' admit he laid her. I warned her, yes I did. 'Stay away from the boys,' I said. Warned her a thing like this could happen. But don't worry yourself none about it. Me and Arthur, we'll take care of 'er, raise that baby like it's our'n."

Papa and Arthur got in just as the orange ball of a sun dropped into the gorge. They'd bagged a deer and some quail, but Papa was quiet-like, not himself. I guessed Arthur'd told him. He didn't hit the ceiling. Instead he seemed kinda sad.

A light snow was falling next morning as they cleaned and dressed the deer and birds on an outside table. Strips of venison were cut thin for drying. The rest was covered with oil, vinegar, and herbs. Aunt Mary put on a large pot for boiling water and spices. When it commenced bubbling she dumped the dressed quails in along with new potatoes, dried leeks and peppers. She cracked eggs and dropped them one at a time into the steaming pot. Met got sick and went behind the house to puke.

The day before we left I asked if we could take the mule and wagon and go up Utah Mountain where Mama was buried.

"Ain't a bit o' use, honey," Aunt Mary said. "I been over there time and again. Your mama's grave ain't nowhere to be found. Somebody's done took her stone, moved it somewheres else, another grave I 'spect."

"I'd remember the place," I said. "I know I could find it. I know what it looks like, just like it was yesterday."

"Thought I would too, honey. But I'm telling you vines is growed all over that burying ground. It don't look the same."

I wanted to cry. They didn't want to take me to Utah. It was too much trouble. I ached to see that mountain, the creek, if our old cabin was still there. Nothing had gone right. I was ready to go home.

"Why cain't you stay, Sippy?" Met padded behind me whimpering like a spoiled puppy as I rolled my clothes and stuffed them into the borrowed carpetbag. "Why cain't you move back to Waynesville?"

"What would I do? I got a job in Maysworth that pays good money and a place to live. Who do I even know in Waynesville anymore?"

My brown serge dress was rumpled and the ecru silk collar would not lie flat. I brushed the stringy strands of my once Mary Pickford curls and pulled them into a tight bun at the nape of my neck.

"You know Uncle John and Aunt Evie."

She was a child again, pouting and pleading.

I shook my head. Evie I hardly knew. Uncle John still worked at the tannery where I vowed never to go again. Just thinking of the dead-animal odor like to have made me sick.

Saying goodbye to Met was the hardest thing I'd done since leaving Waynesville years ago. But Papa wanted to see his brother before we left Waynesville and we had to allow time for that. Arthur let me off at the depot while he and Papa went to see John at the tannery.

Settling onto a wooden bench, I shivered in the icy blasts from the depot's swinging door and savored the tangy smells: apple-scented pipe smoke, pungent bootblack, roasted chestnuts on a string, dried herbs gathered from hilltops and sold for every known ailment. Mama, Met, and I used to come at midday with ginseng root Papa dug from the hills and dewberries picked early that morning. We got to know other peddlers while all of us waited for the shrill whistle of the next train rounding Holcomb's Gap loaded with tourists anxious to buy our wares.

Papa strode in and flopped beside me, "Don't 'spect I'll be wanting Mary's bag lunch fer a while." He seemed in good spirits, laughing about his and Arthur's tannery visit. "I swear that odor like to've took me over, even my hair."

He got his comb out and raked through graying red curls. "John and Evie's fine," he said. "France and Raymond's both moved out, got jobs. France done took himself a wife."

"France married? He ain't but...but nineteen." In my mind France Wright would always be twelve.

Our trip home was long with nothing we wanted to discuss and too much to think about. I couldn't broach the subject of Met. It was too painful. What could we say? There was enough guilt all around.

I looked forward to seeing Doreen much as anything in my life. Even her run-ins with Grandpa would remind me, "This is how it is with family, and it's okay." I daydreamed of Saturday trips to Sweetland for Cherry-Berry ice cream sodas, to The Ideal and The Lumina to see Charlie Chaplin or Mary Pickford or Doreen's favorites, Mabel Normand and those funny bumbling Keystone Kops.

Thinking on it made me smile. I closed my eyes and began humming "Down By The Old Millstream."

"What's that?" Papa asked.

"Oh, just our latest Victrola song. I know all the words to it."

Chapter 19

P resident Wilson's still vowing to stay out of the fray," Grandpa exclaimed from his parlor chair. "I declare 'the professor' ain't living in the real world. Krauts' U-boats are sinking our ships. Now Kaiser Bill's trying to get Mexico to declare war on us. *Mexico!* Would you believe we ain't even ready for *that*. Be 'Remembering the Alamo' all over again." Grandpa rattled *The Gazette*'s pages loudly and shook his white head. "What's it gonna take, for heaven's sake?"

Mrs. Callaway looked up from her tatting. "Now Papa, don't get so riled. You're getting too old for that."

"Listen to me, Elizabeth Dorcas Spencer, it's time folks in this country got stirred up."

A knock at the door caught us off guard.

"Who could be calling at eight o'clock?" Mrs. Callaway wondered aloud.

She knotted her tatting and snipped a thread as Etha jumped up from a losing game of Backgammon with Naomi.

"I'll see," Etha yelled on her way to the door.

"Yeah, he's here, come on in." She opened the door to a dark-haired stranger.

The tall young man walked directly to where Grandpa was sitting and extended his hand. "Remember me, sir?"

Never one to admit forgetting names or faces, Grandpa stammered as he rose from his chair, "I...I do seem to recall your face, yes."

"I'm J.D. *Newell*. You went with me to the police station to turn myself in...three years ago. Remember?"

"You...you're the one that set fire to Sudie Hailey's house!"

"Yessir. I'm sorry to say I did that...that awful thing." His face reddened as he clasped and unclasped his hands. "I'm a changed man, Mr. Spencer. Served my time at Central Prison, paid my debt to society. I want to thank you for pointing me to Jesus. I joined a Bible group in prison. Wrote Mrs. Hailey and begged her to forgive me."

"Did you hear from Sudie?"

"Yessir, I did. Still got that letter. I've read it so many times it's come apart. That wonderful lady said she forgave me *long* ago. Said her life's turned around, too. She's helping other people come to know the Lord."

He turned and looked at the rest of us.

Grandpa pointed to Etha standing next to him, "My granddaughter, Etha Callaway. These others are my daughter, Libby Callaway, another granddaughter,

Doreen, and some of our roomers. Can you sit awhile, J.D.?"

"Oh, no, no sir. I just came to say thank you, and ask for your help. I...I want to enlist in the Marine Corps. They say my crime's a 'waiverable offense' and with good recommendations the Marine Corps might take me. Got no family to speak of. I believe the military life would suit me fine."

"Well, I suppose you've learned a thing or two about discipline. I guarantee the Marines'll have you toeing the line, if they're anything like I hear. So you're wanting a letter of recommendation?"

"Yessir."

"Come on to the kitchen table and have a seat. We'll see what I can do."

J.D. Newell followed Grandpa to the kitchen while the rest of us looked at each other.

"I'll make a pot of coffee," Mrs. Callaway said, padding along behind.

While the procession moved to the kitchen, Doreen threw up her hands and sighed loudly. "Well, of all the nerve! The nerve of *that man* coming here to ask for our help. Up to me, I'd order him out of this house."

I thought of Sudie Hailey, her fingers burned to nubs because of this man, J.D. Newell. Still it was so like her to forgive him. Tomorrow I'd write, tell her about this and ask how Ada and Kizzie were.

J.D. Newell soon made his way back to the front door. "I'll write you, sir," he said, "let you know what happens."

Grandpa extended his hand again. "Please do. Our country needs you, J.D. And our prayers will be with you."

Doreen bided her time waiting for J.D. to be clear out before lighting into Grandpa.

"How could you do that? That man burned Sudie Hailey's house down. Burnt her fingers clean off her hands! He's *got no call* coming here begging for help."

"Doreen Lydia, have we failed you, darlin'? You need to learn forgiveness. Next to love, forgiveness is the greatest virtue."

"I love and forgive those that *deserve* it. J.D. Newell's not on my list."

"*Jesus* is our example. He died for the undeserving."

"I don't care. I hate that man and always will for what he did to Sudie Hailey."

Before falling asleep I talked it over with Mama:

"J.D. Newell was a mean man—burning down Mrs. Hailey's house—but he served his time and acts different, even looks different, says Mrs. Hailey forgives him. How could she—when he hurt her so bad?"

"Christians oughta have forgiveness in their hearts. Didn't Jesus forgive every single one of us? Sudie Hailey's only doing what her Lord expects."

"Not Doreen. Do' won't forgive him."

"Give 'er time, honey. She'll learn."

"The Lord Jesus, He's with you and little Noble right now?"

"That He is. Now go on, sweet girl, get your rest."

———

On April 6, 1917, America declared war on Germany, and on April 7 *The Gastonia Gazette*'s headline blazoned the news.

"Ready or not, here we come," Grandpa exclaimed, and I thought I detected a veiled smile.

"What's it mean, Papa?" Mrs. Callaway asked.

"Well, Libby, like some of us knew all along, Professor Wilson's 'peace without victory' didn't work." His head was bobbing all the while. Kaiser Bill and the 'Krauts' would face dealing with the likes of us. "Right now we'll keep doing same as we have been—helping the Allies—'cept be more open. I expect, if we have to, we'll call up troops, train 'em and send 'em over."

Forty years younger and I could see Grandpa up front in a recruiting line.

In May the Selective Service Act was passed and beginning June 5, all men between twenty-one and thirty-one had to register. Within weeks millworkers were signing up and leaving for army camps before being called, some saying army life beat breathing lint the rest of their lives, others just itching to be in the fray. Women were getting the weaving jobs they'd always wanted and knew they could handle. Posters urged Americans to "Work or Fight."

Sweetland Ice Cream Parlor, ever on the lookout for eye-catching slogans, began naming sodas and sundaes after front-page news. Banana splits became "Navy Boats." "Nuts to the Kaiser" were nut sundaes. Banners of red, white, and blue hung from windows and behind the counter.

Doreen and I were sharing our Cherry-Berry ice cream soda when we caught sight of Freddie Fletcher alone behind a potted palm. Doreen parted two fronds.

"Hey, Fred, where you been? Ain't seen much of you lately."

I hunkered low, not anxious to renew his acquaintance since the box supper incident, though I had to admit he'd behaved himself. Hadn't looked half-bad, either, in his Sunday suit, hair parted and lint combed out.

He pushed the palm aside. "Funny seeing y'all." He looked close to mature in a stiff white collar and bow tie, but his voice was cocky as ever. "One more day and you won't find me in these parts."

"Yeah?" Doreen raised her eyebrows. "What do you mean?"

Freddie got a kick out of being mysterious—like the time Loray Mill went on strike and I hadn't heard. Laughed like I was a *dumb ox.*

"I done joined up," he said. "Army needs me. Posters say so and I believe 'em. Better'n spending every waking hour fixing warpers. Suit me fine if I don't never see the inside of Loray again." He spooned a great gob of chocolate ice cream into his mouth.

I perked up, stretching to look him in the eye. "Freddie Fletcher, sixteen ain't old enough to enlist."

"I'm *seventeen*."

"Still ain't old enough."

He laughed. "I just told 'em I'm nineteen and they never asked for proof."

Smart-aleck Fred had done it again.

"Where you going?" Doreen asked.

"Camp Jackson, South Carolina, 81st Division. Call 'em *The Wild Cats*. Getting the train outta this cotton mill town tomorrow."

He scraped the sides of his bowl and licked the spoon, his tongue reaching all corners like polishing silver.

"Want us to write you?"

"Sure. I'll send you my address soon's I get one. To Mrs. Callaway's on Main Street. Glad I saw y'all."

We left to catch the next trolley home. "What'd you think about Freddie?" Doreen asked.

"They say the Army'll make a man out of you," I said. "It'll take some doing."

She laughed. "Now, S'lene, quit looking for all the fellas to be Winfred Gentry. There's only one and he's taken."

"And the best woman got him."

After a cold supper served from the buffet, Mrs. Callaway left Beulah in charge of the kitchen while she went to a meeting to help organize a Home Demonstration Club for Gaston County.

Beulah washed and I dried. She didn't trust anybody else to get the plates clean. "What kind of club is that?" I asked her.

"It'll take place of the *tomato clubs* they got now. Lib wants to learn the best ways to can and pickle. That's mainly why she's going. They got agents paid by the government to show women how to do everything under the sun using the latest methods. Ain't *that* something!"

"Mrs. Callaway could teach folks herself. Knows more'n anybody I ever saw." I opened the china cabinet and carefully deposited a stack of plates.

Beulah looked around to see if we were alone and lowered her voice. "Did you hear Alma's back?"

"Alma Keeter?"

"Yeah, got herself a job at Mays Mill, wants to come back to Callaway's."

I didn't know what to think. We heard she'd never go back to Gus. Grandpa Spencer didn't approve renting rooms to men or women who'd forsaken their marriages, and Mrs. Callaway went along with it. Till now it had not been a problem.

Mrs. Callaway still wasn't home when the phone rang. It was my night to answer. *Where was Etha?* I waited. No one budged or seemed to even hear. I took a deep breath, went to the hall, and lifted the earpiece. "Hello, hello."

"That you, Sippy?"

"Yeah, Papa."

"Had to let you know 'bout Met. Met's got herself a little girl, named 'er Emily. You're an aunt and I'm a grandpapa."

"Is she all right?"

"Met's too little to be a real mama but, yeah, they say she's fine."

"Aunt Mary'll see to her and the baby."

I dared not say what lay deep in my mind that worried me ever since our trip to Hazelwood. After all, there was nothing either of us could do. Not now.

From the parlor came strains of "Don't Take My Darling Boy Away," with J. Philips and Helen Clark. War songs were all the rage and Doreen spent every cent she made that week on three new Victrola records.

"*Shhhh!*" she said as I walked in. "I'm trying to make out all the words."

When my eyes smarted and hot tears welled, I must've looked like the woman in the song whose darling boy was taken away.

Doreen stared like I was crazy. " S'lene, are the words *that* sad?"

"Ain't your song, Do'. It's...It's Met. My baby sister's got a baby herself, a little girl. I can't believe it. How'd you feel if...if *Etha* had a baby?"

She hugged me. "So sorry, hon."

The parlor was clearing out, roomers heading upstairs. I was glad. By then I was bawling out loud.

"I feel bad, like somehow it's all my fault."

"Stop that. Ain't your fault and don't never think that."

The song ended but the record kept going 'round and 'round, away...away...away...Doreen rushed to grab the needle up. She put on a second record. "Keep the Home Fires Burning" was sadder than the first.

"That one's all the way from England," she said. "It's what they're singing over there—*Keep the home fires burning while our hearts are yearning...*"

I was ready to bust out crying again when in walked Etha. I grabbed her and hugged her tight.

"What'd I do?" she asked.

Chapter 20

Fabric orders poured in from the Army to Cramer Mills, new name for Mays Mills, just as male hands were enlisting or being drafted. To gear up, boys under eighteen and women shifted to the vacated jobs. Increased demands meant overtime, but no one shirked. Patriotism had caught on. Hard work was how to do our part. "Do it for *Our Doughboys*, for the *Old Red, White, and Blue*."

Early on a Monday I was startled when the overseer tapped my shoulder.

"Selena." His voice was shrill above the racket. "Know how to tend warpers?"

What could he mean? "Ain't never done it," I said.

"Well, you been spinning and spooling long enough. I think you're ready to handle a warper. Ain't hard. Mainly need to keep on your toes, watch 'em real good."

He explained how thread was put on warps which were then taken to the weave room. There the yarn would be woven into cloth.

"Come on, I'll pair you up with an old hand."

I followed him to the warper room, scared as a stuck pig, praying each step of the way. "God help me" burst from my lips as we approached the frames.

The rest of my day I spent running in circles, trying to keep threads moving onto the warps.

That night I dragged home and fell into bed without so much as combing lint from my hair. Next morning when the mill whistle blew, I wondered if I'd make it. I did, and the next day, and the day after that. As time passed the job didn't get easier, but the warpers quit throwing me into the heart-gripping fear of that first day.

"Tending warpers is the hardest job I ever did in my whole life," I complained to Doreen.

"Don't worry, you'll get the hang of it."

"I got the *hang* of it all right. It's...well—did you ever lead a mule pulling a plow? No, I guess you ain't. I have, and a warper's just as stubborn. It balks same as a mule. And like guiding that plow, you gotta walk and walk and walk just to keep it going."

"*It* balks, *you* walk. Sounds like poetry."

The Warper

A warper's like a stubborn mule,
That balks, and balks, and balks.
The fool who tries to run the thing
Walks, and walks, and walks.

Just when I've got it going,
Just when it's getting tame,

It throws a fit right in my face
And spoils my little game.

But I must work, not cuss or shirk;
I know my job full well—
If I'm not good while here on earth,
I'll run one down in Hell.

We laughed till we cried coming up with the rhyme, but I swore it was more truth than poetry.

"Miss Whitesides, *Mrs. Gentry* now, will never see this one," I vowed.

"Don't show it to Grandpa neither."

"Didn't he tell us *hell*'s mentioned more times in the Bible than *heaven?*"

"Yeah, honey, but your poem ain't scripture."

———

After talking to Mrs. Callaway, Alma moved into the newly-built dormitory for single women millhands.

"Ain't bad," she told me on our way out from work one day. "Ain't home, neither. The boardinghouse—now that'll always be home to me. Everybody there's same as family."

I understood, even sympathized, but Grandpa laid down the law and had his reasons. Rules were rules and shouldn't be broken.

"Gus joined the Navy," Alma confided. "Ain't never been on a boat before."

"Why the Navy?" I asked.

"'Join the Navy and see the world,' is what they promise 'em. Furthest away Gus ever went was Raleigh, on our honeymoon." Her eyes were dreamy, as if pulling a scene from the past.

I thought of the album she showed me and Doreen not long after the two were married. Beneath their picture standing in front of Central Prison, she'd written "We're shackled now, too." It wasn't true and I wondered why. Did Gus fail to measure up? Where were all the knights in shining armor, the Winfred Gentrys of the world? Would I find mine? Doreen claimed Mr. Gentry was 'one of a kind.' I disagreed. Would a good God break the mold?

Our first letter from Freddie Fletcher was to both Doreen and me, care of Mrs. Callaway's. He apologized for not having written, said he'd had no time.

"Boot camp's another word for breaking your will and seeing how much you can take," he wrote. "We've marched till our blisters got blisters. We eat hardtack and drink water from canteens. 'You'll thank us for getting you ready,' they yell at us. 'This is how it'll be in France.' I'm lean, mean, and hard as a rock. If I live through basic training, I'll get to come home a few days before being transferred."

The letter didn't sound like the Freddie I knew. His words were reflective, the arrogance missing. Even the name on the return address: Pvt. *Frederick R. Fletcher* suggested a person of status, not Freddie, the warper fixer. Frederick R. Fletcher—*Sir* Frederick R. Fletcher, *Esquire,* or *The Reverend* Frederick R. Fletcher. Possibly someone political, *Senator* Frederick R. Fletcher. Ladies and gentlemen, I'd like to introduce our distinguished *mayor,* Mr. Frederick R. Fletcher.

I answered right away giving him all the news I could think of: how Grandpa was heading up a Red Cross drive and asked all us boarders to help, how I was learning to tame the once dreaded warpers. "Bet you don't miss them one bit," I wrote, thinking he'd figure the Army not so bad after all.

His next letter was addressed to me only. "All furloughs are canceled," he scrawled almost illegibly. "Our group's got orders to a brand new camp in New Jersey—Camp Merritt. I'll write from there with my new address. Please keep on writing. Your letters *mean more than you'll ever know.*"

That was flattering, also a little disturbing. His mother lived in Gastonia and I wondered if she might be writing the same news I did. Till one day at work Alma confessed she'd known Mrs. Fletcher a long time.

"The woman can't read or write," Alma shouted above the machines' roar. "She depends on Freddie for everything. Somebody has to read his letters and write hers. Can you imagine? *Second-hand thoughts.* Getting somebody else to put your thoughts down on paper."

It was not something Freddie would tell. He was too proud. But knowing made me write more often

with longer letters. Alma had given the perfect op-
portunity and I asked, "Do you write Gus?"

She seemed to ignore my question and I wondered
if she'd heard above the weave room clatter. Dare I
shout it out again?

Finally, hands free, she turned, looking me in the
eyes.

"What else *can* I do, S'lene? They're shipping out
to who knows where, maybe into the thick of it. He
can't say where or when." She shook her head. "Writing's the least I can do."

Well, how do you feel about that? I wanted to ask.
But Mama taught me not intrude into other folk's
hearts without an invitation. Working the same floor
we saw each other every day. If Alma wanted to tell
me more, she could. She was like an older sister, and
being an older sister myself, I understood that some
things are best kept to yourself.

Nothing surprised me more than when Alma
came to me one day.

"Gus wants a picture of me," she said. "I'm going
to Shuford's and have one made."

Shuford's Studio was well-known for its glamour
photographs. In their window portraits the girls all
looked like movie stars, and the men were handsome.

"Still got your Kodak? I could take one of you."

"Selena, sugar, he wants one to show off to all his
buddies. I gotta look real good. Why don't you get one
made, too, send it to Freddie. Come on, we'll have
fun."

We talked Doreen into going and she had Naomi fix our hair before we left. Mine was tangled for body, then combed over a large rat pinned at the nape of my neck. I looked like I had twice as much hair. Doreen's red curls were tamed into waves with a wet comb with a long corkscrew curl hanging in front of each ear.

The three of us spent Saturday afternoon at the studio where we took off our shirtwaists and put on smocks. Rouge was brushed high on our cheeks and dabbed heavily on our lips. Our brows were tweezed and arched with pencil.

The attendant handed me a mirror, "What do you think?"

Was that really me? Or was it Mary Pickford?

"I like it," I said. She fastened a lavaliere around my neck.

Smocks were removed and our shoulders draped with silk fabric. I was handed a bouquet. With baskets of ferns as backdrop, I took my turn on a stool in front of hot bright lights.

"Turn slightly to your right," the photographer hollered, his head hidden beneath the camera's black hood. "Don't smile and *don't* look at the camera. Think of that wonderful man in your life, how pretty he'll think you are."

The remark almost brought a smile. Instead I looked down as if sniffing the nosegay.

"Hold that!" Light burst with a loud *whoosh*.

"Good, good" he said. "Let's try one more to be sure," and we did the same thing again.

Alma was so excited about Grandpa heading a Red Cross drive.

"I want to help," she told us. "It's the least I can do. The Red Cross is doing so much for 'our boys.'"

The fact she was no longer a boardinghouse resident didn't matter.

Grandpa was so touched, he mentioned it at Saturday night's supper table.

"Alma Keeter's one of the smartest women I know. I can sure use her help. Fact is, what I wanta do will take all the help I can drum up from everybody that's willing."

Forks in midair, every head turned his way.

"We're putting on a stage show," Grandpa said, stunning some of us to the point of almost choking on our food.

Before we recovered enough to ask what he meant, he went on.

"Oh, I know what you're thinking. I've always preached against Vaudeville and movie shows. Well, this's different. Ain't about Douglas Fairbanks or Charlie Chaplin or none of them Hollywood types. No, it's about how to make the most money for the Red Cross. Box suppers are fine, but a theatre full of people'll bring a lot more money."

First to get over the shock was Mrs. Callaway. "When are you talking about, Papa, and where? Maysworth School's got no auditorium. And we sure can't use the church."

"I know that, Libby. What do you take me for? First thing I did was get the place. It'll be The Ideal Theatre."

"The Ideal?" Doreen laughed so hard I was afraid she'd be sent from the table. "*The Ideal?* I can't believe it. Why would the owners do such a thing?"

"Ignorance does not excuse disdain, young lady," Grandpa said, "Obviously you don't have the facts." He was drawing great pleasure from our astonishment. "If you'd been reading the Red Cross column in *The Gazette,* all of you, you'd know The Ideal already sets aside days when part of their receipts go to the Red Cross. Like this Friday, September 28, thirty percent of their take for *Madcap Madge* with Olive Thomas, the most beautiful showgirl in America, will go to the Red Cross."

I could hardly believe my ears; Grandpa speaking of Olive Thomas, the most beautiful showgirl in America! We sat dumfounded as he made an X on his plate with his knife and fork letting Beulah know he was finished.

He leaned forward, lacing his fingers like when he asked God to bless our food. "All this is to say, yes, they're letting us use the theatre for a stage production—free of charge, I might add, except for heating and lights. They got us down for Saturday, December 29. That's three months away, three months for us to come up with a show that'll be a sellout."

Zombie-like we pushed back our chairs and filed to the parlor, wondering how it could come about.

"Well, I be dog," Doreen managed. "You could've knocked me over with a feather. I didn't know the old man had it in him."

Excitement replaced disbelief as ideas were tossed around.

"Hey y'all," I said. "We got lots of talent right here in the boardinghouse. Etha's been in plays at school."

"That's right," Doreen admitted. "And she's good, even if she is my sister. Her drama teacher, Miss Adams, really knows plays; the best ones, funny ones, knows where to get 'em from. We could ask her advice."

"Not bragging, but I can paint scenery," Naomi piped up. "I've done murals. It ain't that different."

"Mama can make costumes," Doreen offered. "All she needs is a picture and she can cut her own patterns."

It was shaping up before our eyes and we convinced ourselves we could actually bring it off. With the mills running twenty-four hours a day, seven days a week, all of us were working full time, sometimes overtime. But for this, we could give up Saturday and Sunday afternoons.

Grandpa talked with Miss Adams and she ordered a three-act play called, *The Old Maids' Convention.*

"It's hilarious," she promised, "And we don't need men—all female roles. The lines aren't that hard.

Scenery's easy, too, card tables for props. It all takes place in a hotel ballroom."

Miss Adams volunteered to help but recommended her best friend to direct. "I think Fran'll donate her time for such a good cause," she said.

Her friend directed the musical, *Madame Butterfly*, at the Opera House.

"Fran can get the best from nonprofessionals. She'll have those girls doing things they never thought they could."

We were on our way.

———

"Mama," I shared that night, *"Grandpa surprised us all with plans for a stage play. He's never done anything like that before."*

"Don't never put people in a box." Her voice was clear as when she sat by our open hearth telling Met and me stories about Lords and Ladies in Londontown. *"And don't think old people can't have fresh notions."*

I smiled remembering when Granny went with us to Haywood County Fair and rode the Ferris wheel. She was excited as we were, and like Grandpa Spencer was about a stage play for the Red Cross.

The next day a letter came from Freddie Fletcher postmarked Camp Merritt, New Jersey, with a snapshot of him sitting on the barrel of a large gun. The envelope had been slit and sealed back up, and the letter was short as if scribbled hastily.

"We're shipping out," it said. "Can't say where or when, but nobody gets to go home. Keep writing to this address. May take a while but I'll get your letters someday."

The address on the envelope had an APO number. I knew what that meant. He was headed overseas, maybe to France.

Doreen was in the parlor playing our latest Victrola record—"Smiles." It was peppy, easy to sing with. The second line went, *There are smiles that make us blue*.

"Here's a smile that'll make you blue," I said, handing her Freddie's picture.

"Must've been taking lessons from Mona Lisa," she said. "Looks like he's thinking: 'Well, so help me if I didn't get caught sitting atop this gun.'"

"I hope he sent one to his mother. Wonder how she feels about him going overseas." I was thinking I should go meet her, see how she was getting on. Alma knew where she lived. Maybe the two of us could go.

On Monday a new posting was tacked inside the door of the mill: GASTON COUNTY'S KILLED AND WOUNDED IN ACTION. One name was beneath the "Killed in Action."

I shuddered. "Dear Father in Heaven—it's started already—where will it end?"

———

Efird's full-page ad in *The Gazette* got my attention.

"Look, Do', new fall coat-suits low as $12.50! Coats—silk plush, velour, and plaids starting at $1.98."

"I need new clothes! Lemme see that."

Belk's'll never beat *these* prices: new fall waists, petticoats, low as forty-eight cents. I want a plaid coat. Need one. Be perfect with my serge dress, my shirtwaists and skirts. I'll call it my birthday present to myself."

"I can't believe you, S'lene, gettin' so vain. First glamour pictures at Shuford's, now a birthday present to yourself. What happened to that little mountain hooger turned *linthead?*"

"She worked hard and got paid."

"Every Saturday's practice time for the play. We got no time to shop."

Wages were up at the mill with salaries ranging from $1.50 to $6.50 per day for men and $1 to $4 per day for women. Who'd have thought in a million years we boardinghouse girls would be making money faster than we could spend it? It was both frustrating and exhilarating for this soon to be seventeen-year-old.

But Granny used to say, "Where there's a will there's a way."

I hardly hesitated, "We'll skip dinner, take the noon trolley to town. If we're a little late for practice, who'll notice, we're not the stars."

Doreen and I were spinsters in the play, but Miss Adams chose Alma for the starring role: a grouchy, gregarious, man-hating old maid. Alma's voice carried. No doubt it came from years of hollering above the clatter of mill machinery. Her easily heard and understood reading of lines earned her the part. Doreen was envious. Not me—I never wanted the limelight.

Etha was playing her antagonist, an untrained waitress who foils Alma in every scene, causing Alma to plead with management to fire the bumbling waitress. When Etha *accidentally* dumps a tray of beverages into Alma's lap, the audience is well-primed for payback. The *accident's* perfect timing would bring applause and roars of laughter.

Our practice hall was the Red Cross workroom where tables were piled with yards of outing to be cut into pajamas for military hospitals. Much of it would be assembled in the workroom; the rest taken home by volunteers to sew and bring back. We carefully avoided disturbing the project and stayed well shy of another reminder of a nation at war—three thousand yards of surgical material donated for bandages and stacks of surgical dressings sent by the Mt. Holly Chapter.

Doreen and I took the trolley to Efird's on Saturday soon as we got off work. I bought my red and black plaid coat, then we hurried across to Belk's where for $1.50 I purchased a red felt hat with black headband that matched my coat perfectly. Doreen bought two waists and a petticoat. No way we were skipping Sweetland, not when we faced it directly across the street. A soda jerk concocted our "Tipperary Berry" ice cream soda with two straws to go, and we hopped the next car to the Red Cross Hall where practice was well underway. Stares and a few frowns greeted us.

Etha snarled. "So what's more important than our play?"

"I needed a new coat," I said. "There's a sale on."

Doreen gave me a hard look. "You don't need to apologize to Miss Know-It-All. Etha's getting too big for her britches."

Etha smirked dramatically.

What an actress! A lead role in the play had gone to her head. Etha was perfect for the part and funny, but it was changing her, and I didn't like what I saw.

Next day I wore my new coat to church over my serge dress, then to practice that afternoon minus the hat.

"I'm crazy about my new coat, Mama," I said in reverie that night. *"It's the most I ever paid for one. But it makes me feel pretty, like Mary Pickford in 'White Roses.' 'Member I borrowed Naomi's coat to wear to the mountains last year? Now I've got one just as pretty—prettier."*

"You're mighty lucky to have it, honey. 'Member how we wrapped ourselves in blankets *on Saunook Mountain 'gainst all that snow and ice, how we wound strips of cloth for leggings?"*

"How could I forget, Mama? I had to leave my doll, Nellie, 'cause we couldn't tote nothing but ourselves and Baby Noble down that freezing cold mountainside." Tears welled in my eyes and I dried them on the pillowcase.

"That doll's here," Mama said.

"Nellie? You mean Nellie's there with you and Noble?"

"Sure. This is heaven, Sippy-gal. Jesus made heaven perfect. Nellie's right here waiting."

On Monday I couldn't resist. Folding my old gray coat, I placed it in Mrs. Callaway's Red Cross box to be sent to the *suffering Belgians,* tied my head with a red scarf and put on my new plaid coat. At the mill I hung it carefully on a rack in our cloak closet and hurried to the warper room. When the mill whistle blew at 5:00 p.m., it wasn't there. Why would somebody move my coat? One rack at a time I looked through the closet. It was nowhere to be found.

Alma saw me searching among the wraps. "What's wrong, sugar?"

"My coat. My brand new coat. I hung it here this morning and it's gone!"

Methodically we searched among and under all the wraps, finally concluding it just wasn't there.

"I don't know what to do," I said.

"We're going to the mill office. You can report it stolen."

We hurried to the office where I filled out forms, but in my heart I knew it was gone forever. I loved that coat too much, I thought, now it's gone. I was getting worked up. Why did this happen to the things and people I loved most? The office loaned me an old cape from *lost and found,* one somebody thought so little of they didn't bother to look for it, and I trudged home.

Doreen was fit to be tied.

"Selena, honey, we'll find that coat. Somebody took it. Somebody's got your coat right now and we're getting it back!"

"How?"

"I got friends, you got friends. We'll all be looking for that plaid coat."

She got sheets of paper out and wrote in bold block letters at the top of each: Have you seen this coat?

"Now write on each one a description of your coat." She handed the papers to me.

Hot tears stung my eyes as I described my coat in detail.

"Dry up," Doreen scolded. "Dead or alive, we're getting that coat back before the trail gets cold."

The thought made me smile as I dabbed my eyes. "Silly! You've seen too many William S. Hart movies."

On Tuesday one of the "missing coat" descriptions was posted in every mill section. A few "sightings" were reported and one seemed to fit perfectly. According to several witnesses, a girl named Carrie Long was seen wearing a plaid coat home on Monday that fit my description. Doreen's sometime boyfriend had a date with Carrie for a matinee movie on Saturday.

"Carrie's a little racy," he confided. "Expect the unexpected, but I can't believe she'd stoop to snatching a coat." Still he decided to "stand her up."

"If she asks what happened, maybe the truth'll come out."

Instead he came to watch our practice session at the Red Cross workroom.

A mental image of Carrie all dressed up, waiting for her date that never showed, bothered me. Mama would never approve of such a ruse. *Serves her right, though,* I thought. Maybe she'll be sorry, send the coat back, say she only meant to borrow it.

A letter came from Freddie: "We're fighting 'trench warfare.' Can't say where but we're bound to be close to the front. But don't worry—my trench is like a little home, coziest nook this side of the 'pond.' The heinies are so dug in we can't see 'em, just their gunfire. At night the fireworks look like the 4th of July. Only this ain't no show—it's real. France has got to be freed from the Kaiser. Looks like it's up to us Yanks.

"Thanks for the picture. You're the prettiest woman hanging in our space. One of my trench buddies says tell you he's coming back 'wearing the Kaiser's moustache.' Picture that! Me, all I want's for this lousy fight to end."

Chapter 21

D oreen's latest disc, "Over There," sung by Billy Murray, was playing on the Victrola. Irving Berlin's new song was the biggest hit yet. Everywhere we went, we heard it. There was even a version by Enrico Caruso. We knew all the words and sang along. *Over there, over there, send the word, send the word over there, that the Yanks are coming*...It was thrilling and so true.

What can we do? became a catch phrase. Liberty Bonds were advertised in *The Gazette*, the trolley, the banks, store windows. A group of patriotic citizens including Mr. and Mrs. Winfred Gentry established and financed the Soldier's Recreation Center in Gastonia. It was furnished and opened free to every doughboy and sailor.

Stuart Cramer, Jr., our mill owner's son, graduated from West Point and his unit was bound for Europe. Many from Gaston County were drafted, others signed up: rich, poor, mill hands, merchants, bankers. Gregg Cherry, an attorney, organized and accepted command of Company A, 115th Machine Gun Battalion, and Major Alfred Bulwinkle became an officer in the Field Artillery. Some were leaving never to come back. The list on the mill door grew.

Gaston County now had more mills than any other county in the country—ninety mills with a million spindles. With the mills running twenty-four hours a day to provide war materials, the need for more workers was great. Once again mill trucks were sent to the mountains for what seemed an endless supply of greenhorns willing to become lintheads. We were happy they were coming.

ESCAPE

My heart is such a wanderer,
With me it will not stay;
While I'm hard upon a task,
My heart is far away.

And to my heart I often say,
"See all this work I do?
This I must do, that I may go
Someday along with you."

But such a stubborn heart have I,
A pain it will not bear,
Nor linger in a dreary place,
Although I'm burdened there.

And when the day is very bleak
With oh, so much to do,
My heart is on a sunny hill,
Beneath a sky of blue.

Saturday was Corned Beef and Cabbage night and Papa came for supper bringing a *date* with him, a newcomer fresh out of Haywood County. She reminded me so much of Clemmie I wanted to say, "Watch out." Instead I told them about my stolen coat.

"Go see that gal," Papa said. "Confront her."

"How can I go up to a stranger, tell her I think she took my coat?"

His date smiled sympathetically, looking so much like Clemmie I had to look away.

"Why not?" he asked.

"I been thinking, maybe I oughta ask Grandpa."

In fact I'd thought about it a lot. Grandpa knew what Jesus would do in every situation. Chances are he'd even preached a sermon on it.

After supper a group gathered with Doreen as she sorted through her latest Victrola records. As usual Grandpa settled far away as possible—the opposite end of the parlor—to smoke his pipe and read.

It was my chance to get his attention. I'd always been a listener when he voiced opinions or gave his warnings, but never the one who asked for help.

"Grandpa, can I get your advice?"

He puffed away, blowing apple-scented circles in the air. I was nervous and he knew it.

"Sit down, child." He pointed to the ottoman in front and I perched on the side.

"Somebody stole my brand new coat," I blurted out, feeling every bit the child he'd just called me.

"How do you know that?" He could've slapped my face with the same effect.

"Because it's gone! It's gone and I think I know who took it."

"Did you see them?"

Why did he seem so unsympathetic? He was quibbling as only Grandpa could.

"No. But some friends of mine saw her wearing it. It's *plaid*, red and black plaid. I'd know that coat anywhere."

"Must've taken some kinda nerve for this girl to be *seen* wearing your coat."

"What should I do?" I was having guilt feelings about my own stolen coat.

"I can tell you what Jesus said to do."

Oh, God, I thought, he's going to suggest something I can't possibly do. And I'll have to sit and listen while he preaches a sermon on it.

"Tell me, Selena, this person you say stole your coat, is she a Christian?"

"I don't know. I really don't know her at all."

"All right, let's assume she's not. Jesus' command is to *Christians*, but may apply to anybody." He placed his pipe on the yellow-stained ashtray atop his smoking stand. Then he pulled the worn leather Bible from the table opposite and opened it.

When his eyes caught mine, I knew I was a congregation of one. I stared at the floor and waited.

"In chapter 18 of Matthew's gospel," he began, "Jesus' disciples come asking who'll be greatest in His kingdom. Jesus lets them know His followers should be humble, not proud. He teaches them humility and how to deal with others. Starting at verse 15:

> 'If thy brother shall trespass against thee, go and tell him his fault between thee and him alone; If he shall hear thee, thou hast gained thy brother. But if he will not hear thee, then take with thee one or two more, that in the mouth of two or three witnesses every word may be established. And if he shall neglect to hear them, tell it unto the church; but if he neglect to hear the church, let him be unto thee as a heathen and a publican'."

"You're saying the *victim* should go to the person who did them wrong? *I* should go to this person who stole my coat?"

"This is not Aaron Spencer saying that. *Jesus* is saying that. And He's saying to go alone."

That night I agonized, sleepless till turning in my thoughts to Mama: *"How can I do what Grandpa says? I don't have that much nerve."*

"Jesus'll help you, honey," she promised. *"Jesus helps His children do the hard things."*

———

Carrie Long worked the same shift as me, only in the spinning room, so I used my lunch break to look her up. The spinning section was a familiar place. As soon as I entered the large room, a peace came over me. Even the gentle roar and rattle of machines gave me comfort I was doing the right thing.

I paused beside a busy spooler, waiting for a chance to speak. "I'm looking for Carrie Long," I shouted close to her ear. "I was told she works in here."

She gave a quizzical look. "I'm Carrie."

My mental image of Carrie was of a blonde, devil-may-care shrew. What I saw was a dark prim petite, smaller than me in a starched gray pinafore. Her pale blue eyes were enormous.

"I'm Selena Wright," I said. "I...I lost my coat." How could I say, *you stole my coat?* "Someone told me you have one exactly like it."

Well, there it was in so many words—*you stole my coat!* I wanted to run and hide.

She didn't flinch. "Watch my machine," she told a boy who looked all of ten years old. "I gotta take a break."

"Come," she yelled above the racket and took my arm. We headed for the toilet. There the noise lessened and we could talk above it.

"So you're the one," she said. "You're the one who thinks I took your coat, the busybody who started those rumors."

"Friends said you wore one home that day, a coat just like mine."

"What you did was make others believe I was a thief. Has anybody ever done that to you? I hope you know how it feels."

"But my coat, where is it? *Somebody* took it."

"It wasn't me, I'll have you know. You've got me afraid to wear my own coat!"

"Will you wear it tomorrow? Let me see it?"

"Gladly. Now I've got to get back to my job."

Next morning I came to work early, headed straight for the spinning room and waited. When Carrie came up wearing the plaid coat, I like to have choked. It was *my* coat, exactly the same!

"Here it is," she said. "Take a good look, my new coat I bought on sale at Efird's." She took it off and handed it to me.

At last here it was, my brand new coat, so familiar, so beautiful. Sunlight streamed from the windows falling on the colors. I fingered the fabric and swallowed hard. It was red and *blue, navy blue,* not red and black like mine.

"This is not my coat," I said. "I'm so sorry. I...I thought you'd taken my coat. But this is not it."

She stared at me, the wide blue eyes full of disbelief or maybe it was pity. I didn't wait to find out. I was so humiliated. I didn't have my coat, and I'd hurt someone who'd never done anything to me. I ran to the elevator and went back to my floor.

———

Saturday was an important rehearsal day for the play and it was also my birthday. When Doreen, Etha, and I walked into the Red Cross workroom, the others began singing, "Happy Birthday to You" and I broke into sobs. They'd passed the hat before I got there and were giving me what they collected.

"By Christmas you oughta have enough to buy a new coat," Alma said.

This was all her doing. And it was too much. Tears poured again as I hugged her tight.

After weeks of not hearing from Freddie, four letters came at once and I opened them by order of date. "Got my first letter from Etha," the second one started. "Thanks for giving her my address." She'd told him she was the star in a play to benefit the Red Cross.

It didn't bother me that Etha'd written Freddie. I knew mail call was the highlight of a soldier's existence—the more letters the better. But I hadn't given his address to her. She'd never asked. The thought of her sifting through my personal things, finding and reading *my* letters disturbed me a lot. I recalled the time she told Freddie which box was mine at our box supper in Loray. She knew it would make me mad and it did. Now she was sending him letters and hadn't told me. Why?

By Christmas I had my new coat, but it was not plaid. The plaids were gone from Efird's racks. It was a burgundy velour and matching muff, with a wide belt and oversized buckle. The price was $8.95. I couldn't wait to view myself in the Lumina Theatre's gilt full-length mirror. Posing this way and that, I felt luxurious.

"My birthday and Christmas gift all in one," I told Do.'

"You're chic all right," she admitted. "Mary Pickford should be so lucky to have one like that."

Mary Pickford was playing at the Lumina with Mack Sennett in *Three Sisters,* and Pearl White's serial, *The Perils of Pauline,* had started at the brand new Cozy Theatre. The Cozy's ornate lobby and its grand player piano with automatic violin attracted all the young crowd even though admission was fifteen cents. One could easily forgo peanuts or an ice cream soda for a Cozy Theatre ticket, but Doreen and I had no time, not with the play two weeks off.

Miss Adams and her friend, Fran, were perfectionists. No one dared goof or forget a line. We practiced our lines at work, shouting above looms and warpers and the hum of giant exhaust fans. Scenery'd been in place at the Ideal for weeks behind asbestos stage curtains. *The Old Maids' Convention* was down to the wire.

December 22, a week before the play, with rehearsal slated for the theatre itself, Alma suggested it was a good time to visit Freddie's mother. She lived two blocks from the theatre. We'd hop an early trolley and take her a gift box of hankies.

Inside the trolley I pointed to a brand new ad right by the window:

SEE THE OLD MAIDS' CONVENTION
Funniest comedy
this side of Broadway

IDEAL THEATRE, GASTONIA
DECEMBER 29, 6:00 P.M.
ADULTS: TWENTY CENTS, CHILDREN
UNDER TWELVE: FIVE CENTS.

All proceeds benefit The Red Cross.

"Hey, Alma, look—we're celebrities."

Beside it an ad showed a ruddy-faced man with his cheek puffed out:

IT AIN'T TOOTHACHE! IT'S CLIMAX!

And below it the trolley company warned:

PLEASE DON'T SPIT ON THE FLOOR—
REMEMBER THE JOHNSTOWN FLOOD.

We mounted stone steps of a duplex apartment to a tiny porch painted glossy gray. At one end potted plants, dead from the cold, drooped brown and dry. An iceman's card hung inside the door pane alongside a blue star honoring Freddie. We knocked and waited.

"Come in, girls. Take off your coats, stay a spell."

Mrs. Fletcher was skinny as a rail, stooped with dark graying hair. Her small brown eyes with circles beneath darted this way and that, as if trying to probe what our visit was about. She motioned us toward a frayed settee. "You girls work in the mill, do ye?"

"Yes, Ma'am. Both work at Maysworth." Alma handed her our gift. "We cain't stay, Mrs. Fletcher. We're fixing to rehearse a play, to make money for our Red Cross Chapter."

Mrs. Fletcher seemed slightly confused and I guessed she was hard of hearing.

"Used to work at Loray, myself," she said, "till I took sick with this hacking cough. Doctor said if I didn't quit I'd end up plumb coughing my lungs out."

A fit of coughing seemed to prove the very words and sent her wilting into a chair. She laid our un-opened gift on a table.

"This was so sweet of y'all. Thank ye." She pulled a scrap of mill-end from an apron pocket and wiped her eyes and mouth.

I faced her using my loudest voice, "I been writing Fred, Mrs. Fletcher."

"Oh, yeah. You're *Selena*. My Freddie says he likes you, likes you a lot. I kept all my letters he done writ."

She opened the table drawer and took out a stack of letters tied with lacy pink elastic, "Can you read me one?"

"Me and Alma can't stay. Rehearsal starts in twenty minutes."

Alma eased the top letter out. "If your clock's right we got time for one."

"No, no." Mrs. Fletcher took the letter from her and pulled one from the center. "*This* one. Read this one."

While Alma read aloud, Mrs. Fletcher slipped another one out and handed it to me, motioning me to open it. Familiar words and phrases, things he'd also written me, jumped from the pages.

"Wait," she whispered, a finger to her lips, "*Shh-hh.*" And I realized she wanted that one read aloud as well.

I shook my head.

"Don't worry, Ma," Alma read, a phrase repeated about every line. "Them Fritzie's toy cannons ain't no match for ours. Limey flyboys keep strafing them bozoes every day. Glad they're on our side. They're something else. Army chow ain't nothing like yours, but I guess it fills us up. Red Cross keeps us in cigarettes and gum, but it's hard to keep our stuff dry. Rains cats and dogs in these trenches almost every day. I keep fags and matches dry inside my 'tin hat.' Stays on my head day and night, so don't worry. Army gave us a English to French dictionary. We can 'parley' a little French if we get lucky enough for 'skirt duty.' All I learned so far is 'parley vous Francais, Chevrolet coupe.'"

Mrs. Fletcher tittered at his joke, coughed hard, then tittered again.

"Don't worry none about me, Ma," Alma continued. "Take good care of yourself. Your son, Freddie."

Mrs. Fletcher pointed to the letter I was holding.

"I'm sorry," I said. "We don't have time." I handed the letter back and she took it reluctantly, slowly folding and returning it to the worn envelope.

"Maybe y'all can come next week," she said.

We nodded, knowing next week was play date itself. "'Bye, Mrs. Fletcher," I said. "I'll be sure to tell Freddie I met you."

"Bye, bye."

We let ourselves out and closed the door quickly against the biting cold. I pulled my belt buckle tight and stuck my hands in my muff.

"Hard to leave 'er like that," Alma said.

"Seems so lonely."

"We'll go back; when we got more time to read the letters."

"Yeah. Looks like they're all that matters to her," I said. "I'll tell Fred he needs to write more often."

Chapter 22

Two days before our big event, Grandpa told us it was a sellout.

"Free publicity did the trick," he said. "Downtown businesses, *The Gazette,* trolley people, word of mouth. Folks support a good cause. And we're giving 'em a dynamite show. Got four free tickets left."

I told him about Mrs. Fletcher, how lonely she was. He pulled a ticket from his shirt pocket and handed it to me.

"Give that brave lady this with my compliments."

"Reckon I'll call the Gentrys," I said. "See if they can take her."

"Guess who else is coming—Sudie, Sudie Hailey. Ada, Kizzie, too, they're big girls, now. 'Bout grown, according to Sudie. Libby invited her; she's fixing a room for 'em right now."

Beulah was clearing away dishes. "All right, Miss Beulah," Grandpa said, snatching his pipe from the plate. "Let me get outta your way."

In the parlor Doreen opened the Victrola and placed the needle on her latest record. *Pack up your troubles in your old kit bag and smile, smile, smile,* the lyrics challenged. *Smile* seemed to be the theme of all the songs. But smiling didn't come easy with headlines about German U-boats sinking our ships and poison gas warfare, and with families getting telegrams about lost loved ones. Making the world "safe for democracy" was taking its toll. We all knew somebody on the mill door's casualty list. Each addition brought groans, "Oh, no! Not *him*."

Though the news was grim, the weather wintry, and snow forecast the night of our play, we believed it must go on, no matter what. It was our patriotic duty. We were doing our part.

At showtime the theatre was packed, a light snowfall adding to the excitement, as if God were throwing handfuls of confetti. A two-man slapstick routine primed the audience before curtain time and by the end of the play's first act, applause exceeded all expectations.

"Gastonia needed to laugh, and *The Old Maid's Convention* provided the vehicle," Monday afternoon's *Gazette* would glowingly report.

Mary Pickford couldn't have taken more swooping bows than Etha. She was ecstatic. Bouquets for her and for Alma came from the Winfred Gentrys and Sol Green of The Shoe Hub. Sol was there near the front with his wife and small son.

Success made us giddy—we were stars. We took bows till the curtain came down a third and final time.

Then Grandpa strode out to address an audience still on their feet.

"Thank you, thank you everyone!" He held his hand high like preparing to pray. "You're all so kind and we appreciate your great support for our Red Cross Chapter. Now I want to extend an invitation to any and all who will to come to Maysworth Baptist Church tomorrow morning at eleven. I'm preaching the message, one we should all heed. 'Nuff said. Goodnight and thank you all."

Grandpa was full of surprises, but those of us backstage were too excited to give his invitation much thought. Miss Adams had us stay in costume to greet those leaving. We lined up in the lobby, nodding, hugging, shaking hands with any who wished before they spilled to the icy street. Young playgoers headed straight to Sweetland Ice Cream Parlor for steaming cups of cocoa and bouillon.

Those of us going to Callaway's Boardinghouse in Maysworth crammed standing room only into the next trolley east. Mrs. Callaway and Beulah had worked all afternoon fixing a late meal to celebrate the successful play and to honor our overnight guests, Sudie Hailey and her daughters, Ada and Kizzie.

The buffet table was decorated with red, white, and blue with "Happy New Year, 1918" strung between tall candlesticks. Sliced turkey and ham for sandwiches, Dixie relish, Mrs. Callaway's own watermelon rind pickle, potato salad, ambrosia, and Jeff Davis pie with whipped cream awaited us, to be washed down with cranberry shrub from her big punchbowl.

When I finally snuggled into my nightie and lay down, my arms and legs felt like lead but my head was spinning, reliving our play's every scene, every line, every bow.

Doreen's kinky curls had sweated and dried and sweated again till they smelled like a wet cat on the pillow next to mine. She wanted to talk about who came to the play.

"Did you see Marvelee? *Pregnant!* I swear, if she ain't big as the side of the house. And that husband—what a rube! Looks like he just stepped out of the cow pasture."

"Did you see Sol Green and his wife?"

"*Hah!* Ain't a bit pretty, is she? They say she's rich. Must be why he married her. Don't matter one speck to me; he can have her. Saw Miss Peeden. She's still nice. Ain't seen her since my last day of school."

"Did you see Mrs. Fletcher, Freddie's mama?"

"You mean that old woman with the Gentrys? Looks too old to be Freddie's mama, and so skinny."

"She's got lung disease and a bad cough. I feel sorry for her, Freddie in France and all."

"She don't look a bit good."

On her cot that replaced the trundle bed Etha claimed was too small and made for babies, she was snoring away. I no longer thought of her as a little sister to protect. She'd become assertive, almost brazen. I couldn't forget how she snitched Freddie's address without asking. Doreen was breathing deep, well on her way to sleep, too.

Not me. Images from our performance kept flashing before my closed eyes: Etha and Alma with bouquets, bowing, people standing, applauding, not wanting to leave.

"We did it, Mama. I was so worried it wouldn't go well, but it did. Everybody did good."

"You were good. Don't forget that, Sippy-gal. You were good."

———

"Get up, S'lene, you sleepy-head."

Doreen pulled the pillow from beneath my head. It seemed I'd dozed off only minutes before, but the sun was pinkish bright on snow-laden trees outside and kitchen sounds rose from downstairs. The whole house would be going to church. With Grandpa preaching it was not just expected, it was duty. Breakfast would be simple and early, out of the way in time for Beulah to go if she wanted to.

Always well-attended, today's eleven o'clock service was full of visitors. We sat our usual place and looked around at back pews that were filling up early.

"If the sermon's too long, folks back there can get up and leave," I told Doreen.

She nodded. "I'd sit back there if Mama let me."

If it weren't for her mother, I doubted she'd be there at all. According to her she'd spent a lifetime listening to Grandpa's sermons not from the pulpit, but from his armchair and, given the chance, could preach them herself.

I squeezed Do's arm. "Hey, looka there!"

It was Alma in a new green outfit with matching hat. She could've been a model straight from the pages of January's *Needlecraft*.

"Well, I'll be dog, she's not Baptist."

"She thinks the world of Grandpa. And he thinks a lot of her."

"Oh, yeah?" Doreen sneered. "Why wouldn't he let her come back to the boardinghouse then?"

"*Shhhh!*"

The chairman of deacons was at the lectern giving a Sunday school report. When he finished he offered a short prayer and announced hymn 264, "Onward Christian Soldiers."

"We'll sing all four verses after which Mr. Aaron Spencer, Associate Pastor, will come and bring a message titled, 'The Power of Forgiveness.'"

He went to where Grandpa was seated in a throne-like chair and shook his hand, then came down and took a seat in the first pew. With martial chords blaring from the pipe organ, we all stood to sing.

After the last verse Grandpa rose from his chair and went to the lectern. His hair and beard were whiter than ever in the lighted pulpit, diffused sunrays from a large stained glass window creating an aura. His pin-striped suit and string tie gave a look of gentility and wisdom. His appearance was charismatic, he knew it, and took full advantage of the fact.

"First I want to acknowledge some people, people important to this congregation," he said, pushing his glasses further onto his nose. "I see Mr. Stuart Cramer, here by my invitation. Thanks to him Maysworth villagers are like a big happy family. He understands how important it is to worship God in a beautiful sanctuary, and we have him to thank for this very building. Mr. Cramer's important to the war effort, too; just back from Washington where he serves on the production engineering committee of the Council of National Defense, the war service committee of the American Textile Industry, and the advisory board of the Treasury Department. Mr. & Mrs. Stuart Cramer, will you please stand."

When the Cramers stood, applause rippled across the sanctuary and they bowed slightly before sitting down.

Grandpa was doing what he did so well—getting the congregation in the palm of his hand. With every eye on him, he reached in his pocket and pulled out a letter, holding it up.

"This letter's from a young man known very well to someone else worshipping with us today—Mrs. Sudie Hailey. Sudie, will you stand."

Surprised, Mrs. Hailey rose slowly.

Grandpa grinned. "No, I won't ask you to come up here this time."

Mrs. Hailey smiled shakily and sat back down.

"I just want to tell you this letter's from Corporal J.D. Newell, the man who burned down Sudie's house, scarring her hands for life, yet whom she *forgave*. The 'healing power of forgiveness' not only gave Sudie peace—it redeemed the life of a young man headed for destruction. Listen to what he says:

> We're in the thick of fighting, but I'm not afraid to die. I know I'm ready. Years back I did a bad thing to a wonderful lady, Mrs. Sudie Hailey. But she forgave me. God's forgiven me, too, and saved me. Thank you for leading me to Jesus, 'cause I know if I die, I'll go straight to be with Him. Keep on writing, sir. If I make it back to Gastonia, I hope to see you."

Grandpa reached in the same pocket and pulled out another letter and held it up, "This one's from me to J.D. It's never been opened, came back to me two days ago stamped 'Deceased.'"

He paused, giving time for reaction as he stared at the unopened letter. "I went to see J.D.'s nearest of kin, his aunt, and she told me yes, she'd received that dreaded telegram. J.D. Newell's gone to meet his Maker."

Dramatically Grandpa sniffed and took out his handkerchief, wiping his nose.

"So you see, today I'm preaching *forgiveness*—not just God's forgiveness to us but our forgiveness for one another. For you see, beloved friends, *we do not know what tomorrow will bring*.

"We're a nation at war, a great war, a world war, and we don't know what the year 1918 has in store, nor even what tomorrow may hold for any of us."

I thought of Carrie Long, what hard feelings I had for her when I thought she'd stolen my coat, how quickly I walked away when I discovered my mistake. Why didn't I ask her forgiveness? Was it too late?

"If you have your Bibles, turn to Colossians, chapter 3, verse 12 and following," Grandpa continued. I found the scripture and read along:

"'Put on therefore, as God's elect, holy and beloved, a heart of compassion, kindness, lowliness, meekness, longsuffering; forbearing one another, and forgiving each other. If any man have a complaint against any, even as the Lord forgave you, so also do ye; and above all things, put on love which is the bond of perfectness. And let the peace of Christ rule in your hearts, to the which also ye were called in one body; and be ye thankful.'

"The apostle Paul had never met the people he wrote this epistle to, but it came at a time when they needed such caring advice, and it speaks to us as boldly today. We cannot have peace, brothers and sisters, or receive God's forgiveness if we're not willing to forgive. Are you harboring unforgiveness? Is there a person you need to get right with before you can get right with God? Can you truly pray, '...Forgive me *my* trespasses *as I forgive others* their trespasses against me...'?"

There was a long pause as Grandpa stared to his left, to his right, and down the center of the congregation. Many were shifting, looking down, looking around, crossing and uncrossing legs. I thought of Etha, how I'd come to almost despise this one who used to be like a little sister. Was it because she snitched Freddie's address, or was it really envy that she was such a good actress? Whatever it was, it ate at me, when Grandpa was saying we should have peace, the kind that Sudie Hailey had.

Doreen looked down at my hands as I twisted my handkerchief into knots.

"What's the matter?" she asked.

"Nothing."

Grandpa closed his Bible. "While our brother here leads us in singing all four verses of hymn 74, "Out of My Bondage, Sorrow, and Night," I'm asking any who need the Lord's forgiveness, or who harbor unforgiveness in their hearts for another, come down and confess that right now—don't wait. If you have ill will toward a brother or sister, get up, go to that person while we sing—ask their forgiveness. Remember, we're not promised tomorrow, so get things right today."

Grandpa came down from the pulpit and stood in front of the communion table as we opened our hymnals and started to sing.

From the corner of my eye I caught a streak of green moving down the aisle to the front. It was Alma. She went to Grandpa, her shoulders shaking as he embraced her. They bowed their heads, talking and praying. I could wait no longer. Etha was standing directly in front of me and I tapped her on the shoulder.

She looked back in surprise. "What?"

"I'm sorry I've been so mean to you lately."

"Mean?"

"You took Freddie's address from my drawer and it made me mad. I'm sorry I got so mad at you, will you forgive me?"

"Next time I'll ask."

Etha was Etha. I had to accept her as she was, spoiled by a house-full of grownups.

By the hymn's last verse, couples were kneeling at the altar clasping hands while the organ continued to play. Alma went back to her seat and others waited to speak to Grandpa.

Finally he signaled the organist to stop. "We must not quench the Spirit that's working amongst us today," he said. "I want everyone to move to the sides of the sanctuary. Form a big circle, holding hands."

People worked their way to the outer edges making room for merging bodies and clasping hands. The Cramers were directly across from me and I saw them searching Grandpa's every move, as if caught in a Baptist ordinance totally foreign to Episcopalians.

"For our benediction, let's join our voices in "Blest Be The Tie That Binds.'"

I was dizzy with exhilaration and conviction.

The next day I got to work early and took the elevator to the spinning room. I waited by the door till Carrie Long got there.

"Carrie, Carrie," I yelled.

She was wearing her plaid coat. "What?"

"I forgot to tell you how sorry I was to think you'd stole my coat. Will you forgive me?"

She looked surprised. "Just don't ever accuse somebody when you don't know what you're talking about."

"I won't."

Chapter 23

On January 8, 1918 President Woodrow Wilson made a speech before Congress which ended with Fourteen Points, a program for world peace and, as he saw it, "the only *possible* program." *The Gastonia Gazette* gave his points front page coverage with editorials praising the message.

Grandpa, ever the critic of "our Democrat dove of a president," had gradually softened his opinion of "the professor" and his conduct of the war. He thought Wilson's Fourteen Points made sense, the only fault being "the impossibility of it ever working."

Grandpa shook his head as he read the *Points* aloud.

"Democracy cain't be forced on other nations," he declared. "Look at history. We cain't make 'em peace-loving. Cain't make 'em fair-minded. More's the pity."

On an inside page was a sketch of a soldier in a foxhole, rifle drawn, bursts of smoke over his head. Below was a quote from a poem by Alan Seeger, killed in action according to the story:

I have a rendezvous with Death
At some disputed barricade,
When Spring comes back with rustling shade
And apple-blossoms fill the air—
I have a rendezvous with Death...

In Maysworth daffodils were trumpeting an early spring. Beneath stalks of yellow-budded forsythia, crocus blooms defied their icy beds. Across the tracks where we liked to stroll on Sunday afternoons, trees were leafing out and clumps of grass were greening. Few of the fellows who used to walk the paths with us remained, most drafted or recruited, while some like Freddie and Gus Keeter were "over there" in the thick of it.

Beulah stayed late several days mopping floors and throwing rugs over a double clothesline to beat. The parlor rug, too big to take up, was sprinkled heavily with salt and swept with her strongest broom. Mrs. Callaway hired two boys to scrub the front porch with lye soap, wash the windows, and repaint the swing. The next day they clipped hedges and pulled up vines, then swept the backyard with yard brooms, burning all the debris.

The smells took me back to our cabin on Utah Mountain. In spring Mama would build a fire under her iron pot to boil our bedclothes, adding slivers of homemade soap. With a strong wooden stick she stirred them and punched them down in the bubbling froth.

Word came that Marvelee had her baby, a girl. Alma took off for Bessemer City the next Sunday morning and came back with good news.

"She had an easy time," she told us. "And guess what! She named that young'n after *me*. I can't imagine why. Little Alma Lee Ledbetter, cute as a button. You oughta see that Jonah, proudest papa."

Alma was back at the boardinghouse. It started with *The Old Maids' Convention*. Grandpa was so pleased with her performance he couldn't quit talking about it.

"I knew we could count on her," he said. "That's Alma—give her something to do and she does it right."

But it was the sermon Grandpa preached on forgiveness that brought her to the altar, made her "see the light," she confessed to Doreen and me.

"I married Gus 'for better or for worse,'" she said. "When it got worse, I forgot that. Now I know love changes, everything does, so do people. But Jesus can help me love Gus a new way, a different way. Gus needs me. I know he does. Always has. I just couldn't see his side of it."

"What about when he gets home?" Doreen asked.

"We'll live together as man and wife. He knows that. I told him. Says he sleeps better now, even in enemy waters. Claims he's not afraid." Her voice caught.

I clutched her arm. "Well, we're mighty happy you're back."

"Yeah, we never wanted you to leave," Doreen said.

Alma asked if I wanted to visit Mrs. Fletcher again. "She's dying, you know," she said.

"Who told you?"

"A good friend, a neighbor, said she coughs up blood, got too weak to even get out of bed. Don't eat nothing, don't want it. They sent for a doctor and he said she shouldn't be by herself. The neighbor stayed two nights. After that they had to hire somebody. Freddie's allotment barely covers it."

"Sure I'll go. Saturday I have to work overtime, but I could go Sunday."

As usual Etha was listening. "Freddie may come home," she said.

"What? He may come home?" I wondered how she knew more than me. "What makes you think that?"

She pulled his latest letter from the pocket of her pinafore and traced her finger down the page.

"I may come home on hardship leave," she read. "Ma's dying and ain't got nobody but me..."

"Can they do that?" I wondered aloud. "Freddie's right on the front line."

"His ma needs him, S'lene," Etha replied angrily. "His ma needs him *bad*."

Alma patted her shoulder, "Don't get so worked up, sugar. We don't need one of your hissy-fits."

The very word seemed to bring one on. "I swear to God," Etha shrieked. "None of y'all understand me. Freddie's the only person that does."

She stomped out of the room.

Alma looked at me and threw her eyes to the ceiling. I was still puzzling over Etha's letter from Fred. Maybe he didn't kept tabs on who he'd told what.

———

On the porch of her little apartment, Mrs. Fletcher's potted plants mimicked her condition. Ravaged by winter, no amount of nourishment would ever revive them. Alma knocked lightly and turned the knob. It wasn't locked so we stepped inside. A Negro woman stood in the parlor, hands on her hips, her head tied with a blue bandana.

"Can...Can we come in?" Alma asked.

She nodded and we followed her to the middle room. The smell of camphor smarted my nostrils. Mrs. Fletcher lay, eyes closed, an asafetida bag tied around her neck with a string. Her tiny hands were clasped across her breast just like Mama's when she lay in her coffin in Granny's front room.

"Ain't long for this world," the Negro woman murmured.

Etha insisted on coming with us and we couldn't very well say no. She hung back while Alma stared at Mrs. Fletcher's hollowed face, cheekbones translucent in the light of a smut-stained window.

"I'm so sorry," Alma whispered.

"Yeah. Got nobody but that boy."

The woman leaned toward Mrs. Fletcher and brushed hair from her forehead. She patted the thin splotchy hands.

We stood waiting as if expecting Mrs. Fletcher to open her eyes and say, "Stay awhile, girls, and read me a letter."

I thought of Granny, how she lingered at death's door for days. Better to go quickly, Papa always said. "Get on to that place where there'll be no more tears, no more pain."

Etha started sniffling till Alma stared at her, putting a finger to her lips, "*Shhhh!*"

I motioned maybe we should leave.

Alma shook her head no, and walked to the parlor. She opened the drawer of a table and pulled out the stack of letters tied with pink elastic and handed one to me.

"Read this one. Then I'll read one and we'll go."

My throat constricted as I scanned the familiar handwriting.

"Don't worry about me, Ma," I read aloud from the first page. "These trenches ain't exactly home, but my buddies and me make do. Our cooks do what they can, but I sure miss your cooking—can't wait to taste a mess of your collards with corn dumplings on top. Red Cross keeps me in cigarettes. Keep mine dry in my 'tin hat' and it stays on my head day and night. Don't worry neither 'bout them 'heinies.' By the time this reaches you we'll have 'em on the run..."

Mrs. Fletcher's eyelids quivered as if her eyes were trying to open. Etha sucked her breath in.

The voice was barely audible.

"The *other* one," she rasped. "The *other* one."

"Dear Ma," Alma began the favorite letter. "Don't worry about me..."

On Tuesday Alma's friend called to say Mrs. Fletcher had died and that Freddie was on his way home. He'd mentioned my name, wanted to see me. With ten days of leave, he'd have so little time.

———

Mrs. Fletcher's neighbors were caring and generous, and all had come to pay their respects to "her boy, Freddie." The tiny icebox was full. The kitchen table, the cabinet-top, sideboard, even a makeshift table of two orange crates were filled with bowls and platters of food.

Fred looked good in his uniform, shoulders broader, his brown hair neat, ruddy face clean-shaven. He was quiet and soft-spoken at the gravesite, whispering to friends and relatives, so unlike the Freddie I once knew as a fixer in Loray's spinning room. Now he moved about easily, mixing with mourners, assured and in charge.

"Get yourself some food?" he asked.

"A little. I'm not very hungry."

He took my hand. "Come with me," and he pulled me into a small bedroom, bolting the door behind us.

A barracks bag lay open on the floor next to a neatly-made bed, and on a wall hook hung a heavily-starched uniform tunic.

"I...I gotta talk to you," he said, taking hold of my shoulders. He pulled me to him hard and tried to kiss me.

I stiffened, turning my head.

"You must know." His voice was husky. "I care for you a lot, Selena. I gotta report back by the 27th. Ain't got much time. I...I want you to go with me."

"What are you saying?"

"I'm asking you to marry me."

Had I led him to think I liked him this much? I wanted to run, to be anyplace but here. "I...I can't do that. I got my job."

His face crumbled, tears forming. He got his handkerchief out.

I'd seen Papa cry once, when Mama died. It tore me up.

"I'm sorry, Fred. I like you as a *friend*, but I...I'm not ready for this. I'm sorry if I made you think I was."

"You don't understand, Selena. I...really *need* you. I need somebody to love me. I thought you did. Will you *wait* then?" He wiped his eyes. "Will you wait for me? Be my sweetheart?"

"I'll keep writing if you want me to."

"Give me a kiss. Please, sugar."

I let him kiss me on the lips, and I knew beyond a doubt that Freddie Fletcher could never be the man of my dreams, never be my knight in shining armor, my Sir Charles Brandon.

I opened the door to the gathering of friends. Doreen and Alma were just outside, smug, smiling. *I'll have to set them straight,* I thought, *this is not what they think.*

"Freddie wants a wife," I confided on the trolley home. "I'm not the one. He'll have to look somewhere else. I'm not ready for that."

"He's lost his ma and he's lonely," Alma said. "God knows that's not a good reason to marry. I found that out long ago."

She stared out the window as if searching for meaning among passing trees and telephone poles.

"I think he's scared," Doreen said. "He's gotta go back to the fighting. He's gotta face all that."

"Well, I hope he finds somebody," I said. "I'm not that person."

Grandpa and Mrs. Callaway were already home from the funeral and supper was being fixed for a sideboard buffet. Beulah placed a stack of plates by the food. There were few takers. No one who'd been to the funeral was hungry, having sampled the well-prepared dishes.

"Where's Etha?" Mrs. Callaway asked Doreen.

"Thought she came back with y'all."

"She was still there when we left," her mother snapped. "Oh, that girl. She'll be the death of me yet. I think the Lord sent her to be my 'thorn in the side.'"

Beulah said nothing as she brewed a big pot of coffee. Alma, Mrs. Callaway, and I sat down to squares of bread pudding with butter sauce.

"Gus's ship's coming to Norfolk for repairs," Alma said. "He wants me to meet him there before they go back out."

"Will you go?" Mrs. Callaway asked.

"I guess it's time for me to face up to being the wife I promised to be. God willing, I'll go. I have to be there waiting since they can't give the exact date."

She toyed with her pudding, then took a bite.

Mrs. Callaway squeezed her arm. "We'll pray for you, honey."

The front door banged closed and we heard foot-steps racing up stairs.

"Must be Etha." Mrs. Callaway got up, visibly tense.

Soon Doreen came down and went to the coffee-pot. "Had to get out," she said. "Mama's giving Etha the devil."

"No one in the house understands me," rang out clearly before our bedroom door slammed hard, muf-fling their voices. Etha's stomps told us we'd best stay downstairs till things calmed down.

Half an hour later Mrs. Callaway was back in the kitchen wringing her hands.

"That child's driving me crazy. I don't know what to do with her."

"Give 'er time," Alma said. "She'll come around."

"I wonder."

Doreen showed no patience at all. "Etha's hopeless," she said. "Absolutely hopeless. I'll be glad to see the day one of us is gone."

I shuddered, thinking of Met. "Don't say that, Do.' She's your little sister."

Like Etha, Met had been a handful, but if I'd kept her with me, looked after her myself, maybe things would've been different.

When we left for work next morning, Etha was up, getting ready for school, mad as a wet hen, but tight-lipped about the spat with her mother. She didn't go down to breakfast. That night when we got home, we learned she hadn't come home from school.

Mrs. Callaway was frantic and Grandpa was on the phone to Maysworth Hall for Single Women, trying to find Miss Vera Elliot.

"Etha Callaway never came home from school," he said when he finally reached her, his voice echoing throughout the house. "Do you know where she might be?"

He kept nodding his head while Mrs. Callaway paced back and forth. "Thank you. Thank you very much, Ma'am."

"She never went to school," he told Mrs. Callaway. "Miss Elliot assumed she was sick."

Mrs. Callaway was fit to be tied. "Where can she be, Papa? Where would she go?"

"Calm down, Libby. We need to go about this logically. She's somewhere and we'll find her."

"I shouldn't have said the things I said last night. God help me. Now she's gone."

"You did what any mother would do. Etha's rebellious and we have to deal with that. Don't go blaming yourself."

Early the following day Grandpa went to the police and reported a missing girl. Before noon Alma's friend next door to the Fletcher home in Gastonia called to say she'd seen Etha there.

"There's no mistaking," she told Mrs. Callaway. "I went over to pick up my platter and she came to the door." She knew Etha well, she pointed out, from her part in *The Old Maids' Convention*.

Grandpa and Mrs. Callaway took the next trolley to Gastonia and came back with a surly defiant Etha.

"I love Freddie," she kept shrieking. "I love him and he loves me. And I'm going to Camp Merritt with him. He's got my ticket."

Grandpa grasped her arm tightly and spun her around. "You're not going anywhere!"

Mrs. Callaway was crying, shaking her head. "Etha, Etha, honey, why are you doing this to us?"

"I'll tell you why, Libby," Grandpa said. "We've pampered this girl too much." He took Etha by the shoulders. "Listen to me, young lady. If you quit school, you'll have to get a job just like the others. You'll pay your room and board here."

"I'll never work in that cotton mill jail," Etha spat out. "I'll never be a *linthead*."

"It don't matter where you work, but you'll work. You'll work for your keep."

Grandpa's face was red, even to the bald spot on the back of his head. His hands were trembling. I'd not seen him so angry since that Sunday years back when he found Doreen working for Sol Green at The Shoe Hub.

Short of tying her up, there was no keeping Etha from leaving. Two days later she was gone. Six days after that she was back home, cynical and moody, with little to say about her visit to Camp Merritt.

When a letter came addressed to me from Freddie, I slipped to Alma's room to open it. "It's *you* I really love," he wrote, "Always have and always will."

I tore the letter to shreds and threw it in the trash bin.

Chapter 24

E tha got a job ushering at the Cozy. The Cozy Theatre was the newest and best in Gastonia. They provided her a uniform, but the pay was peanuts unless you counted all the shows she saw free of charge.

"I get to see them all," she bragged, though we knew it was never beginning to end. She saw just enough to spoil it for the rest of us.

"Make her hush, Mama, " Doreen complained, "I don't wanta spend fifteen cents to see a movie I know the ending to."

"Etha, honey, don't tell how it ends."

But Mrs. Callaway either couldn't or didn't make her stop. Etha sat at the supper table and told the whole thing, acting out parts like Sarah Bernhardt.

"*La, la, la, la, la, la, la,*" Doreen hollered at the top of her lungs while heading to the parlor, where she turned up the volume on a Sousa march to drown out Etha's voice.

Undaunted, Etha went into details to anybody who lingered long enough about how Pearl White in *The Perils of Pauline* survived her latest cliffhanger.

"Pauline's got hold of this big rock over a nasty raging river."

Playing the hapless Pauline, Etha clutched the air, "Help! Help me!" then turned to those still listening: "What you don't see's Pauline's hero reaching down for her. You don't see his hand, but it's there. Next chapter he yanks Pauline up just as that big ole rock gives way and splashes into the river."

Etha was also learning to run the projector, she bragged, and helping change reels. I was glad she liked her job. I never mentioned letters that kept coming from Fred swearing his love for me. My own letters told about friends, our jobs at the mill, what was going on in Gastonia, never about feelings or his relationship with Etha. I didn't know what that was and didn't want to. Etha was young, impulsive, a child in many ways. She could be Met: easy to take advantage of, easy to lead down a primrose path:

GARDEN OF FOLLY

In a garden whose old gray wall
was twisted, broken and ready to fall,
a rose as pure as new fallen snow
sprang forth from debris to grow.

A youth whose heart knew no care
found the chaste rose blooming there.
Ruthlessly he plucked the stem
and dragging tendrils after him,
down the road of folly he went—
Ah, foolish youth in pleasure spent.

Yet scattered behind him in the path,
sweet buds sprang forth - an aftermath.

The rose he carried on his way,
withered white, soon turned to gray.
Her tender heart, pure as before,
was crushed upon life's threshing-floor.

I thought of sending my old teacher, Mrs. Gentry, a copy of my poem, but decided not to. She'd want to know who "the rose" was. She liked to study poetry, to find meanings behind lines I'd rather not explain.

Still the words, etched in my brain, wouldn't quit, like the lyrics of Doreen's favorite records. The broken one—*Sweet buds sprang forth, an aftermath, sweet buds sprang forth, an aftermath.* I loved the line, an image of good springing from evil. It was something Grandpa liked to preach on, and a thought I liked to dwell on.

Aunt Mary's letters told how sweet Met's baby girl, Emily, was.

"She's so *darling*, Sippy-girl. A *good* baby. God Himself had a hand in that."

I wanted so much to see little Emily, but with the war on and the mill running twenty-four hours a day, I didn't know when that would be.

"A boy's been calling on Met," Mary wrote. "A good boy. Don't know what'll come of it, but if he asks for her hand, me and Arthur's ready to say yes."

I wasn't prepared for such news. It brought home the fact I no longer had any control. Mine and Met's paths had gone separate ways, and it appeared the gap would never close. Best I could hope for was to stay in touch. It's what Mama would want:

"Mama," I whispered into my pillow, *"If Met marries, she'll have her own family. They'll come first. I'll be out of her life completely."*

"She'll always love you, Sippy. You're her only sister. Met grew up too fast. She's gotta make the best of that. Let Mary and Arthur handle it."

I went to sleep thinking of the morning on Utah Mountain when Mama, Met, and I picked wild daisies in a field, weaving them into chains to go around our necks. Met wanted her chain to last forever, but when the stems dried and the links began pulling apart, she started to cry. Mama gave her hers, only to have the same thing happen with it. Mama hugged her and laughed.

"Daisy chains don't last forever," she said. "The only thing that lasts forever is our love for each other and God's love for us."

Late in August Alma's plans were firm for her trip to Norfolk. Her train ticket was bought, a hotel room prepaid and waiting, her clothes pressed and laid out, ready for packing. She was so excited.

"I'm wearing my green coat suit and hat," she said. No surprise there. She looked better in it than anything she'd ever owned.

Doreen, Naomi and I pooled our money, bought a black lace teddy and sneaked it into Alma's valise when she wasn't looking.

"Never noticed a thing." Naomi snickered, shielding her words from Alma.

"I'd love to get a picture of her unpacking that," Doreen whispered.

"What y'all laughing 'bout?" Alma asked.

"Oh, just don't forget to take your Kodak," I told her. "We want proof you were there."

"Lord, sugar. I don't 'spect they'll let you take pictures of *The Delaware*. Gus said enemy submarines attacked her twice and she dodged their torpedoes. The 'gerries' would love to know how many guns and torpedo tubes *The Delaware's* got, how big and fast she is."

"Well, who wants to see his old ship? We just want one of you and Gus," Doreen said. "Tell him to pose in front of the ocean. The 'gerries' already know how big *that* is." We laughed.

Mrs. Callaway went with Alma, taking the early morning trolley to Gastonia's train station. Beulah was sniffling all the while she hurriedly fixed breakfast for us first shifters.

"What's the matter with you?" Grandpa asked.

"I...I got this *bad* feeling."

"Speak, woman. What kind of feeling?"

"Don't know, Mr. Spencer. Can't explain. But when I got up this morning, the sun was casting streaks across my wall like I reckon I ain't seen since the day my Joe died."

She hurried to the pantry and stayed till she got back her composure. Grandpa had little patience for what he called "superstitious signs and omens."

"Beulah," he said when she came back out. "Don't put your trust in 'signs.' Put your trust only in the Lord."

"Yessir."

———

*Oh! How I hate to get up in the morning. Oh! How I'd love to remain in bed...*The lyrics were funny and we needed to laugh, with news from the front so gloomy.

Doreen turned up the volume and pulled back the parlor rug. "Watch this," she said. "Learned it from a girl in the weave room. She was showing me this step when the section-hand come up behind us. Scared us both to death. 'Y'all can't dance in here!' he yelled. 'This ain't no barn and it ain't no hall. Y'all got work to do.' We scooted 'round that loom busy as bees. Then soon's he got in the elevator, she showed me again."

Doreen cranked the Victrola and put the needle on one even peppier: *Good morning, Mr. Zip-Zip-Zip, with your haircut just as short as mine.* She stepped back with her right foot, then her left, a quick step to the right, quick close with the left. Soon she had me, Naomi, and Etha dancing alongside her.

"See this *man* in my arms." She circled her arms high, pretending. "He's doing just the opposite of what I'm doing. It's him doing the leading."

"What d'you call this?" Naomi asked, huffing.

"The *Fox Trot*, honey. It's the latest. You can change it every which way—just so's you're in time with the music. Watch this!" Doreen spun and kicked, spun and kicked.

Grandpa, who didn't approve of dancing in any form, got up and went to the kitchen. Soon he was back with a cup of coffee, picked up his book and pretended to read. I saw him peeking over the rim of his glasses, but he didn't say a word.

———

Next to *The Gazette's* front page listing of the war's growing casualties, was a report from General "Black Jack" Pershing requesting fresh troops for the battle in France. His plan was for a grand American offensive, a push he hoped would defeat the war-weary Germans and end the "war to end all wars."

We took in stride Meatless Days and Wheatless Days, and working overtime for "our boys," but in July when Sweetland Ice Cream and Confectionery Parlor was closed by Food Administrator C. B. Armstrong in a dispute over using more sugar than regulations allowed, it was the lowest of blows.

"Why *summertime?*" Doreen asked. "Where else can we go for ice cream sodas? C. B. Armstrong's a mean old man."

But September brought good news; Sweetland had settled and was back in business. Doreen and I watched Ramon Novarro and Geraldine Farrar in *Joan, the Woman,* at The Lumina, then got our Tipperary Berry Ice Cream Soda with two straws. We couldn't hang around. Alma was due in from Norfolk and we were meeting her train.

"Here she comes. Here she comes." The whistle in the distance sent shivers down my spine and when the giant engine chugged in, hissing and spewing, we searched for Alma. She stepped to the platform wearing the same green coat suit and hat she wore when she left, but something was different. Her suit was rumpled and dusty, her face ashen.

"Alma, Alma!" We waved and hurried to where she stood.

I hugged her and she leaned hard against me. "I'm tired, sugar," she said, "*so* tired."

"What's the matter?"

"I don't know—I'm sick, let's go home."

We sat wordless on the trolley, Alma's head resting on my shoulder. At home we hurried her up the stairs, when blood began spurting from her nostrils.

I screamed. "Oh, dear Lord, please help her!"

Alma grabbed her nose. "Hush, hush. Just let me lie down."

Blood streaked down the front of her green suit as she stumbled and fell across the bed. Her hat tumbled to the floor.

"Get Mama," Doreen yelled, and I ran down the stairs.

Mrs. Callaway came with a bucket of water and rags.

"You'll be all right, honey, just try to relax," she told Alma, calm as Granny always was. "It's a bad nosebleed. That's all it is."

Wringing a rag she placed it across Alma's nose, pressing. She placed a hand on her forehead and I knew she was thinking it was something worse.

"Let's get these clothes off her."

We took off Alma's shoes and got her out of her jacket.

Mrs. Callaway whispered to me, "Go find Papa. Tell him we need the doctor."

I grabbed the green jacket to rinse out. Grandpa was in the kitchen sipping coffee, *The Gazette* spread in front of him.

"It's Alma." My voice shook. "She's sick. Mrs. Callaway said get the doctor."

Grandpa shoved the paper away and rushed into the hall. "Where's she?"

"Upstairs, in bed." At the landing we could hear Alma heaving.

"Dear God in heaven." Grandpa yanked his hat from the hall tree and hurried out the door.

When the doctor came he took one look at Alma, reached in his bag and pulled out a mask. Quickly tying it on he scrounged, coming up with three more, and shoved them our way.

"Put these on and keep 'em on while you're in this room. This woman's highly contagious."

He gave Mrs. Callaway a bottle of large white pills. "Get one of these down her three times a day if you can."

"How can I, doctor, the way she's puking? It's pure bile." She set the pills on a table and replaced the poultice, draping it over Alma's eyes and nose.

"Quinine's the best we can do," the doctor said. "Come out to the hall."

"Is it 'the grippe?'" Mrs. Callaway asked.

He took off his mask and shook his head. "There's a deadly sickness going 'round the camps. First case I've seen here. If she makes it through the next two days, she might stand a chance."

"What are you saying, doctor?"

"I'm saying it's serious, and fast. Try to keep her comfortable, but keep this door closed, keep her completely *isolated*. And wear a mask! I'll see myself out."

Downstairs Grandpa grabbed his arm. They exchanged a few words and the doctor left.

Mrs. Callaway put on her mask and went back into Alma's room.

Next day Alma's face was puffed out and blue-tinged. We took turns sitting by her bed. She was breathing hard, her breath raspy as my old cat, Nelse's, when he purred, only Nelse was awake and happy. Alma didn't open her eyes and I wondered if she could hear me.

"Alma, Alma, honey, you 'wake? Can you hear? It's Selena."

She didn't move or open her eyes. Her breath started gurgling deep in her chest. I went to get Mrs. Callaway.

When we walked back in, there was only the gurgling, till finally, no sound at all.

"Alma, Alma!" Mrs. Callaway listened to her chest. "I can't hear her breathing." She felt Alma's pulse at her wrist, in her neck. "Dear God above, go get Papa. Be sure and take him a clean mask."

When Grandpa came in he knelt by the bed and stretched his arms across the slim form that was Alma.

"Eternal God," he prayed, hoarse with emotion. "Receive this your beautiful creature, this one made in your image. Thank you for her life, for letting us know her and love her for a little while." His voice broke as he went on. "Take her sweet spirit to be with you forever, and someday may we see her again in that wonderful place you got prepared. Help us who are left behind to grieve aright, knowing we, too, have the same blessed eternal hope. Amen, amen, and amen."

He stayed like that a long time, not lifting his head.

Mrs. Callaway and me were bawling out loud when we went down to the parlor to tell the others.

I didn't sleep that night. I talked to Mama for what seemed hours: *"How could God let this happen?"* I asked. *"Alma was so sweet, so good, so loving. She and Gus had made up and everything was going to be all right."*

"This world's not our home, Sippy. It's just a journey-ing place. Some leave early, some late, but all journeys come to an end. Alma's is done and she's here with the Lord."

"Is she happy, Mama? Is she happy there without her husband, without us?"

"She's got her baby now."

"She's got little Augustus?"

"Just like I got Noble. Our sweet little babies are right here. They help make heaven heaven."

The thought made me smile.

BRIGHT TICKET

If Love is a virtue,
I qualify
To enter Heaven
Bye and bye.
I'll say to Saint Peter,
"Hail, kind sir!
I have my ticket—
Love's my fare."
He'll open wide
To Streets of Gold
His ticket was love
In days of old.

Our straw bosses let Doreen and me off to go to Alma's funeral. She was buried in her green coat suit we'd rinsed out and pressed like new. I took Doreen's hand.

"This cain't be real," I said. "I'm gonna wake up and find Alma standing right here with us."

"You cain't just shut it out, S'lene. She's gone. You gotta accept it. We won't never see Alma again."

Gus stood alone in the haze of early autumn. His uniform was rumpled from a hasty trip, his eyes swollen from tears that no longer fell. He was silent, stoic, and I wondered how he could take this latest blow.

Marvelee was there in a gray coat suit and black turban. Alma Lee slept on her shoulder, sunny blonde hair wreathing her head. We went to where they sat on a folding chair and embraced. No words passed our lips.

Chapter 25

Mrs. Callaway hired a man to haul away and burn Alma's mattress and clothes. She opened the window to her room, sealed the door and put a black bow on it. Passing by, I couldn't bring myself to look at it.

By October we'd learned the nation was in the grip of a deadly epidemic: the Spanish Influenza. There was no known cure and no sure treatment. With no place to hide, even the rich could not find safety.

In Chicago, *The Gazette* reported, Billy Sunday called the disease a German trick.

"There's nothing short of hell they haven't stooped to do since the war began, darn their hides!" he ranted.

Surgeon General Rupert O. Blue decided against a general quarantine. People had to take measures on their own. Families with the disease were asked to remain in their homes, others stayed there too scared to leave. Some in Maysworth and Gastonia barricaded themselves inside.

"Seems Mr. Blue's leaving it up to local folks to cope with a national problem," Grandpa complained, reading *The Gazette's* front page. "They tried vaccines. Not one of 'em's worth a plug nickel."

Since Alma's death he brooded, obsessed, afraid one of us would be next.

In Maysworth all public places, the churches, school, finally the mill itself, closed. "Go home and look after your loved ones," they advised. The doors were locked to all but a chosen few who met daily at the mill office.

"What should we do, Papa?" Mrs. Callaway asked.

"No new boarders. Everybody here stays here unless they get our permission. If anybody has to go out, they wear a mask. No place to go anyway, with everything closing up."

Merchants nailed up barriers, serving customers through the door one at a time. You had to wear a mask to ride the trolley.

Everybody had their own treatment ideas—from camphor bags around the neck to lying in tubs of onions, from finger bowls of disinfectant to killing germs by blow torching water fountains.

Stuart Cramer, Jr., came home to help his father deal with the crisis in Maysworth. He was put in charge of all able-bodied millworkers willing to canvass door to door. Full wages were promised volunteers.

Against Grandpa's advice, Doreen was bound and determined. She and I signed up right away.

"Who could say no to Stuart Cramer, Jr., handsomest man in Maysworth?" she said.

I agreed. "It's what Mary Pickford would do in *Ramona*. Besides, beats sitting home."

Neighborhoods were divided up to list the needs of stricken families and pick up prescriptions. With only one doctor in town, we were told to do what we could. I was paired with a middle-aged Mrs. Fortner. We must've looked strange in our medicated masks, and strangers weren't welcome anywhere. We ourselves could be germ-carriers.

As we approached our first house, Mrs. Fortner grabbed my arm.

"Wait, Selena. Before knocking we need to pray."

She prayed for everybody in the house.

More than once doors were cracked, then slammed in our faces before we could say anything. In some homes whole families were sick, nobody able to help the others or come to the door. At one house I knocked.

When no one came, Mrs. Fortner opened the door, "May we come in—we're here to help?" she hollered.

From camphor-heavy dankness, a shaky voice answered, "Jimmy, Jim-boy, that you?"

We followed the voice to a room where a woman was curled on a daybed, a croched shawl over her arms. Her shoulders shook, her eyes panicky.

Mrs. Fortner pulled a worn quilt from the bottom of the bed and tucked it around her. "We're here, honey, we'll help you."

"Jim-boy—where's my *son?*" A fit of coughing made her reach for a can on a table.

Mrs. Fortner held it while the woman spit up blood and phlegm. "I'll tend her, Selena," she said. "Go look for the son."

I went to the hall and found a second room. A young man stared at the ceiling from his tousled bed.

"Are you all right?" I asked.

He didn't move. His eyes were glassy, his hand icy cold. I felt his wrist. *Oh dear God,* I prayed—he's gone! I rushed back to where Mrs. Fortner was.

She shook her head and whispered. "This dear woman's dying. Her lungs have shut down."

My knees were like jelly. "Her son, he's dead already. Oh, Mrs. Fortner. I gotta sit down." I reached for the gritty floor as things got black and my knees gave way.

When I came to, Mrs. Fortner was mopping my face with a wet cloth just like Mama used to do. "I'm all right, I'm all right," I insisted. I was so embarassed to be such trouble.

"Both of 'em's gone," Mrs. Fortner said calmly. "I'm putting an X by this house number. We'll get the wagon to come for 'em, God rest their souls."

When Stuart Cramer, Sr., learned the extent of the problem in Maysworth, he set up a kitchen where great basketloads of fresh-dressed chickens were brought from Cramer Farms. With Stuart, Jr., in charge we covered all of Maysworth delivering hot chicken soup, bread, and vegetables to the sick and needy through a half-open door here, a window there.

Sometimes we knocked and set food on a porch to be picked after we left.

The disease hop-scotched, spending itself one place, moving to another stronger than ever.

> *I had a little bird*
> *It's name was Enza.*
> *I opened the window*
> *And in-flew-Enza.*

The ditty made its way across the country like the sickness itself, and children skipped rope to the sad little rhyme.

Late in 1918 the war was winding down according to *The Gazette*, the "flu" having done its part worldwide by sapping the strength and will to continue. In Maysworth and around the nation "The Spanish Lady" was into her finale. Mills reopened. People unlocked their doors and ventured into the crispness of early November.

November 7, a false Armistice was prelude to the real thing. And Monday, November 11, the day after my eighteenth birthday, mill whistles hooted like a dozen approaching freight trains and kept it up for hours. Workers poured from Cramer Mills. Church bells rang, fire bells rang, as the whole town took to the streets screaming, jumping up and down. "THE GREAT WAR ENDS" Monday afternoon's *Gazette* declared in bold two-inch letters. Germany had surrendered unconditionally.

"C'mon, let's go to Gastonia," Doreen shouted above the Maysworth hoopla. We squeezed onto a packed trolley and took off for Main Street. Crowds blocked the tracks, forcing the trolley to stop where a snake dance formed. We jumped off and hitched onto its tail, dancing to the beat of drums.

Flags flew everywhere. Old Glory, along with the Union Jack and French and Italian tri-colors, streamed from automobiles, trucks, wagons, anywhere you could stick a flag. Police stood around watching till a stray bullet broke a window on the seventh floor of the First National Bank building. Nobody got hurt, but police issued orders forbidding hardware stores to sell any more ammunition.

Doreen and I hooped and hollered till the wee hours when the last trolley, jammed with drunken revelers, left for Maysworth. We fell into bed in our clothes and slept till almost noon.

With the war over and the boys coming home, the Spanish Influenza, nearly forgotten, hit hard in a third wave. Reading the news, Grandpa sighed disgustedly.

"All Mr. Wilson gave a hoot about was the war," he said. "He's the only one could do something and what did he do? Not a blamed thing! Don't seem to bother him folks are dying by the thousands, more'n from the war itself, more'n died in the *Black Death*."

When early 1919 a report came President Wilson himself suffered a mild case of flu while negotiating the treaty at Versailles, Grandpa shrugged.

"Guess the man found out just how widespread the sickness is."

Etha was excited Freddie would soon be home. She kept singing along with the record, "Oh Johnny, Oh Johnny, Oh!" substituting her own words: "*Oh, Freddie, Oh Freddie, how you can love. Oh, Freddie, Oh Freddie, heaven's above.*"

Doreen tried hiding the record, but Etha complained to her mother and out it was yanked from the hall bookcase.

"Freddie's bringing me a souvenir from France," Etha bragged. "I think it's perfume. That's where they make it, you know—*oui, oui,* Paree. *Oh, Freddie, Oh Freddie, how you can love...*"

I didn't let on he'd promised me the same thing. I dreaded the thought of telling him again he was not the man of my dreams. While the war was on I couldn't bring myself to do it. Now the day was coming.

The list of those killed and wounded in the war was taken from the mill door. Thirty-four from Gaston County had died, but of the hundreds who left to serve their country, most would be home, looking to get their old jobs back.

Gastonia, the place Papa called Boomtown in 1912 when he, Met, and I arrived, had grown beyond belief in those seven years. The county's population was now 51,000 according to a report in *The Gazette*, with more that 21,000 dependent on the cotton mills for their incomes. Business was booming. My favorite spot to shop, J.M. Belk, had become the largest retailer in the area. Renamed Matthews-Belk, they were building stores in surrounding counties.

On a Sunday afternoon when Papa called to say he was leaving Gastonia for good, I wasn't ready for that kind of news.

"Again, Papa? Why? I thought you liked your job. You're making more money than you ever did."

"I suppose Maysworth ain't felt the pinch yet, honey, but just wait, it will. Mills're slowing down. Ain't gettin' orders since the war ended, and they're taking it out on us. Done let Donnie go."

"Who?"

"Donnie, you met 'er."

"Oh, the woman you brought for Corned Beef and Cabbage."

"That's the one. Let 'er go, dozens with 'er. Cut me to four days, myself, 'stretched' me like I ain't never been stretched before. I ain't taking it. Folks're madder'n hell. Union people done come from Charlotte, stirring things up same as they did over there."

"Where you going?"

"Back to Hendersonville. Say they're hiring."

"Our little family's gettin' mighty spread out, Papa. Met's gone, now you."

"'Tween jobs, I'm headin' to the mountains, see Met and that baby. Little Emily needs to know she's got a grandpapa."

Papa's complaints weren't the first I'd heard about Loray's Yankee millowners. Unlike the Cramers and other local owners, natives to our region who built homes here, Loray's owners never got involved with civic projects or social undertakings. They weren't known for sympathizing with workers' gripes, not around to see unrest. Turning a profit was their aim by whatever means it took. Thinking on it scared me. Sudie Hailey was treated unfairly, but when she complained and joined efforts to unionize, she became a victim herself, one I'd never forget.

By summer "our chickens were coming home to roost," as Papa would say. Workers were being cut, recent hires mainly, those who'd answered the war's demands. Doreen and I had our hours cut, with workloads the same.

Mrs. Callaway's roomers and boarders were leaving one and two at a time till she was forced to let Beulah go.

"Dear friend, I'll miss you sorely," she told Beulah. "I hope the day ain't far off we can call you back. In the meantime, please come back and visit."

She loaded Beulah up with food they'd canned together and gave her a cherished bone china tea set.

"Where'll you go, honey?"

"Goin' to my sister's farm out close to Belmont," Beulah said. "They can use another hand. Tobacco's comin' in. I 'spect I'll be tying it, puttin' it up in barns same as I did as a child."

We all took turns hugging Beulah till she wiped a stray tear with the back of her hand. Toward noon a mule and wagon stopped out front and Beulah loaded her belongings and waved a last goodbye.

On a Sunday evening Etha screamed, "He's home, he's here, Freddie's here!"

When I came down he was on the porch, Etha hanging onto his arm. Out front sat a Model-T churning away like a butter churn.

Grandpa and Doreen stood glaring at Fred and Etha through the screen door.

"You're not welcome in this house, Mr. Fletcher." Grandpa's voice carried all over the house.

Fred shrugged and started down the steps.

Etha pulled him toward the car. "C'mon, Freddie. Take me out for a ride."

He glanced back. "Hey, anybody else wanta go? I can take four."

Grandpa walked away disgustedly.

I looked at Doreen. "Why not? Let's go."

"Let me drive, Freddie," Etha shouted, running to the open car door.

He laughed. "Ain't giving driving lessons, not to the likes of you. Get in back."

He motioned me to sit up front.

We went down every dusty road till we got to Scoggins' Deadend. Freddie backed into a steep incline when the car stalled and started to roll. He jerked on the brake, throwing us forward.

"*Whee,*" Etha hollered, perching her chin on Fred's shoulder. "Can I crank 'er, Freddie. C'mon, let me try."

"Sit right there, dopey." He jumped out. "Make sure that brake holds, Selena," he yelled, and cranked her till she sputtered and caught.

At the boardinghouse I opened the door to get out when he grabbed my arm. "Stay, Selena. We need to talk." Over his shoulder he said, "Alone."

Might as well to've slapped Etha's face. She jumped out huffing, and slammed the door hard.

Fred drove to the churchyard and parked. He took my hand. I braced myself, looking away.

"I'm reenlisting," he said. "I hate Gastonia, everything about it. Ain't nothing in Gaston County but cotton mill jobs and farming and nobody'll ever get rich at either one." His voice changed, husky and low. "Selena, honey, won't you change your mind...about us, about getting married? I love you enough for both of us."

He put his arm around me, his cheek brushing mine.

I stiffened, pulling my hand from his grasp. "I'm sorry, Fred. You deserve somebody that loves you. It's not me. I'm...I'm really sorry."

He pressed his lips together, his jaw tight, as he put a gift box of perfume in my lap. Without a word he turned and drove back to the boardinghouse.

"'Bye, Fred," I said, opening the car door, "and thanks."

He put the car in gear and drove away fast, not looking back.

That night he called Etha on the telephone and talked an hour.

"Freddie's reenlisting," she told us afterwards. "He likes the Army. He'll *never* work in a cotton mill again if it's the last place on God's green earth. That's exactly how he said it. 'Me neither,' I told him."

I thought about my job. There were a lot worse things a person could do. I earned money, I paid my board. Like Mama said, and I believed it—God was watching over me:

LIVING STANDARDS

It's not working in a cotton mill,
Nor the kind of folks you know.
It's whether you're made of clay or dirt
That makes your standards low.

It's not the way you clothe yourself,
Nor the way you do your hair—
It's the kind of life you're living,
And the way you say a prayer.

It's not because you're having fun,
Nor the kind of jokes you tell.
It's the things that hurt your fellowman
That send your soul to hell.

Chapter 26

At the supper table on Monday Doreen complained about a group of people who came to the mill and watched her spool, writing stuff down.

"'Efficiency experts' the second-hand called 'em. I get all my ends tied up; that's when I can rest a minute, get a drink of water or something. Couldn't do it, not with that bunch watching every move I made."

"What's 'efficiency experts?'" I asked.

"That's what I asked him. Said they got the job of deciding how much a person can do in an hour, and that's what they expect you to put out. If *you* can't, somebody else *can*. They'll take your job and give it to them."

"Papa called that 'stretching.' That's why he left Loray. They want you to do more work in less time but at the same wages."

Mrs. Callaway was edgy as always when we complained about our jobs, or anything else. She liked to remind us we were lucky to have a job, what with people in China starving to death.

"Have another biscuit, Papa," she said, passing a basket of her big-as-cat's-heads buttermilk biscuits.

"Thank you, Libby, I think I will. Pass the molasses."

From the day I moved into Callaway's Boarding-house Grandpa'd made it his business to know where each of us was and when we'd be home. He had strong opinions leaving little room for argument. But since Alma died he'd backed off. Not once, after preaching her funeral, had he filled the pulpit at Maysworth Baptist. Was he sick? Getting old? I couldn't help wondering. When Etha got back from her trip with Freddie, he made her go find a job. Now he ignored her, as if she were beyond control and that was that.

Doreen wasn't finished with her suppertime speech. I'd not seen her so fired up since she threatened to march in the streets with the suffragettes.

"They could take my job, give it to somebody else," she snapped her fingers. "Just like that. That's what the second-hand claimed, and who's he? Well, four years ago that rascal was sweeping the spinning-room floor. Sweeping the floor! All he knew how to do. But if you're male, hang around, pal. Quick as a billy goat can butt, you'll be telling some woman what to do and how to do it. Ever seen a woman get to be boss? Even straw boss? Ain't gonna happen!"

"Doreen, honey, you need to calm down," Mrs. Callaway warned. "The others might not like your comments."

"Maybe the men don't. But us women? Hey, didn't we just get the vote? Marched for it, went to Washington for it, got thrown in jail for it, and for what?" She smirked. "So *men* can run for office!" Her face glistened like a tomato beneath her sweaty red curls.

I fought the urge to stand and applaud. Instead I hunkered, chasing two peas with my fork, waiting for Grandpa to say he'd heard about enough. When he cleared his throat I figured it was coming.

"Loray's going on strike," he announced, calm as saying it might rain. "The United Textile Workers is over there right now recruiting members, calling for action. Some here at Cramer Mills are walking out sympathetic with the cause. I talked with Mr. Cramer himself. His hands are tied."

Every eye was on Grandpa as he wiped his mouth, folded his napkin and laid it next to his plate.

"I think it's time for us to go." It was as if he'd rehearsed this little speech, making sure it had the right impact.

"For God's sake, Grandpa, what're you saying?" Doreen asked. "*Us who?*" She glared at him like he'd lost his mind. "Are you talking about *leaving* Maysworth?"

"That's exactly what I'm talking about." He looked at the other boarders and me. "But what Aaron Spencer and Libby Callaway decide don't need to affect any of the rest of y'all. Your jobs are what you need to think about. There're other boardinghouses, other places to room."

We hadn't been served such a shock since Grandpa announced we were staging a play for the Red Cross. Maybe this explained his moods, his aloofness. Doreen hadn't suspected, nor Etha. Like Met, Etha'd never kept a secret. All she thought about now was what might affect her and Freddie. This news probably meant nothing to her. For me it meant everything.

Naomi was our oldest roomer, had been with us since right after the move to Maysworth. "Where you going, Mr. Spencer? And when?" she asked.

"Good questions, Naomi. And you have every right to know all we can tell you. Come to the parlor and we'll explain as best we can."

Grandpa picked up his plate, raked the scraps into the slop pail, and stacked it beside the dishpan, the way we all did since Beulah left.

Grandpa'd talked to a fellow named Brown, a native Gastonian who'd pulled up stakes and moved to Rosemary, North Carolina. Mr. Brown had a big family and got them all good-paying jobs in one of Rosemary's five mills.

"The mills're local owned, local run. 'Same folks that own 'em run' em,' Mr. Brown told me. Said they're building houses, well-built houses, fast as they can. Workers can't wait to snatch 'em up. Everybody's happy, everybody's well-paid. So much so the unions don't bother to come calling."

"Tell 'em why we plan to go, Papa," Mrs. Callaway said.

"Like every village, what they need's another good boardinghouse. That's where we come in. Got a real good offer, one we couldn't turn down. Mr. Brown guaranteed we'd never be sorry."

When we went to bed Doreen was too worked up to sleep. "What happened?" she asked. "Why'd things change? We used to like our jobs."

"Ain't about making workers happy," I said. "It's all about the mills making a profit."

When she finally settled into heavy breathing, I lapsed into reverie with Mama: *"What should I do, Mama?"*

"Ain't we been down this road afore, honey?"

"You mean 'cause I said Mrs. Callaway treated me like a daughter, and Grandpa was like my own grandpa?"

"Sure. With me in heaven, Met and your papa gone, who else you got? You're mighty lucky they treat you like family."

"Then I guess I'll go with 'em to Rosemary. I love you, Mama."

"Goodnight, Sippy-gal."

Keep Your Face Toward the Sun

Keep your face set toward the sun,
and work and work and work.
No task has ever yet been done
by one who dared to shirk.

Though ill winds may blow your way,
discouragement sands may blind you—
Keep your face turned toward the sun,
for the shadows lie behind you.

Black clouds of despair may rise to view,
the sun, still bright, is shining.
The clouds that shut it off from you
have a radiant silver lining.

So work and hope, till the task is done,
till you've trod your hardest mile,
till victory's crown through work is won—
then sit you down and smile!

Chapter 27

As a farewell to all her boarders, friends, and especially the Windred Gentrys, Mrs. Callaway fixed a corned beef and cabbage supper fit for King George himself. She served it buffet-style since all guests could not be seated at the large oak table. The overflow went to the parlor, balancing plates on our knees. For dessert there was Jeff Davis Pie and chocolate layer cake with orange-glazed pecans on the side and her prize-winning watermelon rind pickle.

After washing and drying Mrs. Callaway's primrose-patterned china, we stacked all of it on the table. Each piece was then carefully packed with two thicknesses of newsprint and placed in wooden boxes. All her personal belongings: china, silver, Grandpa's smoking stand, the Victrola, even the aspidistra were boxed up and hauled to Gastonia's freight depot to be shipped to Rosemary.

"I reckon we'll give 'em all a thing or two to do at Roanoke Junction," Grandpa said.

Mrs. Callaway looked at him. "Roanoke Junction?"

"Yep, that's where all this stuff's going including us," he said. "Roanoke Junction, that's Rosemary's railroad station. Close to the Roanoke River. Dangerous river, they tell me, with rapids that'll sweep you away."

Mrs. Callaway shook her head. "Reckon I'll stay away from that."

Naomi moved to Mays Hall for Single Women. Alma's room, fumigated and aired for months, was opened, only the frame of her bed reminding us how horrible her death had been. The boardinghouse was stripped of all that made it home, and our bags were packed, ready for the trip.

On the morning we were to leave, Etha was not in her bed. Pinned to her pillow was a note:

> Freddie sent me a ticket. I'm on my way on the P&N to New Jersey. Don't worry, Mama and Grandpa, little Etha will not be "living in sin." We're getting married right away. Sorry, Doreen, your little sister beat you and Selena down the aisle. Ha, ha! Maybe you'll meet your "knights in shining armor" in Rosemary. Etha.

Etha had finally done something that, in my mind, meant she'd reached a degree of maturity–she'd kept a secret. I was surprised how calmly Mrs. Callaway took the news.

"The Army always provides for its dependents," she said. "And Fred need never worry about drawing his pay."

Grandpa puffed hard on his pipe and didn't say a word.

Two hacks pulled up in front of the boardinghouse. We loaded them with our baggage and ourselves, and left on the winding road to Gastonia's depot.

I looked back at the two-story, cream-colored boardinghouse with its wrap-around porch and big rocking chairs, now turned and leaning against a wall. Oak and maple leaves fluttered to the ground with a colorful finality.

I strained to catch a glimpse of the woodsy trail beyond the tracks where, in a sheltered spot, purple flowers once drank from a pool.

Photo Gallery

"He's the best I can do," Alma said,
hugging the grave monument.

Gastonia, NC 1914

A friend of Selena Wright's
at Camp Merritt

New Jersey 1917

James W. Wright
Selena's Father

Age 36, circa 1918

Selena Wright (lower left) and her
boarding house friends

Gastonia, NC 1918

"An old sweetheart" friend of Selena's

Gastonia, NC 1918